Copyright @ 2023 by Dr. Humpry

All rights reserved. No part of this publication may be reproduced, distributed, or transmitted in any form or by any means, including photocopying, recording, or other electronic or mechanical methods, without the prior written permission of the publisher, except in the case of brief quotations embodied in critical reviews and certain other noncommercial uses permitted by copyright law.

Chapter 1.

The room exploded with a thunderous eruption that fiercely emitted from Daisy, gripping her fingernails deeper into the leather intensely biting the bottom of her lip. Letting out a heavy exhale as the buzzing loudened. Spine curved to almost a ninety degree angle, anticipation spiked as goosebumps populated her fair exposed skin once he touched her lightly with his fingertips. Eyes were glued shut, body tense, controlling her breath through her nose. Descending her overbite till she consumed her glossy maroon bottom lip. Small parts of her nails filed off as she dragged them along the fine leather caused by the intense feeling scrolling up her body. Slowly her teeth scraped her lipstick off, inhaling the cool air as her mouth widened.

The vibrations turned on and off controlled by him, smirking as he did so. Facing her through the reflection profoundly romanticizing the night's series of events that were planned out vividly in his mind. Distracted by the look on her face as he watched through the mirror, an uncontrollable urge forced him to put the machine on the table. He stood up needing to grab her, both of his hands went up her arched body. The nature of his lustful strength rubbing her shoulders turned the rest of her body into jelly.

The lingering power of his touch dissipated, after his absence she heard a loud clacking on the floor. Daisy's eyes finally opened, her head tilted toward the echoing noise of his hard soles on the epoxy. In the mirror's reflection his eyes already locked on hers as if he was waiting for her to look up. Slowly taking off his black sharkskin suit jacket, not breaking eye contact. The devilish passion from just one look made her legs tremble.

He turned around after placing his jacket down, staring deeply into her eyes. Beginning to roll up his sleeves he sent off a wave of electricity that transferred through her making her quiver desperately longing for his touch. Snapping on his gloves then making his way back over to her.

A black glove grabbed her chin pulling her forward in the chair. She moved up eagerly to his command. The smell of latex, then the taste of it as his thumb hooked into her mouth helped her rise. Pulling her up like a prize from a crane arcade game, he stopped once their lips were on the verge of meeting. Licking her lips, patiently with her head facing up with her eyes wide open filled with desire.

Feeling his wet tongue in her mouth, she was completely lost, all sense or train of thought derailed by oblivion. Daisy's eyes remained closed, warped under his spell, blood rushing through her narrow vessels heating her body up. Sticky saliva stretched as their lips released, looking down to the feeling of his hands on her legs. Her body shifted fiercely after pushing her knees down back into the chair. Making sure she was comfortable he watched her expressions and body language. Massive chills ran rampant up her legs as he forcefully put her in his desired position. Moving her elbows up in the air to rest on the shoulders of the chair, tickled by the latex fingers on the inner part of her arm. Leaning forward into the headrest to make her back curve into an seductive arch. Her obvious gesture for attention did not go unnoticed. A latex hand smacked the outside of her ass cheek, leaving a red print that took a few seconds to appear. Knees begging to twitch, her chin pressed into the headrest indenting the leather, a rewarding smile stapled to her face.

    After switching on the machine an abrupt amplified buzzing transpired. Her body shook with a surprising suspense returning to his desired position. The machine was toned down with a switch, the vibrations muttered at a lower decibel. Daisy watched through the mirror as he looked at every inch of her body, admiring the flawless work of art he had propped perfectly in front of him. Once he caught a glimpse of her satire he shut off the machine, nothing but silence.

    On the back of her head she felt his hand push her head down into the headrest. Unable to see him now, her teeth clenched. The feeling of his hand on her made her body tingle something awful, grinding her teeth as his hand moved up her. The machine was clicked on again, he slowly turned it up to the highest setting making her nervousness heighten.

    The room amplified most when the vibration touched her skin. His other hand of latex moved to the lower part of her thigh. Softly ascending up her leg with a tight grip, every inch he dug in getting closer to her hip bone, leaving her tickled. Once her body squirmed the buzzing stopped. Body jolting from his fingers deep in the inside of her hip. The buzzing started again, trying to stay still, biting, enjoying the bitter sweet pain and pleasure.

    Nervous sweat from her body tightening for a prolonged period of time felt as if it froze in the bleak of the air conditioner. Each time the buzzing started she was both surprised and excited, curling her toes together each time the vibrations touched her skin. Pressing her teeth into her lips trying to stay still, she could smell latex in the air. Her abs were tight, back finely arched.

Daisy opened her eyes putting her head on her arm, her eyes wandered. Noticing next to his neatly folded suit jacket was her pants and delicate red laced panties. The vibrations muffled louder as it touched her behind, she gasped now looking into the mirror. Watching him in the reflection, again like a mind reader he looked up to meet her in the mirror. Licking her lips with puppy dog eyes. Anticipation suspended her thoughts and pleasures. Their eyes were connected in the reflection, the machine was turned on and off a few inches away from her skin. She smiled into the mirror as he played with her. Her eyes shut so he could continue, putting her head into the headrest. He finally pressed it onto her skin. Her teeth buried into her skin, breathing out of her nose, shaking from how constricted her muscles were. A moan opened her mouth. Licking her lips she felt the impressions from her teeth, tasting iron in her mouth from the drop of blood that escaped. The vibrating contained in his grasp, she felt it rub on her skin pushing it deep. Daisy reverted back to biting down harder, drawing more blood as he continued, eyes drawn shut.

Trying so hard to stay still, trying to hold it back she shook vigorously. Breathing intensified, his hand slid down to her ankles with a firm grip. Her eyes flickered, rolling her eyes in the back of her head. Trying rigorously not to shake or react to what he was doing. Sometimes it tickled and sometimes it felt so good that it went numb. Never knowing what feeling was coming next. Muscles were tight, constricted listening to the vibrations feeling every throb. Breathing hard out her mouth left her lips dry. Licking them with urgency arching higher in the air. Touching the right spot made every hair on her body rise.

Focusing at the task at hand he too licked his lips when he saw the array of goosebumps that constantly aroused her body. Watching her body twitch all under control, her reaction to how he touched her turned him on more and more. His hand went back up and down her leg, feeling her muscles tightened. His breath swiftly blew across her back forcing her to spasm, reacting her body went up and down in the motion of a snake. Staring at her with a fierce desire that filled in his dark eyes. The buzzing continued, her fingers clenched into the cold leather, eyes closed tight. A sensation that made her eyes cross uncontrollably, knowing what he was doing with his hands. Naturally gifted in reading her reactions with his every touch. Stopping the machine for a few seconds he could see her smile in the mirror, he kept the machine off waiting for her to lock eyes. Her neck tilted back toward him, her thick luscious lower lip was devoured by her overbite that pressed down.

The machine turned back on and she felt drops of ink hit her back side. He dipped the tip of the gun into the ink, hand on her ass with full attention. Hand steady and swift natural strokes. The little movements she made he had to adjust for. Hovering over the backside of her body more ink droplets dripped on her. Making sure each line was perfect, he stretched her skin. Wiping the excess ink off with a paper towel. Then applying more ink, submerging the needle into the cup of black ink. One more letter and it was complete, the buzzing consumed the entire room with the very last last stroke from the tattoo gun.

Chapter 2.

Wetness on the pillow immediately woke Daisy, springing her eyelids open. It was pitch black, scanning the bed not fully conscious. Only her eyes moved in the seconds of waking from what felt like an endless slumber, her body was weak. Tirelessly moving her hand up toward her face. Drool dripped out of the left side of her lip salvia running down her cheek. Rubbing her hand on the comforter, Daisy laid in her bed facing the shadows. The moonlight crept in, making ghost-like figures highlighted by the branches moving in the gentle wind. The swift shadows moved peacefully as the moonlight shed light upon them making them appear to be alive. Daisy watched them dance on her hardwood floor, feeling a presence in the room.

Bright lights in the distance flashed in the sky. The wind picked up, swaying the branches in a hurry. Faint sparkles fell from the heavens and were magnified by the moonlight rapidly appearing just as fast as they disappeared. A chill went up her body as if she was not alone, Daisy closed her eyes.

Taking a deep breath and recapping her last thoughts of unconsciousness that felt like she was somewhere else. Closing her eyes tightly, trying to go through the confines of time for just another few moments. Feeling the reality in its entirety navigating into a time and space in her mind. As she drifted back, she sensed another being that continued toward her.

Shaking the walls in the outskirts of her imagination, a loud crack of thunder overpowered and impeded her dream state. Her eyes opened to an immediate bolt of lightning through the narrow window above her bed, the glass being soaked by falling rain. The sparkles were immersed in the electricity that lit up the sky. Then the droplets began to fall down with wrath beating on the roof, windows and ground.

Slowly forgetting more and more details of lesser thought. Another loud crack crumbled, relinquishing her mindfulness. Struggling to remember more and more as the minutes passed. The rain continued, as the thunder's volatility decreased. Exasperated, Daisy rubbed her cheek till every bit of drool was rubbed off. Her body moved ever so slightly into a comfortable position on her back, her eyes still glared out the window being pelted by rain. The fury inside of her boiled, getting the feeling that she was not alone.

Restsley Daisy rolled over putting her arm out to the empty side of the bed. Pushing around the covers, digging her elbow down into the mattress pulling her weight up to inspect the other side of the bed. She was alone, unexpectedly looking at the other side of the neatly made bed. Rubbing her eyes back and forth. Once her blurred vision subsided she gave another look to the other side of the bed. Dropping back on her back, she began to rub her forehead trying to realize what was going on. The lucidness of her dream made her body fill with heat when reality set in.

Her solitude was shaken, reaching over on the nightstand to grab her phone, no new notifications, holding the phone for an extra few seconds looking in the corner noticing it was 1:11am. A flashing bolt emerged from outside that did not shake her. Clicking the sleep button on her phone she threw it to the empty side of her bed, flopping back into the pillow. Her cheek struck the wet puddle. Upset, warm and dazed, she spun the pillow flipping it around to the dry side. The comfort of the pillow did not help much, tossing and turning still pestered by the feeling as she tried to get comfortable.

Crossing her arms finally still, she stared up at the ceiling in her peripheral vision she saw the shadows of the branches creating animation throughout the room. Trying to concentrate she was fixated on the two tiered pointed light fixture above her bed. Her eyes shifted to each corner of the unlit light. Angry trying to get the remaining memory out of her head. Another glance over on the right side of the bed where the covers were now unevenly shifted, and the same result. It was still empty.

Laying there listening to the rain hit the roof, rolling from her back to her side avoiding the empty side of her bed, restless. Eagerly trying to find the sweet spot so she could reminisce her lucid thoughts, not able to make out anything clearly now. Seeking to not be alone in confusion, the sense of something haunted her. The sound of thunder in the distance continued every so often while the rain dwindled down as she found her slumber.

The alarm clock startled her at 6am, obnoxiously beeping. She rolled to her side, whipping her hand of more drool, then over searching for her phone. Ruffling around on her nightstand to grab it, finally hitting the snooze button. The remnants of her sleep juice was rubbed into the blanket. Quickly rolling back onto her back, eyes still closed tight.

There she was, back to the place in her mind on the verge of waking yet able to fully fall asleep. Her tire grew, body sunk into the mattress helping to wash her back down to sleep.

Under the covers her leg shifted. Again her leg spasmed like someone had their finger on her control button.

Growing, she now had no control of her body making her grip her sheets. Lingering in the few moments, quivering, enjoying the last bit of her dream. Trying to finish, ready to finish her eyes popped open. The blaring sound of her alarm started in the remaining seconds. Her forehead was hot, feeling more drool down her cheek. Turning slowly, rubbing it into the pillow wanting to look at the other side of the bed. Knowing the truth but still hoping for another outcome. Staring up at the ceiling after shutting off her alarm, getting mentally right for the day.

All done up, fresh out of the car park she was still uneasy. Looks can be deceiving, the sun shone brightly on her blond hairlike that shifted in the air like butterfly's wings as she walked down the street. A black modest dress, glossy heels with azure bottoms, a gold chain over the shoulder attached to a leather pocketbook. The combination of her outfit caught the attention of many on the block heading toward work. Shining in not only gold and diamonds but absolute beauty with a cup of class. Mens heads turned, seeing a perfectly put together woman in their presence. Confidently walking without even noticing the looks from not only men but women, still stuck with the feeling from this morning knowing it was transitory. Not only did the woman watch her with jealousy but they also took mental notes on how to be on her level. Daisy arrived at her morning coffee spot, she reached for the door when a man walking toward the shop rushed to grab the door for Daisy.

"Thank you," Daisy smiled as she entered the building.

As soon as Daisy entered, eyes fixated on her. Relatively quiet inside for how busy it was, the caffeine must not have kicked in. The shrieking sounds of coffee beans grinding, to the far right a man on the piano, playing Motzart softly with elegance. Coffee pungently controlled the room, teasing her as she waited in the long line. The man in front of her was wearing a frayed hoodie watching the news with the volume all the way up.

"The President of the United States sentenced to death for crimes against humanity," said the reporter clear as day through the man's phone.

She remembered seeing this all over all media, Twitter had authenticated documents proving this true from the Justice Department only a week ago.

"Crazy times to be living in," the man turned to her.

"Yes, it has been strange the past few years," Daisy said with a disengaged response.

"Millions around the world are infected with a man-made biological weapon. Governments enforce vaccines that prove to be dangerous, the President ordered to infect its own people in a population control plan," the news from his phone played until he moved to the front counter shutting his foldable phone to order his drink.

Looking up at the menu, seeking a good caffeine option to create the best output of work for the day. Daisy ran her fingers through her silky blonde hair, wrapping the lot of it behind her ear. Searching something different on the menu to pop out at her she lost track of her surroundings staring at all the options.

"Ma,am," the barista said to Daisy.

Snapping her out from looking up at the menu. Daisy stepped up to the counter crossing her arms, unable to decide.

"You know what, surprise me with something delicious with caffeine in it. Anything with caramel, vanilla, chocolate will do," Daisy smiling, then instantly staring down with uncertainty.

Daisy pulled out her alligator skinned wallet, pulling out her black business amex card to pay for her surprise drink. Her long freshly painted aqua nails scratched the numbers of her card before paying as she thought perhaps she made a mistake giving the barista control of her morning beverage.

Heels clacked on the hardwoods as Daisy stepped out of the line to only wait in another line a few feet away for her drink. Slowly her head moved, surveying the shop of anyone who may pique her interest. Carefully controlling her eyes to not impede unwanted attention. Unable to find anyone of interest her eyes fixated on the woman steaming milk, a high pitched noise squealed from the pressure being released from the machine. She watched the vapors evaporate entirely with curiosity.

"Daisy," another barista sternly yelled.

    Excited for her drink she grabbed her coffee and walked off, clicking her heels on the hardwoods. The floors created an echo that grew behind with each step she took. A man at the back of the line stepped out of his way and grabbed the door for her as she exited. Turning left on the sidewalk into the sun rising above the city skyline Daisy grabbed her sunglasses from the middle of her v-cut dress to protect her eyes from the glaring reflections of the skyscrapers. It was a block before she examined the mysterious drink. Feeling the heat on her fingertips, smelling a carmel. At the final crosswalk she stopped waiting for the light to change in her favor, picking the cup up to taste it. Licking the excess cream off her lips, swirling the blend around her mouth.

    Daisy's mouth was immersed with a sweet taste from the caramel with hints of chocolate and finishing with a creamy frothy espresso on the back of her tongue. Suddenly she realized what the drink was, of all the endless lists from the coffee shop. Stopping for a second mid stride though the crosswalk, coming to the conclusion it was a caramel macchiato she took another sip to clarify. Putting her head up in the sky letting out a sigh and continued walking to get out of the middle of the street. Daisy took a breath and continued smirking, ironically enough this is the same drink she always gets. Taking another sip, shaking her head in disbelief, enjoying her usual morning drink.

    After another block Daisy reached her building, she walked through the tall carousel doors holding her coffee close to her chest. The air temperature quickly changed after walking through the spinning door. The temperature cooled from the early morning humidity outside from the morning rays. Once inside her body temperature instantly changed, a slight chill from the massive vent blowing on her at the entrances. Now gladdened that the barista gave her a warm drink this morning feeling the brunt of the air conditioner. Reaching into her purse like a ninja, pulling out her card to swipe her key card to enter then putting it right back into its specific secret pocket all with one swift movement. After passing security Daisy takes her sunglasses off and returns them to hang on the v-neck of her dress.

"Hello," the security guard said as he usually did, never smiling but always polite, per usual trying to engage her in conversation as she waited for the elevator.

Smiling awkwardly at the man guard making small talk till the elevator door rang, the metal doors opened. The hurd of business men and women entered the confined space without heists.

"What floor?" The man in the crowded elevator asked Daisy, looking a little too deep in her eyes.

"Seven, thank you," she said, looking away from his infinite gaze.

Once the elevator beeped at the 7th floor the man put his hand out as the doors opened, guiding her out and he stepped back in the elevator waiting for the closing doors.

A gentle touch on the brushed silver square door handle, taking an extra second feeling the texture that most people that enter her office never even notice. Daisy admired the physical touch of things, submerging her sense in the aesthetics of everything. Daisy used all her might opening the ten foot solid glass door. Turning down her hall, something caught her eye. Daisy inquisitively staring at a giant vase with roses blooming in an array of reds on her secretary's desk.

"Good morning, would you like an espresso?" Daisy's secretary stood up over the huge bundle of flowers to greet her.

Daisy raised her coffee cup up to her face, answering her secretary's question with a simple gesture.

"Anniversary?" Daisy asked politely, admiring the beauty of the tight lucious bulbs.

"No, my boyfriend sent me these as a surprise. I think that he is planning something more this weekend. On our getaway up to his cabin up in the mountains," flaring her left hand up, wiggling her fingers.

"They are beautiful, you can leave early today Ronnie if you want. Get a jumpstart on your romantic weekend." Daisy said, completely distracted touching the tops of the roses as she walked into her office, keeping the door open.

Daisy put her purse on the shelf directly in front of The Book of Law collection, all matching burgundy hardcovers titled in gold. Standing by the window holding her coffee acclimating to the cool office environment. This morning's dream still bothered her, trying to forget it by taking in the beautiful view from her corner office overseeing her favorite bakery on the next block and the two nearby restaurants she often goes to for lunch. The shadows of the buildings were vastly pointing toward the West. In a few hours, after the workday was done her roof served as the best sunsets in the city. She had only been there once when she first started working in the building and one of the partners showed her, he tried to get overly affectionate with her but Daisy politely put him in his place and made it known she was not interested.

Standing at the window her mind drifted off. From sunsets to the roses, daydreaming about the trip to the cabin her security had planned for the weekend. Thinking about her experience in the field of romance never lived up to what her secretary was currently living. The only flowers she had received by a man was on prom in high school, a corsage with different variations of flowers wrapped around her arm for a few hours. The time in college had been committed to study and gaining the knowledge to pass the BAR. Once accepting the position at her firm she remained focused on her work.

Perhaps she has been patiently waiting for the right guy with her faint heart. So busy with her caseloads she rarely got the opportunity for a getaway vacation. Only as young with her family, now vacations tended to be for work. Occasionally she had taken spur of the moment trips with her cousin, it lessened since her cousin was married and now has two children.

The phones rang outside her office, the intercom went off. Ronnie asked her how many hours on a case she logged for her client so she can send it to accounting, forcing Daisy to leave Never Never land.

Daisy stepped away from the window, she sat down putting her coffee on her desk and opened the minella folder on her desk adding up hours logged for billing the client Ronnie inquired about. Squinting as she flipped back and forth, using a giant inkjet calculator to get an accurate number, simultaneously pulling her eye glass case out of the dark wooden desk drawer. The friction of the wood made a sharp creaking noise as she opened the old drawer, brushing the lenses off with a cloth before putting her leopard print boxed lenses on. Trading them for her sunglasses hanging on her chest, the case smacked with a clash after she closed it putting the case in the same spot in the drawer.

Situating, opening more briefs, laying them like a colleague on her desk. Grabbing her titanium pen standing in its holder next to her name tag on the desk, along with her trusty highlighter and of course an assortment of colored post-it tabs. Slowly sipping her coffee as she read, striking neon yellow marks through her pages. Swapping the highlighter for a pen making bullet point notes in her notebook. Her focus was indispensable, no breaks. Sidetracking was not a part of the way she was wired. Fueled by coffee, tea, cookies and candies throughout the day.

"Would you like me to order lunch for you?" Ronnie said, popping her head in.

   Lost in her work for hours, until her secretary just appeared like a demon in the doorway. Daisy shook her head, pulling off her glasses, rubbing her eyes viciously. Seeing blurry, taking a deep breath as she came to.

Daisy got up to stretch walking over to the coffee station on the other side of her floor and prepared herself an espresso. As she watched the espresso drip into a small ceramic white cup she looked through the assortment of snacks. The baskets filled with dark chocolates, nuts, pretzels and oatmeal bars. Grabbing two small bars of chocolate and a bag of pretzels along with her double shot of steaming espresso, she added raw sugar into the cup and gave it a quick stir.

Returning to her desk she took a big chunk of chocolate and dropped it into the cup. Watching it slowly melt and blend into a magical drink that helped her accomplish her work. Snacking on the pretzels for a minute she then picked up the small cup perfectly mixed with 100% dark chocolate like a gift from the gods. Taking a sip of the delicious roast to wash down the salt of the pretzels. Funny how something so small could bring so much joy. The rush began to kick in after her ten minute break.

Grabbing her glasses again, marking though pages, taking notes and sticking colored tabs on documents. Eagerly focused on the task trying to complete her work, at 3pm her secretary knocked lightly on the door. Daisy looked up seeing the excitement in Ronnie's eyes. Ronnie had her bag on her shoulder ready to start her weekend, Daisy noticed she had a box in her hand pulling her glasses down the crease of her nose a tad bit. Without a word her secretary entered the door once Daisy looked at what she was holding. Ronnie walked to her desk, placing the box in front of Daisy.

"I noticed you did not have lunch so I got you a chocolate croissant from your favorite bakery in town. Thank you again, Daisy, have a good weekend." Ronnie said, turning to go on her way to a fine romantic weekend.

Daisy did not even say goodbye, pushing her glasses back up her nose with her pointer finger. She was locked into her work once more and continued to work until her stomach growled hours later feeling her energy depleting, she continued on like usual. Daisy finished the notes for any rebuttal her co-counselor would fire at her on a high horse in court. Flinging her heavy titanium pen across her desk as her belly achingly moaning bringing her work to a definitive closing point. On a hunt for food she looked up and saw the most beautiful thing on her desk. Reaching over to Ronnie's gift, quickly opening the box that was tied with a thin white and red candy cane string that was tied up nicely in the middle of the box both horizontally and vertically creating a cross in the center. Grabbing the pastry melted chocolate stuck to her fingers, each bite of the croissant she chewed slowly savoring all the flavors of her croissant. Licking off the chocolate on her fingers, cleaning her fingers with her tongue she realized most of her diet today was chocolate. Smiling as she took in a tranquil breath.

  Pulling off her glasses, a pair of concave ovals laid on the ridge of her nose. Daisy took a short break, taking the time to lean back and relax, enjoying every bite trying not to think about work. Her quiet mind was disrupted, Daisy put her half eaten pastry down in a flash. A thought pricked her brain, something that she had been contemplating about the case finally sprouted in the back of her mind. Now it made sense after letting it brew in the outskirts of her mind for hours, she rushback to add this genius to her work before losing her train of thought.

  Daisy took small bird bites every twenty minutes or so. Once she finished her croissant she ran through her workload like a bullet train. The consumption of dark chocolate was like a legal version of adderall, her very own cheat code to life. Finding a solid checkpoint, she looked up at the clock. It was 6:30pm, yanking her glasses off to look into the distance past the door. No one was in sight and she decided it was time to leave, organizing all her files neatly away. Daisy put her pen and glasses in their proper places before grabbing her purse, she gathered her belongings and headed toward the elevator.

  After a long strenuous day, a stiff drink was needed. The job of a lawyer is tough, multiple caseloads, trials, consultations and due diligence intertwined with a non stop client list, was a job only for the strong. Tonight Daisy decided to go to a new spot that was on her way home called Half Full. This place had been popping up on posts over facebook and other social media looking a potential hotspot. The reviews online were already outstanding, Daisy used yelp as if it were a bible. Just the reviews would have sealed the deal for her, even without any photos. The photos from the reviews had astonishing hand crafted cocktails poured in stunning glassware then paired with food that looked like it was served by Micholin chefs. This vibe and sophistication was right up her alley. She drove there after work to check it out alone, straying out of her comfort zone. The navigation was directing her and an unexpected ring blared through her speakers, taking control over her GPS. Daisy looked at the red and green dots on her screen, her fingers flipped back and forth singing while contemplating picking up the call from another lawyer at her firm.

"Eeny, Meeni, Miny, Moe

Finally after the fifth ring Daisy reached over and flicked the green button up. It was Jameson, he was always full of energy rambling on before she got the chance to say anything. Jameson often called at this time on a weekday, asking Daisy out for a drink to talk about cases. He did have a tendency to prolong every story, after going on into a frenzy he began sweating with a slight narcissist disorder.

Daisy finally having an opportunity to butt in, she quickly told him she was going off to the new restaurant in town. The navigation was yelling at her to turn! The map was down because of the call and she was forced to hang up the phone to figure out where to go. Pulling up to the valet, she pulled out a $5 bill slipping it into her folded palm handing the cash to the man in the red coat trading the keys for a ticket.

Strolling up to the classic look brick building with tall gates and torches in the courtyard she was already impressed. Eyes drawn at the main wall inside the courtyard, with each step admiring more the red well manicured roses growing up the wall so lavishly. The dark red roses were in full bloom, the stems wondrously woven under and over the white painted wood frame that held this mystical masterpiece in place.

Walking inside the first set of double doors, through the glass she saw what was to greet her upon entry. A grand dark stained staircase curled down as the last few stairs widened significantly, a warm lit gothic chandelier in the open foyer as she put her hand on the handle of the second door. Walking though the giant castle-like doors she was assisted by a short brunette host with her hair in a ponytail that welcomed her and asked about her dining preference for the evening.

"Thank you, no table for me. I am going to the bar."

The hostess complimented Daisy on her cowhide heels with the vibrant shade of azure on the sole of feet, a synopsis of walking in the sky.

Walking to the bar on the old oak flooring, clacking with each step. Perhaps it was too early in the night so the noise of her heels echoed, drawing the restaurant's customers off their meals, cocktails and conversations to draw their eyes on Daisy. The illusion was that she was a star walking making her way through the bar, a rare sight to see. Not only were eyes magnetized to her because of her hard sole heels, it was also in the manner of style and pure beauty Daisy effortlessly aspirated. Paired with her accessories that complemented her all too well both men and women looked as she made her way to the bar. Daisy did not really notice until the man on the right side of the bar stared for a bit too long, making it uncomfortably obvious. Taking that sign to serpentine she veered off to the left, rather than sitting on that side of the bar where the man would definitely engage her in small talk and possibly ruin her already pleasant experience.

Daisy found an open spot with an empty seat on both sides of her, it was directly in the middle of the curved bar. Once in her stool reaching into her purse to pull out her phone to check emails to ignore the man still staring like a deer in headlights, seeing him in her peripheral vision. The bar was dimly lit, a huge island amassed in the center of what seemed like endless rows of liquor stacked on the shelves. Giant bottles of wine enough for twenty or more people to enjoy stood as a statement piece with signatures written in silver sharpie in the biddle just behind the register. On the right side of the cash register there were dozens of different bourbons, ryes, and whiskeys from all over. Daisy did not recognize most of the bottles but was very curious about where they were made and what they tasted like. Daisy just became a fairly new connoisseur of these darker liquors finding a new taste for sweet and smokey aged bourbon.

At 7pm the bar was not dead nor crowded surprisingly, looking around at a cloud of joy that surrounded every customer sitting at the high top tables. To Daisy's left there was a beautiful view of the lake, though the side window. The windows were surrounded in bricks, and in the center of the wall was a wood burning fireplace built with Montana ledge stones. No need for a fire today, the day was as beautiful as ever in the mid 60s. She became distracted by the bar's interior design looking around fascinated like a child. Touching the beveled countertop of the bar, rubbing her fingers on the smooth stone and admiring the waterfall countertop at the corner of the bar where the wait staff picked up drinks. Allured by the light gray veins of the stone flowed throughout the bar. Distracted by the restaurant design she looked down in front of her and realized she did not have a drink, no less a menu.

    Feeling drafted from the side door that opened multiple times in a short interval, couples and parties were coming in. Within no time the bar area was full. Voices grew louder giving the bar area a completely different vibe overpowering the music. Looking around trying to flag down a bartender, no one was free behind the bar. One young man was filling ice, the other was talking to guests opening a bottle of wine.

    Daisy took her free time while the bartender was busy to continue looking around at the decor, eyeballing the walnut high top tables perfectly lined up in the dining room. Glancing over at the back side of the restaurant checking out the sconces she was suddenly struck by the man walking out of the back. The existence of life stood still, evaporating all matter Daisy was captivated. He was carrying a full sized silver keg to the bar. The man was wearing a black dress shirt with the top two buttons undone and his sleeves rolled up with no wrinkles. He had slicked back hair that shone brighter in the dim light as he approached the bar. His neatly kept beard had him looking rugged and mainly like a hunter. Permanent marks all over his arms, ruptures in his skin blended made him stand out more profoundly hiding more behind his ironed black shirt.

Daisy was tuned trying to make out the tattoos he wore on almost every part of visible skin as he neared. He carried the keg with awkward ease rounding the corner to walk behind the bar, she watched accidentally staring at him in quite an obvious way. The keg passed the waterfall countertop corner and he looked up catching her staring and gave her a quick half smile. The force of his eye contact was overbearing, his dark brown eyes filled a dazing mystery that she wanted to uncover.
"What are you drinking?" A different bartender, stepping out of nowhere in front of the man holding the keg breaking Daisy's view.
 "Buttery Chardonnay." Daisy responded, blinking repeatedly.

The man carrying the keg waited for his coworker to get Daisy's order first. The tattooed man swayed back and forth in a circular motion with the keg waiting, shaking the beer into a whirlpool. As soon as he had the opportunity to get to where he was going he threw down the keg after Daisy had just ordered and there was a path. The man took a quick breath and put the keg down, leaning over to open the doors to the cooler. He was almost right under her only a foot and a half away, Daisy bit her lip. An empty keg moved out of the cooler, he picked up the fresh one with one hand. Sitting on an empty keg as he moved the line to tap the fresh keg. Daisy got her glass of wine from the other bartender, taking a sip filling her mouth waiting for the man under her to pop his head up. She eagerly wanted to engage him in any sort of conversation, Daisy was very intrigued by this man. He scooted the empty keg back, closing the door the mystery man stood alas then picked up the empty keg.
"How heavy is a full keg?" Daisy yelled over the loud voices that bounced off the brick walls stopping him then leaned forward putting her weight up on the bar.
"150lbs give or take, I make kegs my bitch."

He reached underneath the bartop and grabbed two pint glasses palming both of them in one hand. He pulled down on the tap pouring beer into the first glass that began filling with foam. Once the foam hit the top he started to fill the second pint up. It was a much better pour after the line was cleared and because he put the glass on a 45 degree angle with virtually no foam only about an inch at the top. After he topped off the glass he chugged half of the beautiful pint in two gulps, whipping his mouth of the foam that stuck to the hairs above his top lip while looking right at Daisy.

"My reward," he said, giving Daisy a wink that struck her with such an intensity, he then turned around dumping the full glass of foam into the sink putting both of the dirty glasses into the dishwasher that steamed up once it opened.

  Before she had time to react the tattooed man patted the other bartender on the back, they gave one another a handshake and he proceeded to the back with the empty keg not returning again for the rest of the night.

  This mystery man had been gone for about 20 minutes and she was still replaying a video in her mind of him coming out of the back carrying the full keg. Continuously Daisy kept turning around hoping to see him again, imagining his wink with a genuine smile again. Displaced, she chugged her glass of wine unusually fast, ordering the first martini on the menu that tickled her fancy after reading through the long list of different cocktails on the menu. Thinking that a stiff drink might relax her mind and bring her mind at ease.

"One cucumber mint martini," the other bartender said, promptly placing the drink on a fresh coaster in front of her.

  The drink was delicious and strong, just like every martini should be. She dipped the cucumber garnish into the liquor and took a little bite to add more complexity to the drink. In her mind she was already planning on visiting again. Thinking she would return on Saturday with her girlfriends for brunch. Bloody marys and mimosa with some roast beef hash sounds like a plan after researching the menu online. Perhaps during brunch he may have time to talk more without vanishing. Saturday is a busy night everywhere especially the new hot spot in town, hoping brunch was ideal to get to know him. Constantly on her phone organizing a plan of attack and composing a text for her girlfriends about Saturday, suddenly she was tapped on the shoulder. Excitement filled her body, a feeling of nervousness to turn around then her body twisted around.

"This is a nice spot, good choice." The empty bar stool next to her moved out, Jameson smiled as he sat down.

Daisy's face automatically turned into a frown once she turned, the butterflies flew away accidently feeling disgusted in her stomach and her face mocked her feelings..

"It is, I had a long day in the office. A drink was definitely needed, how was your day?" Fixing her frown upside down to be polite, turning away from him looking back at the bar again.

"These charges are easy to prove, this case is an easy win like Grenada." Jameson went into a long narrative about one of his clients. The client he was representing was suing his business partner for stealing money in a fraud case from their company and laundering into offshore accounts in the Cayman Islands to fund a life he hid. Daisy continued to smile, nodding her head trying to act enthusiastic, sipping on her martini until it went dry. The alcohol began to get hot inside her body, taking off her jacket to get comfortable.

The side door continued to open and close all night as more people arrived forcing everyone in the bar area to talk louder. Jameson continued to ramble on about the client and the case she listened unenthused to his intrusive behavior. Jameson proceeded to go into more detail more so then he legally should tell anyone who is not his client breaking breach of contract ethically as the whisky entered his veins. Daisy looked down at her finished martini examining it, putting her two fingers up in the air flagging the bartender for another cocktail without a word. In the back of her mind she thought loose lips sink ships.

Daisy continued to be pleasant and polite bantering back at the brief pauses in conversation with Jameson to liven up her night. Within another twenty minutes she was done with her second martini. Jameson noticed that something else was on her mind and suggested they get dinner before she got sloppy. Ordering two filet minions medium rare and twice baked potatoes for dinner but first a kale caesar salad with extra croutons to start.

"Easy on those martinis, I don't want to carry you out of here now. One martini is not enough, two is just enough and three is too many. My father alway told me so," Jameson remarked chuckling and took a sip of his old fashion.

The bartender brought them both ice waters with their kale caesar salads. To cool herself down she took a sip of the ice cold water. Taking a bite of the salad she tasted hits of lemon that flavored the dull taste of kale. Daisy was never such a fan of caesar salad because it contained anchovies in the dressing, but after almost three drinks she did not think much into it.

The entrees came out right after the salad plates were removed from the bar. The entrees were beautifully plated on a black oval plate. Daisy ordered a glass of wine with dinner, that was her last drink of the night. Jameson went on about how extravagant the meal was, taking in the carefully measured ingredients that the chef put into the work of art that came from the kitchen trying to examine everything to be perceived as intellectual.

The food was a mondane to the thoughts in her head, Daisy was still unfortunately stuck on the mystery man. A lingering desire of the unknown. Thinking to herself how it was possible that just a wink and a small half smile can make one spiral out of control in thoughts.

"I didn't even get his name," she said aloud, not realizing.

"Who?" Jameson stopped talking for a moment and replied to Daisy's mummer.

Frozen like the cliffs in the Alps with the realization that she spoke this thought aloud out of turn, quickly she pointed her head toward the bartender that has been serving them all night putting another piece of red meat in her mouth that cut in her teeth like butter to act casual.

"The Bartender?" Jameson said his eyebrows raised.

Daisy nodded covering her mouth as she chewed, lucky her outburst played off all too well. Jameson flagged down the bartender and asked him his name.

"Im Chris, nice to meet you guys." The bartender said as he looked back and forth between the two of them.

"Well be in here a lot, it's about time a place of this stature opened up around here. This place has it all." Jameson said, extending his hand out to shake Chris' hand.

Jameson finished his pleasantries with Chris taking another sip of whisky from his rocks glass, then excused himself to go to the bathroom. Daisy cut through the last piece of her buttery steak, dipping it in the delicious house steak sauce fully satisfied.

Placing her fork and knife horizontally on the plate, pushing it away once she was finished glanced in the hazy mirror in front of her in between the shelves of the bar and saw Jameson at the hostess stand. Inspected further she noticed the hostess giving Jameson his phone back. The two of them were flirting hard, and it seemed as if Jameson had secured her number. Jameson tucked his phone on the inside of his left jacket pocket, after he buttoned up his coat tugging down on both sides of his jacket walking away grinning toward the lady before saying goodbye heading toward the lavatories.

Suddenly the bartender that was taking care of them all night stepped in her field of view, he was pouring a beer from the tap in front of Daisy.
"Or were you looking for the other bartender's name who just left?" He said making direct contact with Daisy.

Daisy perked right up, her back straightened upright in her bar stool leaning her back up against the backrest waiting for the answer saying yes with body language digging her elbows into the bartop as Chris reached toward her to grab her empty plate. Picking up her plate and then leaning down on an angle Daisy heard the plate clink as it was put into the bus tub. Jameson returned out of the blue just as Chris returned from putting the dirty plates away. Jameson pulled out the chair and sat down interpreting her desired conversation.

Jameson began to ramble about the case once again the second he sat. The curiosity did not die within her, wanting Jameson to leave so she could finish getting the information she desired from Chris. In her head she began devising a plan to engage the bartender later in conversation to find out his name in a subtle manner. Sitting though the rest of Jamesons rant anxiously waiting.

Jameson's phone rang, he turned to Daisy with his finger up to let her know he had to step outside to take the call and proceeded toward the side door. Daisy looked around for Chris, once Chris saw her alone he walked right back over to her knowing what was on her mind.
"Being a bartender for so long you learn to have situational awareness and become a master at reading people. His name is Jackson." Chris said and began pouring a beer.
"Hhh-Hhhow?" Daisy muttered as her cheeks turned red, sighing with relief finally putting a name to his face.
"Jackson has that effect on people, I saw your face when the pair of you were talking. I also overheard you burst out about a bartender's name, I knew it wasn't me. Jackson is his name." Chris said as he topped off the beer creating a foamy head bringing it over to the server section of the bar.

Grinning from ear to ear in with a slight embarrassment, her cheeks were red and extremely warm. The printer machine went off, Chris grabbed the ticket and headed back to the taps in front of Daisy. Leaning on the tips of her toes on the footrest of the barstool, her elbows on the bartop and shoulders pointed toward the bar showing she wanted to continue to pick Chris' brain the second he returned to pour another few beers that he lined up in front of her.
"My wife says all I do is get people drunk all night, tonight I'll have to go home and tell her I did way more. He will be back in on Saturday," said Chris, walking away giving some happy customers at the bar their perfectly poured beer.

Daisy's head became a human calculator figuring out how many hours were left in between now and then, her mind went into preparation of what needs to be done by then. Going into her phone and putting reminders to book a hair appointment followed by fresh manicure and pedicure. She was online looking for a new dress for Saturday when Jameson came back in from his call. Jameson looked frightened he had to go because his sister's husband was in a car accident. Everyone involved was at the moment to be ok but he had to go babysit so his sister could get more information they refused to tell her on the phone. Being a good uncle while his brother in law gave his silver Amex card to Chris, getting the whole bill.

"Sign for me, just give me the card tomorrow." Jameson said to Daisy and ran off in a flash.

Once Chris returned the check a minute later Daisy picked up the pen giving Chris a 20% tip on the receipt then pulling out a twenty dollar bill from her bag placing it in the checkbook. Thanking him for the information he provided her and to also help him remember her for future visits getting better service, even though it would be hard to forget her first visit in. She didn't mind slipping him extra cash for a job well done, it is something Daisy's father taught her that you take care of the people who take care of you, especially your bartender. Daisy's father was something of an alcoholic having an eclectic knowledge in drinking in bars.

One of the few things that really stuck, she always did because it made sense. Over the years taking care of people came back with its perks. Twenty dollars traded for the help to find out the name of a complete stranger that instantly caught her interest was a fair trade. Daisy finished off the remainder of her very last martini of the night till it was bone dry.

"Goodnight, thank you Chris." Daisy said with gratitude, putting her jacket on then her purse over her shoulder.

Once she was outside she gazed up at the stars and moon, taking a deep breath that was followed by a chill of positive energy. Understanding a glimpse of a spiritual sense of the world that she rarely felt. Euphoria entered her body as she stared up. Walking slower than usual, stepping slowly toward her car taking in the wondrous full moon. Standing at her car after opening the driver side door into the abyss of space hoping for more. Daisy stepped into her car putting the keys in the ignition then pulling away in silence.

Daisy was almost home before turning on the radio, taking in the silence of the night.

"It's hard to imagine, bigger than I could fathom. I didn't know you from Adam, but I prayed for you. I prayed for you. I prayed for you." The country song was playing, Daisy slowed getting stuck at a red light singing along with the lyrics.

A perfect opportunity for her to look up at the sky and as the song said.
"I prayed for you," at that moment looking up into the darkness she saw a laser shooting across the sky.

It was a star flying right above her, a definitive stoplight matching her thoughts. A feeling like never before coerced thought her body leaving her numb.

The light turned green and she continued to stare up at the fast light fading into the distance. The car behind her beeped the horn and so she stepped on the gas throwing her hand up and out the window for an apology. Daisy's foot felt heavy flooring the pedal mixed with booze to the point of speeding.

Returning home she threw on the kettle then proceeded to get ready for bed. In the midst of finalizing her nightly regime the kettle started howling, she finished brushing her teeth, spitting into the sink then whipping her mouth. Staggering back into the kitchen toward the banshee crying.

Grabbing a tea cup along with the matching tea plate before sounding off the kettle. This set was given to her by her grandmother. Daisy put the tea packet into the cup submerging it with boiling water. Accidentally splashing some hot water on her hand as she held onto the cup's handle Daisy flinched. After putting the kettle down she ran her burnt hand under cold water that poured down on the scorched surface of her skin. Her body felt a bit tipsy, head elsewhere. Now trying to find the answer that was haunting her with a sense of rage as her hand throbbed.

Thinking to herself about the shooting star and its purpose if there was such a thing. Cleaning up the mess of water on the countertop, she pondered at all the events of the night. Daisy began cleaning the kitchen trying to distract herself rigorously. Reorganizing the refrigerator, setting up the coffee machine for the morning, wiping down the countertops, then sweeping the wood floors.

The steam rose off her tea, you could hear the wind blow through the windows in the dining room that were wide open. Daisy walked over to the doors double checking if they were locked, walking around barefoot she was distracted by the sink that dripped before retiring for the night.

Taking a deep breath she stood still as her mind became at ease from the distractions for only a moment. Rewinding herself, she entered the kitchen and began fidgeting with the faucet to make the dripping water halt. Once she had finished that task she walked into her room to lay in bed. The second she comfortably laid on her mattress she realized that her tea cup wasn't with her. Shifting her weight out of her bedside, Daisy stood stomping back to the kitchen to grab her missing tea cup. Once her fingers touched the hot cup a picture popped into her mind.

It was Jackson sitting on the keg. Winking at her. Drinking a foamy beer. A bleak smile for a moment then all at once the images disappeared. She turned to dump the tea rapidly down the drain in anger, not even taking a sip. Retreating back to her room, setting her alarm for 6am and viciously grabbing her book. After ten pages she realized she was not paying attention, only reading the words as they emerged, not as they were. Between the lines she was reading into other things, whole scenarios that depicted in her sweet fiction.

What was different about this man?

They hardly spoke to one another. That night it took her longer than usual to fall asleep. After tossing and turning for an hour Daisy reached into her draw, reaching all the way to the back corner to grab a pill bottle. Opening the full bottle, swallowing two white tablets as recommended, washing it down with a glass of water on her night stand. Once they kicked in she was out for the count.

Chapter 3.

At precisely 6am Daisy's alarm began repeatedly beeping. In the distance the yellow glow begins to surround the clouds with the soft singing of the early morning birds that chirped. Morning dew congealed on the blades of grass. Daisy rolled over to silence her phone then turned back around trying to sleep for a few extra minutes, tossing and turning to continue her dream state. The headboard of the bed brushed by her restless hand as she tried to find it, in between dreaming and being awake.

Her head pressed down hard into the pillow shifting her weight. Watching him cutting ramped into a cedar plank salmon with a drizzle of wholegrain mustard cream sauce accented in parsley. Soft elegant music playing over the birds. People all around are laughing over candle lit dinners. In the middle of the room a loud shatter of breaking glass. Her wine glass is on the floor in a million pieces, Daisy turned violently reacting to the clash.

Looking around the room at everyone's eyes targeting her. The people around her stopped having a good time, they froze eyes locked on Daisy. Servers walked around the table to see what broke searching with tenacity.

Daisy looked down and there was nothing, no wine glass in pieces, nothing to be found. The man face that she was sitting with vanished without a trace. Dozens of eyes that were powerfully judging till she felt ill, all of a sudden they turned back to their conversations at their tables.

Daisy got up from her seat running down a hallway into the main foyer through the swinging door to the outdoors. As the door swung she saw a beautiful setting outside. Overlooking the topside of a mountain, a beautiful green landscape at sunset. The man in a suit reappeared in the distance waiting. Daisy got close enough, so close that she could reach out and touch him, the man in the tweed suit felt her behind him. He started turning toward her, just as she went to touch him her alarm clock went off again.

BEEP

BEEP

BEEP

  Quickly hitting the snooze button, Daisy aggressively flopping back on her pillow, closing her eyes to try to finish the dream. Running back to the mountain. Imagining furthermore what she remembered, to repeat and continue this beautiful scene that was vividly painted ever so perfectly. Closing her eyes tightly, wondering back down the rabbit hole. Searching for the swinging door, in her mind, nothing. Only darkness, within a minute she forgot most of what happened. Only remembering the last bit of the dream. The man in the suit on a mountain. Unable to find him she was severely pissed and popped out of the bed, opening her eyes coming back to reality.

  Pulling a white tablet out of her drawer, then getting ready for the day after ingesting. Trying to push out all thoughts of her dream, angry that she was unable to comprehend the signs. Getting ready for the day in the routine she regimented for years.

  Going to the office in the car in complete silence for over an hour. Daisy looked up at the buildings once she reached the city, admiring the architecture as fresh air blew in through the cracked window. Daisy's body was beating to a different drum taking her dream as a sign. Hoping it was an out of the norm good dream. Walking into the lobby with a smile on her face and a vanilla iced coffee.

"Good Morning," she said to all that passed.

  In such a good mood Daisy stepped into her office shutting the door taking a deep breath focusing on the positive. Putting her hand on her head feeling she was getting closer to her vision. Daisy took a sip of her coffee and proceeded to go about her day going through folders of documents and evidence blocking out all other parts of life.

Once she was fully into her work she was oblivious to her surroundings, startled by the abrupt hard knocks on the door. Ronnie opened the door and walked up to the chair in front of Daisy's desk resting her hands on the back of the chair. Ronnie's fingers freshly painted in a light purple hung off the leather chair. Daisy noticed her ring finger was empty after her romantic weekend along with a manilla folder.

"Here are the documents on case IV.10102020.CVC." Daisy's secretary Ronnie said then delicately placed them in the empty corner bin.

"How was your romantic getaway?" Daisy curiously asked, looking down at her nails once more to clarify.

"Well he did not propose, but I think he will for Thanksgiving. Hopefully, we've been dating for almost two years." Ronnie said, staring down at her empty ring finger.

"There is no need to rush it, when the right person comes at the right time everything will fall into place. Forcing something will weigh negatively on the foundation. No need to have a good thing crumble prematurely." Daisy preached seeing Ronnie's facial expression change, trying to shed light on a different form of perspective.

Daisy watched Ronnie fade out.

"Did you eat breakfast? If not, can you pick up something for us?" Daisy said, trying to change the conversation.

Ronnie agreed, shaking her head up and down with acknowledgement swiftly moving in getting closer to grab Daisy's credit card closing the door behind her. Once the door was shut Daisy pulled her glasses out, popping open then snapping them closed, dropping the case back into the drawer.

This custody case Daisy was currently working on was a nightmare, feeling the heat from her client because of the plaintiff who was borderline mental. Taking a quant breath then

Daisy quickly dove into these documents and all the drama that entailed from this particular case distracting her mind off of this man she was dreaming about. Out of sight out of mind, not able to picture him working deeper into the case happily sipping her iced coffee.

This case involved her client Roger who was fighting for split custody with his ex wife. Usually custody cases are difficult filled with ego instead of logic. This one was like someone let the crazy out of a clown car. The opposing party was not just a woman unwilling to budge on simple things, she was an unbearable vicious monster. The betrayal of morals of his ex wife led them to need to go to court far too often and spend large amounts of time and money on things that a judge would easily grant.

Roger's ex wife was the one who has the big issue, extremely irrational and delusional of what's right or what's best for the kids. Daisy personally knew the opposing counsel who was practical and logical, she had worked with him before in the past hoping he would check his client. This woman was constantly talking bad about Roger in front of the kids causing them to start to create an unbiased hate for their father due to their mothers relentless opinion. The woman constantly tells the children lies creating a false narrative. Clear cut case which highlighted extreme control issues mixed with the need to be the center of the kids universe by using scare tactics instilling fear into their hearts.

Roger was a nicely dressed well mannered successful man who had a kind face and a big heart. All he wanted to do was have his children 50% of the time, he could have gone for full custody but did not want to take his kids from their mother despite her trying to turn the kids against him. Rodger's ex-wife Linda tried to keep him from his kids at all cost. Any angle she could prevent him from having his kids she took and followed through with no remorse. Linda did it out of pure jealousy and spite because Roger after a year of separation also another a previous year into the divorce he had found himself a girlfriend. Linda constantly tried to brainwash the kids that dad was not a good person. Planting a seed in their minds that their dad left them when in fact she had run away and kept the kids from Roger months after they had their second child. Daisy always puts herself in the clients shoes to get more of an understanding of their state of emotions and how to play it. It gave her an edge on how to win, an eagle eye into the law. Daisy was purely disgusted by how this woman operated and lived her life being a mother of two children. She was completely unable to understand how a woman could be so ruthless. Linda's main objective was to hurt and prevent Roger's happiness by keeping him from his own children. Daisy could not understand how Rogers' ex Linda did not see that she was hurting the kids, striking a negative feeling of fault in their hearts blaming their own father for a tragedy constructed under insane thoughts.

    Linda displayed standard post traumatic stress syndrome mixed with complete control issues for everything, trying to weigh her kids down to her gravity and nothing more. It was as if Linda got off putting Roger down range in her crosshairs of dismay. Unstable behavior is easy to prove but the psychological conditions of mentally illness are harder to prove requiring a psychological evaluation. This process was more extreme, needing the help of a judge to start the process. If the judge denied their psychology evaluations to prove her issues, he would still get split custody. Linda thought she was right in everything she was doing, no wrongs or mistakes. Thankfully the law does not work that way, in pure delusion. Roger always says, I can not wait for a judge to put that woman in her place. Even Daisy who made a living on defending clients going through custody cases due to a divorce, felt for Roger because of his wife.

    Daisy tried her hardest to never get too emotionally invested into her cases, holding back her empathy and leaving it all at the office. Making the mistake of emotionally investing in one of her clients once cost her unneeded stress and a case of depression. Rogers' ex wife was just caught stalking, harassing, and also trespassing on his property a few weeks ago. The worst part about it, she decided to bring her fury in front of the kids at the time of each incident. Daisy read through the police report she was absolutely appalled, a grueling feeling brewed in her stomach. Looking up at the door for Ronnie to return to soak up the acid build up from feeling disgusted that bubbled in her intestines.

Linda's pattern of not being able to co-parent created repressed anxiety for far too many people. After years of being bullied by Linda, Roger finally came to Daisy after his first heart attack caused from fighting her sadistic ways. The stress of fighting with Linda insanity caused him internal trauma physically breaking him down bit by bit.

All just to be a father, only to be a presence in his kid's lives the cost was literally killing him. Roger was trying to do this without lawyers for several years with no gain. Now that the kids were getting older now able to comprehend what was going on he needed protection against this manipulative vicious woman. No one should have to go through the disgust that this woman has put this Rodger through.

Linda brought new men into the kids' lives and home abruptly after only dating for days. Roger could not do the same for his kids sake trying to teach them values. Linda tried to ruin the relationship with Rodger's current and only girlfriend like it was her full time job. Endless emails and text came to his inbox from Linda lecturing him on how he moved on too soon not seeing the ironic picture of arrogance she painted. The crazy inside her was apparent resulting in a revolving door of men to leave as quickly as they came in. Roger only wanted the kids to have a stable environment on both fronts. Linda had other ideals and a double standard for every parenting practice.

Roger collected tons of documents to prove his case, the stress logging everything was unbearable. Having to keep a comprehensive journal of time, dates and notes of every single interaction with Linda The crazy jumped off the page, so wild that foreign people that had no affiliation to this subject would think it was made up. Mentally and emotionally draining this man who is fighting to be around his children and be a permanent part of their life.

So many of Daisy's cases the man wants nothing to do with the kids or the woman's sole priority is to go after child support. Most cases had their share of drama but this one was over the river and through the woods, a crazy squirrel looking for nuts.

Daisy was by the book, to the letter of the law. This was her hardest case yet by a long shot, holding back her emotions. The man almost died because of the strain, Linda pulled him closer to his demise every day. Courts have not always been in favor of the man, but in recent years there has been some progress. Both Roger and Daisy spent hundreds of hours combining documents, preparing different orders to send to the courthouse.

Leading Roger to stress more, financially he was getting reamed since it is very expensive to have a lawyer pulse having to pay child support and alimony. In the beginning when Daisy took Rodger as a client they tried to do it peacefully, unfortunately they sat down with the opposing counsel for mediation twice getting absolutely nowhere.

The first time Daisy saw Rogers' ex wife she felt as she got a clear picture of what Linda was about. The first appearance into the court Linda came through the large court doors in a skin tight dress and knee high heels, looking like a hooker. Dressing inappropriate to court happens all the time nowadays, men wear t-shirts and shorts, women wear yoga pants and hoodie. In this new delusional era we are living in, a shocking amount of people have no class. Presenting themselves at a low level even in court, made Daisy upset for this generation. What people don't realize is that it does impact decisions by all judges. Linda tried to professionally dress for court looking like Julia Roberts in Pretty Woman. Seemed impossible to imagine but his ex pulled it off. Roger was in a three piece black suit and yellow striped tie looking proper and sane. Little things like that leave a lasting impression on the judge, intelligent people understand this.

You can see the genuine pain on Roger's face being in the same room as his ex. Not once did Roger look at her. Sickened by the grotesque aura that surrounded Linda. When Linda was on the stand Roger looked down at the paperwork, never turning to his left when Linda sat with her lawyer. Roger kept Daisy directly in his peripherals, using Daisy as a shield often joking Daisy was an attorney at wall instead of attorney at law.

When Daisy interrogated Linda she was all over the place, circling around a web of lies. Frantically trying to get her story straight as she spewed fictional stories. Linda's statement was like a symphony rising louder with every lie, lowering in the few moments she was actually telling the truth. Daisy unloaded question after question knowing Linda would lie. Daisy set a perfect trap to create a clear picture of who Linda really was, a control freak and manipulative liar. Roger heard Daisy expose his ex, filled with good notions putting his hands together with relief. After Linda was caught several times, realizing she was lying being stumped by Daisy Linda began to cry, the water works turned up to level ten.

Daisy stopped to let her ball, Linda proceeded to make a fool of herself up on stand frantically crying. The last question Daisy asked was the nail in the coffin for Linda. Swaying the judge's decision in Rogers favor. Roger looked so relieved and happy that it was finally over. In the back of his mind he knew his ex got what she deserved. One slam from the gavel would not be the end to her ruthless crusade sadly. Relentlessly adamant on control, Linda was never going to stop pushing for full control. Gloating that they were solely her children and never their children.

Finally a foot in the right direction for his kids, his heart was truly gladdened. Sadly his mind knew his ex would never stop as long as she had air in her lungs. A mentally delusional person needing to be the dictator of everything without regard of morality, especially restricting access for Roger to have anything to do with her children. Roger left the courtroom as soon as possible creating distance between his ex, he was not able to smile or truly appreciate what had happened yet as long as she was near.

Roger's file went across Daisy's desk just seven months later. Linda had straightened up her act, not been up to her usual nonsense just long enough that in a court of law it was proof that she had *changed*. Only after a short few months the court basically forgets the past if behavior has changed good or bad. Linda's lawyer must have told her that and she followed it out to the day. Daisy and Roger became speed dial buddies once more as the manipulation started more than ever after that day, since the file crossed her desk she has been on top of it trying to help Roger prevail over evil. Now Linda conjured up the idea to go for full custody along with court costs that she incurred because of Roger's refusal to submit to her tyrannical rules acting like she was an outstanding law abiding citizen.

Dismally every time she saw the case number run across her desk it depressed Daisy quite a bit, back to the parade of this wild circus. She took pride in winning the first case for Roger. Doing her best for clients everyday, she felt like she was the balance of the law in a heroic manner helping the innocence. The hardest part was getting the less cooperative parent attune to the orders that are set out. Daisy felt like she was doing her part, keeping kids around parents who loved them or getting manipulated by the law that needed reform. Unfortunately it resonates with her and her earlier years in life.

After reading over some of Roger's case and the new bullshit Linda had pulled for only a few minutes Daisy had a massive migraine. Digging into her egg bagel toasted with cream cheese that Ronnie just brought her in, after taking a big bite and whipping the cream cheese off her lips she put her glasses on pushing through her work for the day fighting her migraine. Looking up after hours, her head was deep in this file, taking off her glasses Daisy began rubbing her eyes. A change of scenery and break was needed to decompress the pressure in her brain. She gathered her things and drove to a nearby coffee club that had a very mellow classy work from home vibe. They served pastries along with dessert like coffee cocktails and light sandwiches for lunch. The creations themselves were a work of art both decadent and delicious.

The decor inside the club was modern with a classical feel, then a strange checkerboard ceiling to uniquely blend it all together in such a beautiful way. There were lots of mystics all throughout the club that mastered a focal factor. A few plants hung off shelves and throughout the sitting area making it feel welcoming and homey. During the day it was a gourmet coffee club and at night was more of a social club for business professionals, the drinks were outstanding and the dinners were always divine. The bar was open all day but many people during the day liked to work quietly by themselves, maybe partaking in having a few drinks while they worked in the afternoon. Daisy liked that aspect of the club, a good place to get a rush of caffeine then use that rush to knock out some work in a different environment getting some fresh perspectives. She was sipping on her strawberry pie cocktail with oat milk, fresh strawberry puree filled with a double espresso under a layer of whipped cream topped with thinly sliced strawberries and graham cracker crumbs.

  Daisy caught herself getting distraught, suddenly she began thinking about the man from the bar some more. Trying to make out every detail of him, she started with his hands, how they were both covered in tattoos of black ink flowing up from the fingernail up. She couldn't make out what the ink depicted exactly, only noticing the bulk of shades. His sleeves were only half rolled up to a length that showed a cluster of tattoos that completely covered the whole of his exposed skin. She could see a few veins popping out in the contrast of the light while he moved the heavy keg with his bare hands. One thing for certain that she did make out for sure, well what all women look at when they check out a man. His ring finger was empty, no band of any kind. Strangely enough it was solid black, definitely darker and solidly filled than any other finger but it was dark. Daisy could swear she noticed his ring finger had a raised surface below the knuckle on his hand. A gold ring on both of his pinky and middle fingers made the empty black finger in between, making it stick out more. Curiously wondering about this man that she barely got a glimpse of, Daisy pulled out her phone remembering to check in with her friend to see when they all would join her to go back to the new restaurant Half Full.

  Sipping up a gulp of her strawberry coffee cocktail through a copper straw she paused taking a whiff of a pungent smell attached to the man who just sat down beside her. Daisy looked over quickly at the man who had his jet black hair slicked back sitting over on the right side of her. Had a navy cashmere long sleeve shirt tucked into light gray pleated dress pants. Looking down, examining him quickly with her peripherals feeling guilty for checking him out.

His marron thatched leather boots rested on the bottom bar metal foot rest, elbows on the bartop leaning forward. He took off his sunglasses, Daisy glanced at him trying to be sly. Trying to be modest but in reality she was trying to get his attention to turn her way. Daisy began playing with her hair with her right hand. She leaned to the edge of her seat to act as she was repositioning for comfort now having a better perspective of him, his hands! Looking directly at his hands the air was sucked out of her lungs, her heart abruptly started pulsating when she noticed his hands were tattooed and his left ring finger was black in between two gold rings. Daisy now felt like a nervous wreck.

    Completely unprepared in disarray of this paradox she unintentionally got herself into. Secretly she was fantasizing about him since the other night, just a few moments before she was trying to picture him and his hands were the first thing that popped into her brain. Now like a premonition he appeared in the flesh. Her body began to feel hot, her stomach became the breeding ground of cocoons that hatched hundreds of butterflies fluttering around in her lower intestine. Daisy was on the verge of sweating, inhaling deeply and exhaling out of her mouth drying out her lips. As she was terrified he looked so calm, cool and collective sitting in complete comfort.

    The man looked back and forth for the barista on duty. The man shifted his body toward her, he saw her eyes lingering in his personal space and gave a sexy half smirk. It was like he knew what she was up to, playfully commending her for her efforts of secret flirtation style because it got his attention. He turned his head looking at Daisy, his eyes were like a tractor beam pulling her.

"Hi," Jackson said, he was saying that to be polite at first but after looking deep in her eyes and getting a good look at her Jackson realized her and his face lit up, changing his tone and demeanor.

"Herd you were asking about me." Jackson said, instantly he turned to the barista that approached catching Daisy completely off guard.

"What's going on Jackson, what are you drinking my man?" Asked the barista resting his body weight on the bartop.

"I'll have a double Irish coffee, thanks Mark."

Jackson turned back to Daisy who was still stunned her lips were numb. She continued to look over at that tattooed man, envious of how calm and collective he was. Her body was completely paralyzed, her eyes were the only thing able to move but they could not look at anything but him. Daisy's blue eyes were fragile looking him over. Jackson smiled as a moment of awkward beauty waiting for a response, he knew he put her in a corner. Jackson could not get over how beautiful she was. On the outside Daisy had a lot going for her, that advantage gave her time to look cute and nervous. His dark brown eyes inspected every bit of her, on the inside at this second she was absolutely petrified, over thinking a mile a minute. Daisy's mind raced around to think of something to say, fumbling to get words to exit her mouth.

"Ohhhh, you're the guy from the bar." Daisy said nearly incapacitated with fear.

"Yes the guy from the bar, the bar you happen to be at the other night."

Daisy smiled and tilted her head, unable to look anywhere else. Jackson looked right back smiling.

"You're Daisy, Chris tipped me off about you. Now I'll formally introduce myself, I'm Jackson."

Daisy stared at him in awe, locking into his dark eyes. He spoke with such conviction, Jackson extended his hand out glowing in confidence. Flabbergasted by her current situation she stared at his hand first. Daisy's brain was frozen but her hand instinctively moved to shake after a moment of lag, she extended hand. Their skin touched, his fingers felt down her soft skin taking his time before locking hands with her. Once their hands locked fierce feelings swarmed her, an unfathomable exchange of energy sparked. Continuing to shake, then holding on for longer than any other handshake they had ever experienced. Jackson smiled looking down at her hand still locked with his. Daisy looked down as well noticing they were still holding on, she did not want to but she released her tender touch.

"Well I hate to tell you that you were uninformed. I did not ask about you." Snapping at him insecurely in defense.

After licking his lips he turned to his left, two pretty blue eyes waited.

"Really?" Jackson responded charismatically leaning in his seat crossing his arms giving her the floor to explain further her argument.

"Really! Your friend Chris is it? He gave your name to me without me asking." Daisy said her cheeks turned red, her guard was up responding back feisty.

"Why would he go doing a thing like that now?" Jackson quickly snapped back putting his hands together in his lap after putting her in checkmate

Daisy knew she could not continue on, he had correct information and was using it to his advantage. Honestly she had no idea why she lied to him, he had an overpowering aura that surrounded him and she did not want to seem too interested. Daisy smiled, enjoying the kind way he was looking, hiding his smirk.

"Hello Jackson. I'm Daisy, but you knew that already," She spat out quickly to try to change the subject, caught like a deer in headlights.

"Yes, I was informed. It is lovely to meet you Daisy." Jackson paused after he spoke looking back towards the bar he nodded at Mark who dropped off his Irish coffee, pulling it in close, wafting the perfect blend of coffee, whiskey and baileys.

Jackson smiled, bringing the hot glass of coffee and whiskey up to his lips. Daisy continued to watch him as he swallowed, opening his mouth to take a breath the steam released from his mouth like a dragon.

Daisy's heart radiated with an odd feeling, her body felt light as a feather. Looking peculiar at Jackson's mannerisms, his scent was consuming her. Thoroughly assessing the idiosyncrasy of his hand, fully shaded holding the tall glass coffee mug.

"Chris may have been exaggerating then." Saying right before indulging back into his steamy coffee, slowly raising it to his mouth like he was on camera. Daisy observed him softly blowing, making ripples in the liquid under a cloud of cream trying to cool it down so he didn't burn himself.

"Exaggerating? Exaggerating about?" Daisy said and straightened up her back viewing his lips wrapped around the glass, bizarrely intrigued.

Jackson licked the whipped cream off of his top lip after a sip, then wiping his mouth with his hand. His two gold rings shone in the light, a bit of steam came out of his mouth as she continued to inspect him. Daisy leered at him drinking to completion till the mug hit the countertop. Placing the handled glass back in the very center of the coaster of the bar Jackson's head was facing the liquor behind the bar feeling her reviewing eyes.

Smiling, he sat calmly, his shoulders square in his seat, elbows still on the bar. Daisy's body was horizontal along with the bar with her hands in her lap wanting to inquire more. Her body eagerly faced him. Daisy patiently waited for his response but Jackson was enjoying the time he was having, he knew she was examining him up and down continuously. Two blue eyes drifted from his boots to the top of his head, then back down the faded shaved side of his head stopping at his bulging shoulder blades.

Jackson sat there knowing exactly what he was doing, adding to her anticipation. Continuing to build up Daisy's suspense as he silently drew her in. Turning her head right at him with full interest, Daisy was hardcore biting her lip making it obvious she wanted him to turn. He put out playful bait and let her chase. Daisy was hooked now, working for his attention subconsciously. After a brief intermission Jackson turned and leaned into her close, with direct eye contact smirking ready with a response.

"Chris said that you were drooling when you saw me, looking like a sad puppy dog after I left." Jackson said holding direct eye contact until Daisy shied away turning red. Jackson didn't bat an eye, not moving an inch and waited for her to look back.

Daisy felt his steady credence, her jaw was still dropped hiding the fact he was right. Daisy looked back wanting to admit he was right and neither of them blinked, they stared into one another's eyes intently. Daisy's wit was halted dead in her tracks having no comeback or explanation. The two did not break eye contact if someone had fired a gun or broken a glass neither of them would notice. They both felt stuck in place at the moment magnetized on each other as if they were meant to collide. Daisy's pearly white teeth emerged, her cheeks started to rise, smiling so hard it began to hurt. Jackson smirked but it was barely seen though his thick dark beard. Though his uncontrollably smile continued to grow seeing her blush, Daisy was able to see a glimpse of Jackson teeth that appeared under the vastness of his neatly kept beard. Daisy grabbed her drink bringing it to her mouth blindly bound by the magnetic gaze. The dead silence staring contest was interrupted by Mark dropping off some peanut butter cookies with a chocolate syrup dipping sauce on the side.

"It's on me guys." Mark said he had been on the other side of the bar watching the two of them light up the whole place with pure happiness.

    Both of them looked at eachother surprised at the pile of cookies in front of them, Jackson put his hand out for Daisy to dig in first. Grabbing the biggest cookie breaking it in half giving Jackson the other half. Dipping her half into the warm syrup, getting as much of the cookie dunked.. Jackson accepted his half of the cookie as his eyebrows flared with her thoughtless action, after Daisy's cookies were dripping in chocolate he took his turn to dip the cookie in. Jackson raised his cookie up in the air, pausing, waiting for Daisy to cheers him. Daisy had her mouth wide open about to put the cookie drizzled in chocolate into her mouth. Before biting down or getting a taste she pulled it out of her mouth. They cheered their peanut butter cookies dripping in chocolate as if they were the finest glass of wine. No clink of the glass yet heads turned to the pitch of the crumbs falling. Chocolate dripping on the counter and down her fingers laughing trying not to make more of a mess or ruin their nice clothing.

"Here are free cookies and good information." Jackson said toasting after touching cookies.

    Daisy's cookie was smothered, she couldn't get all the syrup in her mouth. Licking off her lips, another taste of the succulent chocolate to add to her repertoire. Jackson reached over, whipping a dab of syrup right under Daisy's lip that she missed. Jackson licked the chocolate off his finger as she watched in astonishment. Between the rush from the sugar and watching him captivatingly lick the chocolate that was just under her lips she regained a sense of tenaciousness.

"Well, I told him you piqued my interest, I'm not stalking you! Seeing you here was a coincidence." Daisy said as she took another bite finishing off her half of the cookie.

"Purely a coincidence. Naturally I sat next to a pretty woman with files all over the bar because I knew she would not want to talk. I came here for a quiet drink to get my mind right for my shift. I was going to get your name next time you came into the bar." Jackson said, charmingly hiding his smile with the coffee mug.

"How did you know I'd be back?" Daisy inquired leaning up in her seat.

"I saw the way you looked at me, even for a moment I knew. I've bartended for way too long! I hear and see everything, causing me to pick up on social cues. Able to read people all too well, it's my bartender sense," Jackson made a gesture like he was casting some kind of magical spell from a crystal ball.

The pair of them both laughed for the next hour, time didn't feel like it was ticking. Paused in a wrinkle in time feeling like six hours had passed. After being done with their drinks for quite some time Jackson asked for the check when he saw Mark walk by.

"Jackson, the ladies in the corner took care of your bill." Mark said he wanted to watch Jackon turn, Jackson squinted his eyes in the direction Mark pointed searching for the anonymous payees.

"Oh the ladies got your bill, you must come here often or maybe..." Daisy said.

"The ladies that took care of the bill, they said that it looked like you two were falling in love and enjoyed being around it." Mark said, cutting Daisy's sentence short.

Stunned they both turned to thank the ladies behind them waving after Mark pointed out exactly who they were. Mark gathered up the empty plate of cookies along with the dry mugs taking them back to the dishwasher.

"Interesting day today." Jackson said, pulling out a money clip from his pocket shaking his head laughing to himself.

"Agreed," Daisy said, taken back by what happened in the past few hours, her wet dream from the other night filled retraced in her mind as she watched Jackson thumb through his stack of money with his veiny hands.

"Maybe I should play the lotto, keep this winning streak alive. Free cookies, free Irish coffee and you." Jackson said staring off into the distance deep in thought like he was composing a master plan in one's mind.

"And me?"

"Yes you. Pretty eyes of blue," Jackson spoke like a true poet.

Surrendering herself, letting out a powerful exhale letting out a sexy expressive vibration in the back of her throat causing a low muffled squeal. The notion of his word had a tight grip on her, weighing her down just enough that she would not float away. Without haste effortlessly intruding into her sentiment with his insight of a divine energy. Taking her to new heights by mere words. Honestly it was more than just the words, it was the manner in which they were said that took her emotions through the storm. Daisy's neglected desires stuck on bookshelves in the back of her mind full of dust, were now wide open intuitively. Jackson had surpassed every encounter Daisy experienced with any other human of the opposite sex she met in her life in an extremely daunting duration. Salacious visions preoccupied her as a buildup of tension made Daisy clench the more her mind continued to wander in thought. The pulsating feeling spread throughout her body throbbing with underlying sensations maliciously trying to take her soul from her body. With no inhibition bringing out her inner animal. Waves shook the rocks, her legs in anguish tingling the closer she got to shore, almost through the storm. Having a deep concealed gasp, she hid her mouth. Putting her head down and closing her eyes. Daisy's body constricted fighting it, bringing that surge sensations to a prompt termination. Surviving without being caught, subtle shivers coerced down her spine seamlessly playing it off like she was chilly.

Jackson pulled out a $10 bill from his money clip while Daisy had her moment of solitude. Having the cash in hand trying to get Mark's attention by waving it in the air, but he was too engaged in his work. Jackson let out a high pitched whistle to get his attention, startling Daisy in the midst of coordinating herself back from a close to outer body experience. Jackson put the bill on the bar top after Mark turned his way. Mark finished stacking clean coffee mugs on the shelf, wrapping up his conversations with the other barista then grabbed his phone and keys from behind the register, proceeding to walk to Jackson.

"Thanks for the cookies, they were phenomenal. I don't have a sweet tooth at all but I approve of them!" Jackson said, showing admiration rubbing his stomach that was full.

Mark looked down at the money, his head lowered down then his eyes rose up not moving his head so he was not looking through his glasses anymore but over the lenses looking Jackson in the eyes with a meaningful demeanor. Daisy thought that Mark was mad at Jackson and perhaps he was in trouble by the way he was looking at him. Mark placed his long pointer finger on the cash sliding it on the bartop back to Jackson.

"Watching you two interact is an exceedingly better tip than money." Mark said looking at Jackson then Daisy, praising them both before he walked around to the end of the bar heading toward the exit.

The couple spun their bodies around watching him every step of the way, his long hook earrings pulled down his ear lob with a lego figure that swung side to side as he made his way to the main glass doors. The sunshine was overly bright, Mark disappeared into the shiny rays. The two ladies who took care of the bill were in the head wind close to the closing door. Another wave of admiration was sent their way beaming with happiness.

The pair slowly turned back from the coffee club entrance and caught themselves looking at each other in awe. Incredulous, both in otter shock of the series of events of the last minutes. Shell shocked looking at each other with mystery. Daisy began to feel hot again, her stomach filled with butterflies. Thinking to herself this can not be real, there is no way that just happened. She began to fantasize Jackson taking her hand, pressing his body on her and meeting lips. Getting the same overwhelming feelings she got in her most recent dreams. Jackson noticed Daisy pinched her arm, coming to the conclusion she was trying to make sure this was not a dream.

"No, we are not dreaming!" He said.

Jackson took a long pause, like the inner poet was going to come out again.
"You're going to have to trust me on this." Giving an alluring affirmation as he spoke.

Daisy was all smiles, she was a lot of things at this moment placing her hands on her legs laying them together on her upper thigh only inches from where the waves crashed. Almost able to feel the outcome of the splash.
"Okay."
"I honestly was going to do this anyway but now it seems that the signs from the world are forcing me to ask you out sooner than expected." Jackson said, reaching over and pinching her arm making it very clear again without words.

Daisy completely understood, like they were developing a language all their own. She smiled as her playful mind stirred up.
"Forcing you? The world is holding you against your will to ask me out?" Daisy accurately tried correcting his sentence with a flirtatious spin.

Jackson didn't move, his frame steady without hesitation from her wit. His eyes painted a picture, stern and sound that spoke to her. Trying not to get lost in his eyes, she bit her lip intimidated by his answer. Even though words were chosen specifically from the start he made his intentions apparent with his eyes.

"Yes, it seems the forces of the universe are making it quite clear. Only under these circumstances, I must agree to go out with you for the survival of mankind." Daisy resiliently responded with sarcasm to off put his gritty regard.
"Friday night at 7:30pm I'll pick you up, wear a dress." Jackson unlocked his phone and handed it to Daisy to punch in her phone number.
"Ok, 7:30pm Friday night." Daisy said while nervously putting her number in his phone, her fingers vibrated with each number she punched in.

  Her nerves were spiraling out of control letting him in the door to her life, curious what other new feelings to her body he could bring out. Already his spicy tune had her shivering without physical touch.

  Daisy was putting in her phone number and Jackson looked at his watch. Realizing they had been there for over two hours. Jackson grabbed his phone back when Daisy was done and stood up hinting he needed to leave. Daisy looked at her watch as well after he stood and gasped. Freaking out that she had taken a long lunch break, it was not like her.
"I gotta run, but I will pick you up Friday. It was a pleasure finally meeting you Daisy." Jackson said, making his way toward the door in a slow enough pace for Daisy to follow.

  Biting her lip and waving goodbye, not able to put words together to say goodbye. Daisy gathered all her files quickly putting them in her bag, still stunned at what just happened she was distracted. Still looking in his way resulted in her dropping some of her things since she was not fully paying attention. Taking a deep breath and bending down to pick up the papers off the floor, Jackson bends down helping her, he appears out of nowhere to block out the glare of the sun. She smiled and calmly finished putting the last few papers away into her bag. Walking toward the door together, once they stepped outside the sun hit their skin creating an outer glow. The pair both stopped in the middle of the sidewalk and shifted their weight in the direction they needed to go, both having to go in opposite ways. They locked eyes saying goodbye with no words just by genuine lustful expressions before going their separate ways.

Butterflies flew around in her stomach all the way back to the office. Daisy's realm had become extraordinary walking with determination feeling completely recharged. The intense fantasy personified from manifesting it subconsciously. The vivid replay reeled over and over in her mind, every moment. Scenes were pieced together from her dreams in no particular order, some of the bar, the coffee club shuttered though her mind. Friday couldn't come any faster filled with end possibilities that could come from this one date.

    The work on her desk became less intriguing, for the first time ever her work became mondane. Flipping through pages that looked all the same, blobs of ink on blank paper unable to focus. She had read the same piece of paper seven times and not retained a thing.

    Grabbing an extra espresso and snacks throughout the day to help put her in focus. It felt as if deja vu had consumed her and awakened a different side of her that was always there all along but it was always very shy. Afraid to let it out of the cage, deciding to release her inner animal in her own time for the right reason, not anyone who randomly popped into her life. Completely different thoughts ran rampant through her head, this new reality distracted her mind of her normal obligations.

    New reasoning devoured her mind's livelihood, resonating deeply. The daily routine changed in spirit, everything had enhanced in her. Touching the bushes with her finger tips squeezing gently without snapping the fraile leaves. Taking a break outside in the day after she met Jackson, decompressing in nature from her cumbersome workload. Walking back to work after lunch, Daisy enjoyed the sun beating down on her face feeling it heat up her skin. Taking the last chunk of her break sitting by the river at lunch admiring everything around her. The energy of everything going on around her she was now able to absorb. Taking small bites savoring all of the notes and flavor profiles her prosciutto caprese sandwich had to offer. Daisy stared into the water flowing, watching each ripple sparkling from the reflective sunshine. The shimmering body of water mesmerized Daisy as she finished off her sandwich.

The co-workers in Daisy's office were sparked by her good vibes, more talkative charmed by Daisy's charisma. Coming out of her solitude and breaking away from her shell appearing out of the darkness. In the last week she had become the new favorite throughout her floor bringing homemade cookies as she was inspired to recreate the cookies from the coffee club. It was a huge hit, people continued going on about how tasty they were all day. Adding a chocolate syrup dipping sauce was pure genius.

Daisy began to drink more water and juice trying to dilute her body's need for loads of caffeine. Now waking up early in the morning with the sunrise, outside in her tennis shoes with the morning sun the cool air taking a quick walk.

Flashbacks shuttered through her mind like a set of polarized photos. Her body felt high with no drugs, her skin sleek with no lotions, her mind full with no thought. The sight of her admirer's hands cruised into her vision more than once a day. Different scenarios flew through her brain, longing for his touch. The movie in her mind played in the days that neared their first date with blissful anticipation. The classic cliche finessed her heart as her brain thought it through fully.

The clock struck 4pm in the office, she had been counting down the minutes. Daisy hit the spacebar to pause the music on her computer playing moderately to get her through the day. Gathering her things quickly hopping from cloud to cloud as she left the work, walking out of her building Daisy's smile could be seen from five miles away. Humming the last song that played on her computer all the way to the salon, singing the song aloud.
 "Bottle of red, bottle of white."

This tune was stuck in her head, the instruments and chorus played in her head rent free. Daisy checked into her 4:30pm appointment at the nail salon. She instantly began checking out all the different shades of polish trying to select the perfect color to make her nails pop to grab his attention. Imagining what colors would contrast beautifully with his dark tattooed hands, wanting to touch them once more.

After selecting her choice in polish she began to preplan her outfit selection for the main event in a few hours. Going through the list of dresses she had in her closet in her mind, still humming. After a few minutes her technician was ready for her and called her back to take a seat. Once she sat down she handed the polish across the table. Daisy was suddenly asked a question by the technician, strangely the same words she had been humming in her mind. "Would you like a glass of red wine or white wine?"

Daisy looked up with a blank stare, looking right past her gazing off in the distance. The question seemed convoluted, still singing the line over and over in her head subconsciously. The salon vanished with a single blink, a white tablecloth with two empty wine glasses appeared. Place setting wrapped up on the table and a small white candle in the center of the table. A basket of bread covered with a white napkin over the loaf keeping its heat in, perfectly matched with oil and vinegar sitting beside the basket. Her mind drifted along seeing the waiter come over with a bottle of wine. The white label had some raised texture along the outline with sharp edges. A bright blue foil at the top of the bottle covering the cork. The dark almost black bottle came closer looking like a bottle of red wine.

"Red wine please." Daisy said to the technician, opening her eyes, arriving back in the salon.

The polish covered her fresh smooth manicured nails with Ruby Red. Watching the technician's aptitude with each brush stroke. Sipping the wine while her nails were being colored, the wine was not half bad for a nail salon. Bold flavor with notes of chocolate and berries swished through her mouth leaving medium tannins on the back of her tongue. In comparison her nails were a few shades lighter than the dried grape juice disappearing from her wine glass. Daisy's visions were surreal, dazing off into oblivion. The euphoria filled her body during the visions, always ending on the brink of suspense.

Nails painted check, she began thinking again of what to wear heading back to her place. Strikingly her outfit choice eluded, thinking of every other detail for the most anticipated event. The clock struck 5:25pm as she pulled into her driveway. Two hours to get ready is cutting it close, the bliss she was feeling for days deflated. Nervously spinning around her closet picking outfit after outfit. A black flowered romper was cute and casual, magnifying her curves. The next outfit was a dark green blouse with leather pants tightly gripping her legs. Tank tops, dresses, skinny jeans, dress pants, short skirts piled on her bed creating a mountain of fabric. Emptying her closet she realized that she had no idea where they were even going. Daisy certainly did not want to be overdressed, but underdressed would give a crummy persona of character. Scanning through the clothes touching each one feeling the fabrics texture before deciding. Tags were still on a good amount of items that hung in the closet, never worn or shown off to the world.

    Pushing aside the inferior garments she remembered Jackson did say for her to wear a dress. Daisy grabbed a brand new dress that she had forgotten about and immediately knew this was the one. Walking over to the counter top in the bathroom drawer she grabbed a pair of scissors to snip the tag off clean. After a clean cut right though she placed the scissor back neatly in the organized drawer putting it in its place then pushing on the purple crystal drawer handle.

    The dress was charcoal made of linen that tied around her neck with a gold chain, another gold linked chain attached to the dress dangled freely across the small of her exposed back. Her freshly painted nails complemented the dress wonderfully, her look was somber. Now just hair, wait also heels she thought to herself as she admired her dress in the mirror. Daisy did not wear much makeup so that would be done in no time. Only mascara, eyeshadow and lip gloss was all she really used, all that could be done in about five minutes.

     Looking over at the small digital clock that just turned 6:39pm. Daisy plugged in her Airwrap multi styler and straightener then looked through her heel collection as it heated. Comparing each choice with another rival. White suede zebra print on the left foot and a tobacco leather on the right, assimilation in the mirror. Stepping away with two different heels to go into her jewelry box. It was like a gold and diamond mine, Daisy put in her gold studded diamonds in her ears spinning the backs that screwed in for full security. Once they were securely in her ears she grabbed her double clasped golden diamond tennis bracelet without looking for another possible option for her wrist. Running her fingers through her necklaces that swung on her stand trying to decide, she smelt the smoldering heat of her straightener. Heels clacked on the hardwoods walking back into the bathroom giving a quick look at herself when she passed the mirror of the two different heels still trying to figure out which to wear.

No fire, good! When she finished making her hair soft and straight it was 7:12pm. He could be here any minute realistically, she did not know how punctual he is yet. Hurrying to give him the benefit of the doubt on being on time. The perfume scented the bathroom like lavender, minty freshness filled her mouth as she brushed her teeth returning into the closet once again to grab her final decision of heels. She reached into cubby on the first layer of her tiered heel organizer grabbing a pair that helped contrast her whole outfit, being a new pair that she did not try on yet and honestly forgot she even owned.

Jackson pulled up at 7:28pm in a boxy black 1980s Cadillac Eldorado accented with a lot of shiny chrome around the body of the car. The glossy black paint covered with splotchy water marks that had not dried fully after the car wash he had visited just minutes ago. Stepping out onto the concrete he walked around the car and the sun was shining on him. A large shadow followed him on the way up the brick walkway outlined with large river rock all the way up to the front stoop. Running his hand through his hair making sure it was slicked back and set in place. Stepping up three stairs he saw his faint reflection through the glass screen door.

Knock... Knock... Knock..

Knocking on the door at exactly 7:30pm with a firm beat on the door. Daisy heard the thuds double checking how dolled up she was in the mirror, looking down to confirm if she had matching heels before stepping out of her room. The gold shined, the diamonds gleamed and her skin was glowing. Applying the last bit of glossy flavored maroon lip gloss before heading toward the front door. With each step toward the door she became more nervous. Her hand on the door handle taking a deep breath with her eyes closed, turning the squared knob and swinging the door open to her much anticipated interaction with him. Beginning to get warmer with every inch the door opened.

  Once the door opened, Jackson took a step back ever so slowly seductively looking her up, staring down at her shiny gold glitter heels. Jackson's eyes were drowned with lusted desire until he got to her eyes, stopping at her beautiful gaze.

  Daisy was stunned he looked so distinguished standing there admiring her. The two didn't say anything, but they both said enough with their eyes as Daisy opened the glass screen door. Jackson reached out his hand with complete composure. Daisy looked down and reached out her hand then looked back up in his brown eyes. Their middle fingers touched, sparking an instantaneous connection that melted Daisy. Jackson's wrist spun to have his hand now on top, his fingers slid on her gentle skin, their ring and index finger touched continuing before stopping at the palm. Jackson's thumb squeezed on her pinky then they locked hands. Daisy was consumed by his grip submitting to his direction. Without a word he bound her, setting off an eruption of wild butterflies that scattered around her stomach. Jackson guided her to the passenger side of the car holding her hand the whole way, the sun shining their way. Jackson smiled at Daisy, looked her up and down again leaning to open her door. Leaning in he smelt her perfume, his lip was so close to her ear it sent shivers up her spine feeling his warm breath on her skin. Jackson scented her pheromones pulsating out of her body, putting his hand on the small of her back.

"You." Jackson took a breath smelling lavender on her neck.

"Look." Taking a longer breath in.

"Absolutley fucking gorgeous." Jackson said putting so much emphasis on those three words then licked his lips, his animal instinct wanted to take her right there and then.

Daisy quivered noticeably, Jackson smiled looking at her shake. She smiled with her eyes closed enjoying how he was making her feel. The flame grew into a wildfire.

"Now get in the car, gorgeous." Jackson said, guiding her into the car with one hand on her hip and the other holding her hand.

Daisy sat down nervously reaching under her touching the leather seat while Jackson walked around the car making sure there were no puddles from the waterfall that just took place. Actualizing that rushing to get ready she had missed a certain garment of clothing. Daisy's body was tingling in a way she had not experienced yet. Crossing her legs placing her hands on her knees holding onto her dress. Jackson stared at her through the windows as he approached the driver side door. He was a silhouette in the sun. A loud creak sounded as he pulled the heavy door open. Jackson got in the car and put the keys in the ignition then turned to Daisy smiling, once she made eye contact he winked then cranked up the car. Putting the car in drive then running his hand on the wood grain radio dashboard, his fingers pushed in a cassette. The music that bega to play set an intense vibe mixed with mellow tones.

"We have the same taste." Daisy said.

"In?" He said, looking at her with excitement.

"Your shoes, the color. I have a pair that I almost wore tonight that are tobacco leather as well."

"Did you want to wear matching outfits on the first date? If you want I can turn around," Jackson said with his hand on the wheel ready to turn.

"Negative," Instantly Daisy whispered as her face grew long, hiding her bottom teeth under her bottom lip, pressing her teeth together, her tongue rubbing the roof of her mouth.

"So I have a question for you." He paused looking her up and down.

"Do you have a stylist, or do you just put yourself together this well all the time?" Jackson said, holding the wheel staring off into the sunset.

"My stylist took off today, I did what I could." Daisy said, flicking her hair that was still warm from straightening.

Jackson grin widened rubbing down on his beard with an open hand disguising how hard his cracking laughter was. When the next song came on, he cranked up the volume. The music sounded familiar to Daisy. It was the jingle in her head all day. Daisy was breathless, fulfilled. Her jaw dropped when the chorus started "Bottle of white, bottle of red."

"This can't be real." Daisy said softly as the goosebumps blossomed.

Jackson did not hear her; it was spoken in such a low octave. He began to sing along while Daisy was in her mind not fully comprehending her very reality. Daisy cracked the window, the cool breeze hit her face. The car slowed, eventually stopping for the red light and he was still singing the words. Jackson was tapping his fingers on the wheel leaning back in his seat and put his arm around the back of her headrest. Jackson fingers were in between the metal bars of the head rest. She felt the finest touch in her hair as he got comfortable, forcing her to turn his way.

They were both connected in a silent staring contest. A horn beeps behind them, the light had been green for a prolonged time. Jackon hit the gas, not straying away from her. Her blue eyes grew brighter with the help of the sun. Jackson finally took his eyes off her, placing them on the road even though he did not want to.

Daisy hummed along and really listened to every word in the song. Every song that came on on their drive spoke to her. Jackon parked in the far back in a secluded area of the parking lot by a lamp post. The ignition cut off, the windows were rolled up. Jackson did not hit the unlock button, manually pulling on the lock on the driver side. Jackson stepped out around the front of the car with his keys in hand, holding the key and then put them in the door to unlock her side. The heavy door creaked as he swung it open. Jackson extended his arm assisting her out like royalty. Her glitter heels hit the floor stepping out of the car feeling like a goddess in real life.

Wearing only a dress and jewels, nothing else! Embracing her accidental nakedness holding his hand. She watched Jackson undressing her with his eyes. When the wind blew she felt a cool draft up her thighs. Daisy was on edge but excited for tonight.

"Are you hungry?" Jackson said as he led the way holding her hand to the restaurant.

Daisy nodded her head stepping up over the curb off the blacktop. Jackson held the door for her then quickly maneuvered stepping in front of her to greet the host. Looking around Daisy knew it was an Italian restaurant, the paintings on the walls were filled with classical artwork of fine grapes, white table cloths with wine glass already on the empty tables, a server grinding fresh pepper tableside, gaudy furniture and decor screamed fine Italian dining. Jackon leaned to the host, Daisy only heard the word "King," during their exchange. The place was small, voices echoed throughout the rooms walls. The host took the couple to their table in the corner. Jackson pulled out cash for the host then pulled out Daisy's chair. Jackson sat down back to the wall, within seconds the server stepped over. Jackson pulled out cash already folded, handing it to the server discreetly while the server passed out the menus. The server did not seem surprised, then he greeted the couple going through the lovely specials for the evening.

"Grab you a cocktail to start off then a bottle of wine?" The server said looking back and forth at Daisy ending with Jackson.

"Bottle of red, and a bottle of white." Jackson said, pointing to two different bottles on the wine list.

Daisy bit down on her lip, watching Jackson flick his finger through the wine menu. Once he noticed her stare after he selected the wine he put the menu down not breaking eye contact. Another server dropped off a basket of bread with a napkin over it keeping in the warmth. A tray with oil and vinegar was served on a silver platter with gold foiled sticks of butter. Daisy caught herself breathless again. Jackson put his hand on the table, his ring clinked on the water glass once he grabbed it and took a sip.

"I have to use the restroom." Daisy said feeling lightheaded, warm and overwhelmed.

Jackson stood up with her, not sitting down until she was away from the table and on her way down the hall to the restroom.

Daisy went through the wood paneled door intently getting there as fast as possible, turning on the cold water to the coldest temperature. Splashing some water on her face staring into the mirror right back into her blue eyes. Her hands stayed on her cheeks taking a deep breath.

It was all too real, the constant vivid flashes now happening in the real. Struggling to accept what was actually going on. Is it manifesting at its finest?

Still staring into the mirror, she felt wet as the breeze went up her dress. Daisy began pat drying her face with a paper towel. Touching the mirror to make sure she did not go into the portal of another world. Overcome by the way he moved, spoke and smiled. None of these very details were depicted in her dreams but the way she felt was identical. The magic of his aura left her in a loop.

Walking back to the table Daisy was in the spotlight, Jackson checked her out from head to toe. Standing up once she got neared then guiding her back into her chair, he got very close to her again.

"You smell so good." Jackson said casually sitting down pulling in his chair towards the table.

Daisy's body tingled, not able to look at him hiding her exhilaration. Sitting in her chair under his spell, a few appetizers were then dropped off to the table. Jackson must have ordered them while Daisy was in the restroom. One plate was put down in the middle of the table closer to Daisy. This plate was filled with caprese skewers drizzled in oil, balsamic glaze and a sprinkle of basil. The freshness of each ingredient's smell took over luring her in to try one, stopping when the other plate made Daisy grab her nose. Jackson also ordered fresh raw oysters. The large lipped platter held chopped ice that the shells rested on, a ramekin of horseradish and cocktail sauce was chiseled into the middle of the cubes surrounded in lemon slices. Daisy did not like seafood, the smell brought back memories of the fish that stunk up her house as a child.

Daisy was intrigued that he ordered them. Knowing in the back of her mind they are an aphrodisiac, she thought more in depth cracking a smirk. Even though she did not like seafood the thought of a man eating raw oysters made him all the more masculine.

Jackson reached over under Daisy's chair, she looked down excitedly. Jackson pulled her chair closer to him, moving her a solid two feet with ease.
"That's better," he said as he released his grip from the chair, moving his hand up to grab an oyster.

An intense feeling crept up inside of her after he put her right next to him. She took a bite of the mozzarella and tomato to distract herself from the flood of emotions. It tasted so fresh, perfectly blended together to create an outstanding combination of flavor.

Daisy excused herself again, overwhelmed feeling the bottom of her chair. Luckily this time she had an excuse to go back to the bathroom. Using the oysters as the reason to retreat back to the restroom console herself. Jackson understood assuring her they would be off the table by the time she returned. Daisy looked in the mirror again and splashed cold water on her arms, rubbing them up and down in the empty bathroom. Stomach tingling, legs weightless and her cheeks hurt from smiling so often. Finding a piece of mind, convincing herself to se la via. Enjoy the moments presented instead of overthinking, if it was real. Another breeze shook Daisy. The need to freak out ends here talking herself up. Another woman came into the bathroom, stopping once they locked eyes in the reflection.
"You're a lovely couple. I see the sparks flying everytime my eyes wander to your table. He is a keeper." The stranger told Daisy, the woman went right into a stall while Daisy acknowledged the sign.

Daisy badly wanted to walk over to Jackson and kiss him. As she walked toward the table she chickened out thinking it would be her coming on too strong. Jackson seductively touched her with only eyes, making her fantasize about kissing him more. Daisy noticed the oysters were gone, only the plate she enjoyed was in sight. The waiter came over with a plate of fresh mint from the back once Daisy sat. Jackson took a handful and chewed it up covering the remnants of the sea smell.

"That solves that." Rubbing his hands like he accomplished something great.

Both bottles of wine were already brought to the table, Jackson indicated that they would be starting off with the white wine. The waiter filled up their glasses, placed the white wine in the ice bucket and left after he opened red wine to breathe in the middle of the table.

Jackson grabbed his glass and raised it. They clinked glass, Jacksons glass didnt move toward his mouth it stayed up in the air. Daisy noticed and stopped, taking her lips off the glass looking at Jackson. Daisy was so close to filling her mouth with the oaky wine.

"Here's to the cheek bones hurting from laughing like we are alone yet we're in a room full of strangers, Slainte." Jackson said leaving Daisy stunned frozen in her chair.

Jackson took a sip, finishing off his mouthful when he noticed Daisy's arm was still up. He reached over, pushing up on the bottom of her glass. Daisy took a sip, Jackson pushing up a little more making her guzzle down a mouthful.

Jackson went on asking questions for most of the night gathering as much information as he could refraining from getting too personal about him. The main courses came out, they were beautifully plated. The sauces were so creamy, the food was piping hot. The way Jackson and Daisy looked at one another definitely made other couples jealous. The way the table vibrated with the eruption of laughter controlled the restaurant. Conversing like they were the only two in the restaurant. They did have plenty of space away from any other guests. One empty table in each direction. Daisy thought to herself perhaps Jackson slipped the host some cash to have that happen. A quiet romantic evening came true with the doing of Jackson. The bottle of white wine was empty upside down in the wine chiller standing on the side of the table. Jackson poured a half glass of the red wine to Daisy then himself a full glass. Jackson put his napkin to his mouth covering his cough before taking a sip.

The wine tasted identical to the wine she had a few hours ago at the nail salon with more of a spiced flavor. The bottle at the restaurant was a much better bottle, but it was like she had already tasted it early. She certainly knew why the wine was spicier looking over at Jackson, her bottom lip curled into her mouth. They continued their meal, electricity zapped between them with each bite, each sentence and every smile.

The plates were taken from the table with food still on the plate, they were both satisfied from the succulent meal. The bottle of red wine was still halfway full in the middle of the table. The long candle burning, dripping hot wax down the shaft. Jackson stared at the flame, his elbow on the table and wine glass in the air near his head. Stoically staring deep into the burning flame. Daisy watched Jackson's finger go in and out of the flame skimming the hot wax. Consumed, Daisy imagined the heat. It seemed like he was charging himself to be hotter. She was mesmerized watching his tattooed fingers twirling, twisting in the flame.
"Now are you ready for dessert?" Jackson asked, still playing with the fire, halfway looking up at her. Daisy looked into his glowing brown eyes glaring back at her, his face pointed back toward the candle licking his lips.

Chapter 4.

Daisy rolled over in the middle of the night soaking in her bed. Rubbing her tongue on the roof of her mouth feeling it tickle her sensitive nerve endings. Lightly rubbing her finger tips together on the sheets. Her glowing skin was covered in a light sweat. Her toes tingle, gripping them together tight, pushing the hair out of her face, breathing heavily. The duvet cover was over half of her naked body, one leg bent on top of the covers. Thinking more, warmed her blood. Laying there wishing that dessert was different, having naughty thoughts when he said it. Jackson's hand in the fire illuminating his tattoos in his black striped suit had her still thinking of him hours later unable to sleep.

Jackson put the hook right into her like he tattooed it on her skin himself. Tugging her along in her dreams. He was not in the bed but she felt his presence seeing him in her head. Reminiscing a gentle kiss on the cheek at her door that kept her curious desire afloat. One kiss from a gentleman had her fantasizing for more, wishing his hands all over her body like a gangster. Jackson's hand touched her on her hip, pressing into the curve of her hip bone made her weak in the knees. Teasing her ever so slightly, then saying goodnight. Upset he was not the dessert.

The real dessert at the restaurant was without a doubt the best piece of tiramisu she had in her life, paired with a hot espresso ending the date was still top notch. The night finished with cash on the table and two empty bottles of wine. It was chillier outside after they finished up but they both rolled down the windows all the way. Letting in the natural air, to cool down the heat they burned for one another. The dark sky magnified, lit with hundreds of stars and no clouds in sight.

Clear night, beautiful evening, bellies full, cheeks hurting, it was obvious the night had been more than enjoyed. Jackson made his intent very well known. Leaving Daisy wanting more of everything he did. Daisy rolled over to look at her phone, no new notifications. It was 4am, a bead of sweat dripped down her side and she pulled the covers completely off with her body.

DING..

Daisy's text tone notification popped up in green, it was from Jackson. She rubbed her eyes then hit the power button making the phone fade to black. Holding her finger on the button to unlock the phone, it opened recognizing her fingerprint, surprised it really was him. Opening his message she sat up in her bed quickly leaning on her padded headboard.

"I missed." The green bubble read.

"?" Without hesitation Daisy sent him back a text.

Anticipation corralled, placing a pillow behind her back for more support and getting very comfortable. After a few seconds she had read his text ten times trying to interpret it. Over analyzing the meaning. She looked at the message time, she texted back at 4am in less than 10 seconds. Two minutes went by waiting for a text. Daisy pressed the sleep button on her phone and reached over to put it on the nightstand.

DING...

It vibrated in her hand with a chime just before putting it down. Daisy put it on the nightstand and rolled over to wait, not seeming overly anxious.

DING...

Daisy's eyes opened, rolling over to grab her phone. Finger moved to unlock as fast as possible to open to his double text.

"Did I wake you?" The first text read.

"Haven't been able to sleep." The second text read.

Daisy took a deep breath remembering what she told herself in the bathroom at the restaurant to let it be, not overthink. Choosing to do what made her happy and felt right, despite what was in her head replaying like a broken record. After a final deep breath to clear her mind she sat up excited to text him, not worried about the time or how fast she texted back. Pulling up the covers feeling a chill from being wet as the air conditioner turned back on.

"No, I was just thinking of you to be honest." She replied, smiling knowing he too was thinking of her. Proud of herself for telling him the truth. She did not have a worry about being vulnerable after the way he made her feel since the moment they met and then again when they remet formally. Fighting her own worries and self doubt thinking that they work well together in natural peaceful intense frequency.

DING..

"You were now?" Daisy read his text, her phone was still open waiting for his text.

DING...

"I must have left quite the impression having you think of me at 4am." Jackson sent.

Smiling, her eyes squinted. Daisy was thinking of something witty to send back. Wanting to be playful or moderately sexy. Contemplating telling him what she really felt, all of what she was thinking about. Maybe not too early, she had not known him for a full week yet. Then it crossed her mind of everything else she had been thinking about since him, all the dreams the past few days and even before she first saw him for the first time. The flames were there, the connection was already insatiable.

It was 4am, both of them thinking of one another. Daisy's cheeks are still hurting from laughing all night. She continued to smile with the risk of leaving wrinkles on her face in the future from her overjoy.

Jackson threw the bait out there for her to snatch right up. Testing her with an open ended question. Laying on his dark gray silk sheets he placed his phone down on the side of him. Picking up the book he was reading, opened the page where the $2 bill bookmark remained. Continuing to read, his feet were stretched on top of the white folded blanket at the end of the bed. Shirtless, barefoot he laid with his gold rings and gold knotted chains. Coming out of his wall was a pipe with a bulb on the end of it that curved the light and was warmly pointed toward the bed. The record player was on low, mellow classical tunes for background music while reading, helping him relax. Laying down the cuts in Jackson abs were seen, the dim light and tattoos created texture that contoured the lines. Jackson picked up his phone that vibrated, opening her text that read something he didn't expect her to say.

"You are different. Unique and too well put together. I feel that there is chemistry between us." After reading he began clicking the keys on his phone, a small vibration with each keystroke resting his elbows on his sides.

DING...

"It is obvious we have a connection." Daisy read his text lying back down full of joy.

DING...

"We are going to go on an adventure. As much as I like seeing you in heels and a dress I strongly recommend you don't wear them on this date. Goodnight gorgeous."

Each text was better than the last, hitting her like pure ecstasy. She typed "Goodnight Jackson," then deleted it, scrolling back through their texts re-reading every text from the beginning.

His very first text at 4am, she pondered after rereading. What did that mean? What did he miss? Distracted by the feelings that the conversation that changed course, she needed to know. Otherwise it would bother her all night.

"Jackson, what did you miss?" Texting him one more time.

A list of different answers began to write with bullet points in her brain. The thought of him grabbing her hand slowly rubbing his fingers seductively tickling her finger tips walking into the restaurant popped into her brain, she continued to rub the tips of her fingers in the sheets mimicking him. The way he touched her, the way he looked at her, the way he guided everywhere had her feeling conquered.

DING...

"Your lips." Jackson responded.

Daisy's eyes fixated on his text. After reading that she knew exactly what he ment. Daisy's eyes shut, eyes rolling to the back of her head leaning and arching her back submissively. She licked her lips, throwing the phone on the bed. Her hands descending, slipped down the side of her body stopping at her naked hips.

Wanting to pick the phone back up and continue to text him knowing she needed to stop texting him before the ongoing uncontrollable urge to see him tonight prevailed. A simple text would not fulfill her needs right now. Forcing her mind to go black holding back all possibilities, ceasing evolution of thoughts on the subject.

Taking about twenty minutes to fall asleep, quieting her mind. Excited enjoying how she is feeling at this very moment. Thinking of nothing, seeing a world of darkness her mind wandered off to oblivion. Things would pop into her mind accidently, like the thought of kissing him.

Finally in a relaxed mediated state of mind out of the cloud of darkness something her mom used to say disrupted her momentarily that put her at ease:

"The right guy is worth the wait."

Feeling thankful that she was focusing on herself instead of dating a bunch of wrong guys wasting time. A few guys that tried to enter her life had good qualities but lacked. Daisy never had someone that knocked her socks off like Jackson did. She shared an instant connection with him that was organic. Daisy was breathing deep in and out until she drifted into a sleep state. No lucid dreams that night, no need for it when they were slowly unfolding candidly.

Jackson waited until Friday to text Daisy, driving Daisy crazy all week. She continued to do what she did on the daily yet her heart was longing for him. A literal feeling inside her chest of aching pain. His prompt text was to the point after seven days of being muzzled.

Presumptuously reminding her to dress for adventure not in heels stating the date would require her to be awake early. Jackson sent her an address of a restaurant that was an hour away.

Her heart felt full after reading his text after a long day at work ending her night with a bourbon on the rocks. Sipping on the sweet and smokey liquor getting ready for bed. Brushing her teeth after finishing her second glass. Daisy's body moved loosely, dancing in her white bathrobe swaying to the music while she picked out her action packed fit for the morning. Much easier to pick clothes when she knew what he had planned. Her mind wondered what kind of adventure specifically?

Daisy finished applying her religious lotion and skin routine to finish off her night. Daisy stretched pulling the bathrobe from her shoulders, the moon shone on her naked body. Placing her robe on the leather couch in her room feeling chic as she undressed, freshly lathered shining skin. The blinds in her room were always open, not feeling phased walking in front of them in the nude. There were enough trees and bushes in the backyard making a natural barrier. As she got into the bed the blanket tickled her, before hitting the light on her nightstand she decided to grab her book to help tire her out. Opening the book she smelt almost mold, knowing how old the book was by the pages being so brittle as she then flipped along, Daisy only read two chapters before putting it down and hitting the light. Daisy continued to move as the blanket tickled her body thinking of Jackson.

Daisy got up before her alarm, popping up out of her bed going straight to the stove. Turning the switch to the gas and clicking the igniter creating a large blue flame. Daisy turned down the flame to medium, putting the stainless steel kettle on the stove top to be heated. While it warmed she prepared an empty cup with a fresh black tea bag into a tea cup. Turning to the refrigerator to grab her whole grain bread and popped two pieces into the toaster. The music from her phone was turned on, she danced all around the kitchen preparing a light breakfast. Shimmying around in a baggy shirt she got from the last concert she went to barefoot on the hardwoods. The music amplified when she finished connecting it to the built-in bluetooth speaker above disguised in between the warm bright flood lights of the kitchen ceiling.

Dancing around patiently waiting for the toaster to pop, looking down into the machine's red coils seeing the heat change the color of the bread to a crip. Daisy continued singing along with the music slicing from the stick of butter after the bagel was fully cooked. The kettle howled, steam blowing out the spout cut into the loud music. Daisy filled a tea into a cup that she got from Mexico adding only two teaspoons of brown sugar. With a steaming cup in one hand and an emerald green small plate in the other hand she made her way to her bathroom without spilling anything. Flicking up the switch to both the lights and then the switch to the built in speakers in her bathroom that instantly connected to her phone.

Daisy's bathroom lights were currently brighter than the sun that was creeping up from the East. Faint sounds of the chirping birds outside of her window as Daisy danced right into her tight navy blue yoga pants. Looking in the mirror adding a small amount of makeup per usual, widening her blue eyes thinking about him while applying her mascara. Her body was going to melt once she saw him. Daisy couldn't wait for Jackson to bring her in with his seductive eyes. Daisy stopped and looked at herself once more in the mirror before putting in the coordinates of the restaurant into her phone.

After an hour's drive, Daisy pulled up to the restaurant Jackson sent and even though she had eaten she was now hungry. Ecstatic that it was an old school diner that looked like a train. The silver sides of the restaurant made it hard to miss and with the sun being in the position that it was, it made it very hard to look at because of the rising sun's insane reflection. Walking toward the double doors she was partially blinded. Daisy was putting her hand in front of her face to block the powerful rays. Putting her phone in the waistband of her elastic pants, other hand still blocking out the sun stepping up the staircase.
"I didn't think you would show." Jackson said, immediately Daisy looked up toward the door to a tall figure that spoke from the top of the stairs.

Glaring up at a dark figure, stepping closer finally getting some shade from the overhanging awning above. Her hand finally came down and it took a few seconds for her eyes to adjust. Finally seeing Jackson stared down at her from the top stair once her vision cleared.. The breeze had her hair smoothly trickling back and forth in the wind. Jackson watched her in what felt like slow motion. Admiring every microsecond he could get to look at her. The manor in how he was looking, made her weightless. Staring deep into his dreamy brown eyes stuck in a speechless interaction. Stepping up the last stair with no clack from a heel, yet still feeling like she was on a runway smiling more as she got very close to him.

"I needed a little adventure in my life," Daisy said leaning in, feeling his hand on her lower back pressing her towards the door that he opened for her.

Opening the door to a crowded breakfast spot, barely after the crack of dawn. Walking in they were greeted by two cute hostesses. The two hostesses at the front of the diner were giggling to one another once the couple walked in. In no way shape or form did they try to hide their infatuation with Jackson. The two giddy ladies stared and smiled at Jackson while he asked for a table for two. Jackson soaked in what they were putting off yet unfaced and focused like it was not the first time he had experienced this encounter.

Jackson put his hand on the ledge of the counter, putting his weight down involuntarily flexing his tricep forming strong defined lines. The solid piece of muscle stretched, his veins in his forearms were bulging out of his skin. The bulge went all the way up his arm to the center of his bicep. Jackson had a snapback on backwards, his beard was manicured and he had a black baggy tank top exposing the art all over his skin.

Daisy examined the back of his neck, down his traps to the collar of the tank top. Having a minute to thoroughly appreciate it without making it creepy. Captivated, trying to not make her gleam obvious in his notice. Her eyes making their way down his wide shoulders down to the tattoos on his ribs. Cutting her inspection short with the fit of his tank top concealing her view and breaking her infatuation for a moment.

Jackson turned to Daisy pulling her in closer while the ladies flirted with him. Daisy noticed what was going on but honestly she was not phased nor really paying attention. Knowing exactly why they were doing what they were doing, she had the same feelings as the hostess at this very moment. He warped the room in stunning fashion, more than his look, or charm there was an underlying presence that attracted him to others. Daisy was playing with her hair until she noticed the other two ladies were also doing the same. One of the hostess grabbed two large foldable laminated menus escorting them though the grid of tables.

    Daisy peeked at his skin once more from behind as he followed the cute brunette to the table, looking at what was drawn on the back of his neck. After taking a step he turned the corner of the host stand, her hand was snatched by Jackson bringing her with him to the table. The other hostess behind the counter's jaw dropped down a bit of how smooth and sexy he took command of her hand, continuing watching him take charge of her all the way then he led her into the booth first before sitting down himself. Daisy began to get hotter when he sat down face to face. Jackson's elbows were on the table, hands together leaning forward toward her looking in her direction. She felt like he was in her mind going through her thoughts. Daisy looked over at him, there was so much to look at. Trying not to stare at the ink popping out at her or the veins bulging out of his skin. Rubbing her fingertips on her legs under the table consumed by all of him. Daisy's lips felt so uncomfortably dry due to the humidity in the restaurant.

"We're going to have fun today." Jackson said, then picked up the menu scanning until a word popped out for him to read the full description.

"Are you going to give me a hint?" Daisy said in the sweetest voice playing with her blonde hair controlling her breath.

"Patcientes, gorgeous." He said with his menu up still scanning, Daisy smirked watching his mistic.

    An older waitress approached the table, she had her hair pulled back in a ponytail and walked in all black directly in front of Jackson's field of view. The ladies at the hostess stand had a perfect line of sight to Jackson, they did not neglect to look at him from the front door. The waitress talked directly to Daisy barely moving her eyes, inferior toward Jackson until he spoke up to order after Daisy placed hers. Writing down his order Daisy thought she saw the waitress draw a heart next to his order. Maybe her mind was playing tricks on her, she only saw the motion of the pen. Parched Daisy licked her lips waiting for the waitress to get back with her water and grapefruit juice. Jackson zoned in to his menu then put it down once he had decided, leaving it hanging horizontally off the table.

"I'm starving, I didn't have anything this morning but a shot of espresso." Jackson said, leaning back as his legs were widening in the booth, crossing his arms like he owned the joint.

"I snacked on toast this morning." Daisy said, still licking her dry lips, body began to feel hot, feeling like she was going to perspire as her clit began to tingle.

"Get something to eat, we're going to get our heart rate up and burn some calories." Jackson said moments before the waitress dropped their drinks off.

    Daisy felt dehydrated, hot and now nervously excited grabbed the glass taking a big sip of water accidentally swallowing an ice cube. The feeling of frost descended all the way down her throat, cooling her down only a degree. Daisy continued to quench her thirst till no water remained in her glass. She stole Jackson's water, proceeding to chug half of it. Jackson leaned back smiling watching her while he sipped on his coffee. She was at the edge of her seat, unsure why she was so triggered by him.

    Daisy felt better physically, but she did look up with embarrassment thinking that Jackson found it strange she just chugged water like an animal so quickly. In her defense the glasses of water were skinny, not the average pint size water glasses from most restaurants. Jackson's coffees steamed, he leaned back cool as a cucumber with his arm on the top of the booth watching her abnormally. Daisy grabbed the napkin and whipped her mouth.

"Thirsty?" Jackson said, taking a sip of coffee.

"Uh - I - mhm." Daisy was unable to differentiate words feeling her pussy getting really wet.

"Excuse me." Daisy said getting up to go to the bathroom watching Jackson smirk like he knew.

Now after finishing off almost two glasses of cold water Daisy had a real excuse to go to the bathroom. Again she was soaking wet just sitting there with him, nothing sexual at all happened. Exasperated by the way her body naturally reacted to him, turning into a temple of fertile temptation.

After finishing up in the restroom Daisy walked back to the table, Jackson stood up as she returned. The breeze of his aroma smacked right into her. Taking a big breath in she stood there with him staring into his eyes for a few seconds dramatically before sitting down. His scent went away after she sat down making her eager to get close to him again.

After the two ate Jackson settled the bill at the table and then they proceeded to the front door where Jackson held the door for Daisy as the two hosts gawked at Jackson. He absorbed it and pleasantly said goodbye. Jackson walked her to her car, opening the door for her as soon as she hit the unlock button. Jackson shut the door and walked back to his car without a word. Daisy could not take her eyes off him as he went back to his car, once he started the engine he nodded his head at Daisy in the direction toward the exit. Jackson put the car into reverse, angling it for a straight shot out after putting it in drive to pull straight out of the parking lot and Daisy followed.

The two cars pulled into a gravel parking lot after a few miles. The sound of rocks being crushed by the ton weight of the vehicles continued till they pulled into adjacent parking spaces. Dust clouds pulled up all the sand and dirt making it hard to breathe.

Daisy could see a sign with a map and a trail leading into the woods once she got out of the car getting a feel of her surroundings. Though it was too far away to read anything that would tell her what they were doing. Jackson pulled out a black backpack from the car and put on his sunglasses. Daisy went to her trunk and sat down on the small tailgate that dropped and began applying some sunscreen into her hand.

"Need some help with that?" Jackson said, putting the backpack straps over his shoulders.

Daisy's body tingled thinking of his hands all over her rubbing in the sunscreen deep into her skin with his strong hands. Daisy pushed the cap closed on the bottle instantly. Daisy already knew the answer, her body was saying yes along with her brain. Daisy was muted, smiling and threw the bottle at Jackson with an underhand toss. Jackson caught it with one hand, smiling. He twirled his fingers for her to stand up and turned around. Daisy took a step forward and Jackson approached her back side. Jackson took his empty hand putting it on her hip pressing in lightly and spinning her half way around to sit in his lap. He sat in the trunk of her car. Such a smooth move organically dancing her around to a comfortable position for the two of them.

Daisy had a shiver throughout her body once Jackson's hands massaged the sunscreen into her shoulders. His hands went up her neck rubbing it in with his fingertips making his way to the front of her neck gently rubbing under her throat. When he got back to her shoulders he showed some strength pushing thumbs into her shoulder blades. Daisy's whole body moved down several inches completely under his control. Jackson finished up then began to rub the excess sunscreen down her arms with a firm grip.

Jackson put both hands on her hips pushing her up off his lap. Jackson stood up and closed her trunk door rubbing the excess sunscreen on his face. Daisy stood up, ready to go knowing if he did that for another minute they may have very well ended in the back of the car.
"Shall we." Jackson said, pointing his hand out toward the trail going into the woods.
"We shall." Daisy said her face was still lit up, body loosened up now that the date could be over now and she would be satisfied, blown away and mellowed out.

Walking toward the entrance of the trail Jackson slowed his pace down. Jackson took two steps less to slow behind her, putting his hand over her eyes.
"The adventure is more so a surprise." Jackson said walking toward the dirt path passing a green sign that showed what kind of activity was ahead.

Daisy's expectation grew biting down on her lip. Jackson released the blinders from her face after about ten feet, upping his pace to pass Daisy. Jackson grabbed Daisy by the hand and continued on the trail. The couple hiked up a fairly steep hill for a good mile.

 Reaching the top they walked out of the trail to what felt like paradise. Jackson walked over to the water and looked over the river, consuming the vibrations of nature. Daisy was standing behind him watching her stoic date, it was as he was taking in the environment not only visually but spiritually downloading the data of the electrical currents surrounding them. Grounding down into the trenches of roots below ground his mind seemed intertwined, his body flowing in the same motion as the river. Jackson picked his head up and stared directly up at the sun, eyes wide open charging himself with natural vitamins.

Daisy watched in envy, examining the right side of his arm while Jackson looked out into the abyss. Jackson finished, winked at Daisy then walked over to the dock to pay the attendant. The attendant pulled off a paddle board off the racks placing it in the water. Daisy was a few feet behind him taking in the beauty of the landscape overhearing Jackson cough while dragging a paddle board into the water.

Getting balanced was not hard for Daisy standing and maneuvering the ore like she had done this before. Jackson sat down unable to balance standing up, he blamed it on the weight difference on the boards. The water had a slight chill to it, but was being warmed by the sun. Luckily they were flowing with the water's current, not having to row that much. An absolutely beautiful day, it was hot but not humid with a breeze that stopped them from sweating.

After rowing down the river for a while Jackson put up his hand telling her to follow him, his two fingers wiggling. They turned into a small cove that was nicely shaded by many low hanging trees. Jackson went into his back packs, after unzipping and rummaging around he grabbed a rope out and rowed closer to the branches. Daisy staired and her eyes widened trying to figure out what in the world he was doing. Jackson grabbed a hold of a thick low hanging branch then unraveled the rope. After uniting the rope with the branch he then tied the other end to a plastic rivet attached to his paddle board creating an anchor system. Jackson fumbled in his bag pulling out bungee cords attaching it to his paddle board then pulled in Daisy's board attaching the other end of the bungee securing their boats together.

Daisy was in disarray when she saw Jackson pull out a bottle of white wine out of his backpack after anchoring the boards. Jackson pulled a corkscrew out of his pocket making the cork pop by pulling it out with force, the noise echoed throughout the cove. He poured the wine into two stemless glasses holding them both in one hand. Jackson passed one to Daisy then secured the bottle back into his bag. Jackson's arm remained up, ready to make a toast. Daisy raised her glass as well, not having a chance to take a sip too distracted by him. Jackson took off his sunglasses and looked up at the sky through the trees for a moment.

"Not taking natural beauties for granted, take them in while you can." Jackson said, locking eyes on Daisy.

Daisy's head was tilted, cheek bones raised, pearly whites exposed. The paddles rocked up and down after they clinked glasses from shifting their weight. The white wine was buttery and surprisingly cold. Daisy took a sip, she noticed he continued to look her way. Daisy smiled at Jackson with his glass still up, looking right at her. Daisy put her glass back down away from her lips, waiting looking at him.

"Did you not finish your toast?" Daisy said with adorable confusion.

"I'm just taking in the natural beauties." He said, continue to look at her whole face light up then he took a big sip.

Perfect words worthy of poets to sing rolled off his tongue with ease. Daisy was very taken back by his words.. Jackson eventually reached into his backpack putting his glass between his legs, securing it. She stared at his big arms digging into the bag, his tight skin moved, she enjoyed watching his muscles shift. His wide frame straightened out putting his shoulders back squaring up sitting up after pulling out a plate wrapped in plastic. Pulling back the plastic he exposed a meat and cheese spread on a sterling silver plate. If Daisy was not sure of him then, she would have been after this move. What woman would not like to be surprised by a man of interest that so decadently planned out an exciting date? Getting brownie points that he had brought wine and a charcuterie board and a few more points for packing it with ice packs so the temperature was divine when it was served.

Swaying back and forth with the waves, the two of them had an aquatic picnic. This was definitely a first for Daisy. His creativeness stole her interest, more she was curious what else he had in store. The fine cheese, salty spiced meat stacked on thin seeded crackers washed down with the crispness of the wine blending together for a perfect day.

"So Jackson, how many times have you brought a woman up here?"

Jackson chuckled and finished all of his wine in his glass. Grabbed the half empty bottle topping her glass off proceeding to pour the remainder in his glass. Jackson took another sip looking down at his glass.

"Only you. This idea came to me late at night, like a vision after we formally met in person at the cafe. Popped into my head and it was a fine idea" He said squinting as he looked up at her, the sun beating down on him through the trees.

"Not going to lie, this date is going to be hard to beat." Daisy said as her lips pressed against her wine glass.

"I accept that challenge,." Jackson said with conviction in his eyes.

The cheese and meats dwindled down to just a silver platter, the wine came to an end. Just as they took their last sips of wine a huge bolt of lightning followed by thunder and simultaneously they both began to pack when noticing the wind began to pick up for the past few minutes, the colors of the clouds darkened. Jackson untied the rope from the branch with one fierce pull. Swinging the rope around his hand under his elbow he wrapped it up neatly putting it back in his backpack. After they released from one anothers board they both paddled up river to dock their paddle boards with the wind on their side. Jackson helped put the boards back on the racks after returning, thunder crackled through the woods. Walking back down the hill a strike of lighting lit up the sky through the trees.

Moments after the rain started shooting down like bullets, the trees absorbed some of the drops that fell from the heavens. Raindrops pooled up and slid down Jackson's shoulders all the way to his finger tips. When they came to the end of the trail they both looked at one another knowing they were running out of cover from the trees. They ran through the gravel and small puddles in the parking lot to the driver side of Daisy's door. Daisy did not grab the handle of the door, stopping before grabbing it Daisy turned around toward Jackson. The rain drops ran down her forehead and cheeks dripping down her face, licking the drops off her lips staring up at Jackson. Tasting the salt of the water that cleansed her mouth.

"I have to get back to get ready for tonight." Jackson said standing very close to Daisy, almost pushing her against the car. The rain began to fall harder, they were getting absolutely drenched and not phased one bit.

"Despite the rain, today was pretty amazing." Daisy said, picking her head up letting the rain hit her face then wiping off the water from her eyes, so she could look back at him.

"Well I know a way to make the rain part of an amazing day into a perfect one." Jackson said, then his body shifted down leaning toward Daisy.

Daisy closed her eyes, their lips met, raindrops falling down their bodies, sharing the salty taste that fell from the sky. The thunder roared and bolts of lighting streaked through the sky as if it reacted to the energy transferring between them. Jackson thrusted her back, forcing her back to get soaked leaning on the car. Jackson put his hand on the side of her face, his thumb ran along her jaw with the remaining fingers behind her ear. Powerfully kissing her, making her weightless, pulling her in with his leveraged hand.

Jackson slowly took his lips off hers and they were stuck to each other while he pulled away. Daisy was tickled, pushing up toward him savoring his lips following his body for more as he released his lips from hers. They stood captured by the moment, not concerned by the rain but only on one another. The thunder continued to rumble the area that surrounded them. Jackson grabbed her door for her, Daisy got in her dry car. Jackson peeked his head in grabbing her chin, giving her a quick kiss on the lips. Looking into her eyes saying it all without a word and shut the door.

  Driving back home her thoughts stuck in a mess. Truth be told she was ecstatic, for the first time in a long time. Wiping her arms pushed the water off her skin that dripped down her body absorbing on her cotton seats. Feeling the warm blowing heat from the vents, letting it hit her face warming her. Daisy blasted the heat to help dry her until the car got too humid so she put it on a lower setting and cracked the window to defog the windshield. The country music was not much higher than the sound of the hot air blowing through the vents. Daisy was in her own world, enjoying the drive back.

  As the days went by the two were more open in communication compared to Jackson's previous absences. Not so much via text but on the phone, calling one another when they could for twenty plus minutes a day if they were not hanging out that day. It was like they went into a time machine and they were brought back to the days where people talked to one another instead of sending emotionless texts to banter back and forth. Talking to one another they had no concern for anything else, their focus still on one another miles apart. They both were very busy with work all week and decided to meet on the weekend. Daisy got her fix talking to him every day but still could not wait to see him again in person. Jackson could tell she was really into him by the way she smiled and laughed at him being himself. He continued to reel her in little by little after setting the hook in on her. Jackson invited her to a more personal part of his life, inviting her to his favorite thing to do in the entire world that made him a bit nervous even though he would never tell her. The night before on the phone he told Daisy to dress warm, really emphasizing it. She fell asleep no problem and surprisingly was not haunted by any lucid dreams like the rest of the week.

Daisy stood in the cold of the rink with a sweatshirt and jeans the next day. Happy to be in his presence once more, now learning a little more about him and his hobbies. Every exhale she could see the vapors of water turning to foggy gas in the brutal cold rink. Standing in front of the glass looking at colored lines on the ice. Daisy was freezing, reaching for her gloves that she was reluctant to bring. Trusting his words, especially when dressing for the occasion as he had never told her what they were going to do. Jackson always kept the activities full of suspense. Daisy standing along the boards felt someone tapped her shoulder

"Daisy?"

"Hello Roger, what are you doing here?"

Roger had a big blue bag with white stripes that looked like it could fit a body in it, strapped over his shoulder and two hockey sticks in his hand. Roger looked down at his sticks and equipment pointing out the obvious waiting for her to put it all together.

"I'm a little out of shape and a little old but this game keeps my blood pumping. It also lets out some stresses that you are aware of. The real question is why are you here Daisy?"

"I'm here with my fr..." Pausing and changing her words, quickly rubbing her hand together close to her mouth.

"Freezing, I'm freezing! I'm here to see Jackson play."

Roger's back tightened up and his chin raised, nodding his head before speaking. Then he looked at his watch and his eyes popped open.

"Oh, I see, let me get in there and get ready."

Daisy watched him go into the locker room. Pondering on Roger's mannerisms after she said Jackson's name. Still not knowing little about Jackson, it was a mystery she was yet to solve but actively trying to find more clues.

Freezing her ass she decided to make her way to the lobby to warm up, as she walked she felt a tap on her shoulder for the second time she turned around surprised. It was Jackson, he spun her back towards the ice once she saw him. Jackson extended her arms up in the air,

Daisy was curious what he was doing behind her then she felt him put his jacket on her. Jackson also had a cup of hot cocoa that he handed her after she put her arms through his sleeves.

"Roger said you were freezing this should help, enjoy the game sexy." Jackson pulled out a beanie pulling it over her head and walked off, Daisy's face lit up and a cheeky smile rose up uncontrollably.

"Problem solved." Jackson said, winking right before the door swung shut.

"No I'm not going to get frostbite, thank you," she shouted as Jackson disappeared into the locker room.

      Holding the warm beverage she fixed the beanie on her head and now she was set, warmer and much more comfortable. When he told her to dress warm he should have been more specific and told her dress like the world is freezing over. Thinking about his simple gesture she bit her lip still smiling from when he left, gripping the hot cocoa for survival in the wretched condition. Daisy began searching for a place to sit in the bleachers and she noticed a few women staring at her. They whispered back and forth to one another like they were talking about her too. It was because they just witnessed what happened, seeing her man take care of her needs. They stared at Daisy in envy of what they saw she had, the connection was obvious to everyone, the smiles were genuine.

      Daisy went all the way to the top of the bleachers, remembering in school that hot air rises hoping it will help the blizzard like conditions. Daisy took off her gloves wrapping her bare hands around the cup of hot cocoa to help warm herself up. Holding onto the steaming cup like the holy grail, bringing the cup up to her face feeling the heat on her nose.

      Daisy's body with the help of the hot drink and extra jacket began to acclimate. When the two teams came out she saw Jackson jump on the ice skating around the ice wearing number 11. Thinking to herself that's strange because that's my favorite number also. As the two teams warmed up, pucks sailed across the ice, Daisy saw Roger and Jackson talking. Seemed like they were joking around as they stretched near their bench. By now Jackson must know that Roger is her client of hers.

The puck was getting ready to drop, the two teams lined up on their respective sides. Jackson was the center taking the faceoff, his stick on the ice body low to the ground. Right off the puck drop Jackon took charge, gaining control of the puck. Pushing up ice cutting in between both defenders deking the goalie out and putting the puck in the top left corner. Daisy got up and cheered loudly without thought. Jackson celebrated with his team and as he skated back toward center ice he looked up and pointed his stick at Daisy, she was right in his crosshairs. The jealous ladies below looked up at her following the gratification. At this moment Daisy was proud, frankly not worried about their envy. The puck was about to drop again and the two teams lined up at center ice again. Daisy looked up and she saw the clock, it was only 11 seconds into the game. She pondered about the numbers for the rest of the game. Seeing the number over and over lately, especially every time she looked at the clock lately. All are good signs, angel numbers sharing her favorite number with Jackson was a bit strange.

The game went on as time decayed from the clock, Jackson scored two more times and assisted Roger in scoring one goal. The men skated hard putting divets in the ice, chiseling the ice to snowflakes that sprayed every time they stopped on a dime quickly changing direction. The puck flew through the air with sheer force sliding all over the ice at such a fast pace. The players moved the puck from stick to stick with an effortless look. Daisy had been to a few hockey games with friends, clients and coworkers; they were more for fun and she did not pay much attention. Now alone in the freezing bleachers she really analyzed things a bit more.

Daisy realized it was a tough sport from the brutal weather to the aggressiveness in which each player played and pure strength that the players used, throwing their bodies to bump in the corners fighting for the puck. The puck moved so fast along the ice that it was difficult to keep track of at some points.

Jackson had the puck circling around in his offensive zone passing it up to the defenseman on the blue line. The defenseman wound up his stick and fired a slapshot. The puck shot through the air like a bullet. Roger was in front of the goalie leaving the goalie completely blind. The puck went right past the goalie and bounced off the crossbar making a high pitched sound.

Tiinnnnnnggg

    The puck flew up in the air and Jackson snuck behind the net, as if he knew where the puck was landing. He pulled the puck to the inside of his body as the goalie shifted his way. Jackson snapped a shot that went right through the goalkeeper's legs. Jacksons hand flew up in the air and gave his team including Roger highfives.

    The game ended shortly after that, Jackson leading the team to victory. Jackson was the last man off the ice. Jackson was rigorously coughing when he finally stepped off the ice. Daisy walked down the bleachers quickly to meet him by the door.

"Well I see why they put the C on your jersey," Daisy said, poking up on his jersey at the letter signifying the captain.

    She smirked looking up at Jackson towered over Daisy with his skates on with his pads he looked like a giant out of a bedtime tale. Jackson picked her up by the sides, stepping back on the ice carrying striding around the ice with her in his arms like a trophy. Flying around the rink she felt like a prize. Jackson stopped at center ice putting Daisy down. He leaned down more than usual because of the size difference with his skates.

    Kissing on the solid puddle of ice, she melted into his arm gripping his jersey tight Daisy was immersed in that moment. The horn sounded behind them and they both turned to see the zamboni coming out to clean off the ice. The zamboni driver beeped the horn again forcing the two to get off the ice. Jackson skated Daisy over to the door and placed her on solid ground before stepping off himself.

"Let me shower and we'll go get lunch, yeah?" Jackson said.

"Good I gotta get out of this iglu." Daisy said, running to the lobby for warmth.

Jackson took off his helmet and gloves walking into the locker room watching her quickly move toward the door to the main lobby. Once he rounded the brick corner where all the sticks stood in the dressing room, one of his teammates threw him a beer while walking through the locker room. Quickly popped it open and chugged it down, the team cheered him on. Jackson took off the top half of his gear then grabbed two beers and threw it at Roger. Roger quickly popped it open and drank the beer. This was the team's way of praising the top stars of the night. Jackson pulled off his red long sleeve under armor tight fit shirt, throwing it in his bag.

Unlacing his skates it looked like his body was on fire, the steam seeped off his tattoos. While whipping the ice off the bottom of his blade Roger walked over and sat down with two beers in hand. He cracked it open for him since Jackson's hands were full, placing it on the bench beside him.

"Hell of a game, thanks for setting me up for that one timer to make me look good." Roger said, patting Jackson on the back.

"You were at the right place at the right time." Jackson fired back, taking a big sip of his beer, smoldering in steam coming off his warm body in the cold rink.

"So." Roger said, leaning back relaxing as Jackson undressed the lower half of his gear.

"So, how do you know Daisy?" Jackson said, pulling off his shin pads.

Roger leaned back sipping his beer slowly adding drama to Jackson's question. Chuckling a little to the point that Jackson stopped what he was doing and made a face that would make anyone get to the point as quickly as possible.

"She is a hell of a woman, strong, determined, sexy." Roger took another sip looking off into the distance. Jackson straightened up completely waiting for Roger to further explain.

"You're a lucky guy Jackson." Roger said, smiling.

"How are the two of you acquainted?" Jackson stared right at Roger with a bit of rage.

"Daisy and I know each other threw certain legal matters that I am unfortunately involved in, Daisy represents me. I think you two make a great duo, don't screw her over though she is a lawyer, a damn good one." Roger knew what he was doing getting under his skin and finally broke his poker face busting out laughing.

  Roger walked away laughing. Jackson cracked a small smile and shook his head at the eldest jokester he'd ever known. Jackson knew what was going on with Roger and his ex wife, how he was having a rough time dealing with not seeing his kids. Jackson never met Linda but he got a clear picture of how vindictive she was with the few stories that Roger told him about his life outside of hockey and work.

"Asshole." Jackson said, throwing his empty beer in the garbage next to Roger as he walked back.

  Jackson came out of his shower in a towel tightly along his waist and flip flops, slicking back his hair. With speed dressing and saying goodbye to his teammates, ready to take Daisy to lunch.

  A few tacos and margaritas for a few hours was a fine lunch indeed. They laughed and talked endlessly, getting deeper with their questions but most of all their answers. The more indepth they got the more they both were getting a better understanding of what was truly going on between them. Unfortunately a few hours was all they had because Jackson had to go to work the night shift that night leaving the restaurant a little buzzed.

  A few hours later after getting ready Daisy showed up an hour into his shift to surprise him. Jackson was certainly surprised when he looked up seeing her sitting at the bar. Not realizing at first it was her, it was like he had checked her out for the first time. Putting his eyes on the bullseye knowing what he wanted the moment he saw her.

  Jackson had seen her quickly when she walked in the doorway off in the distance, he thought the woman in the blue dress with white leather heels walking toward the bar was so sexy it should be a crime. Jackson only saw her from a distance and became distracted to take care of another customer unable to make out her face. After going to the well, getting caught up on one side of the bar making bloody mary's and gin and tonics for a couple. Jackson handed the drinks to the couple, cleaning out the shaker in the sink and shifting to the next guest that needed a drink on this busy weekend night.

"Want to make a few drinks for me while I check out some guests?." Chris said, reaching in, grabbing ice below Jackson.

"Yeah what's the order? Cash my couple out too for me while you're at the till." Jackson grabbed the card from the wife of the couple and handed it to Chris.

"Three martini's and two dirty, one wet with a twist, two old fashions and a vodka on the rocks lime."

"Herd." Jackson shouted, going to the well to set the shakers up to whip up all these cocktails.

"Jackson. Blue dress center of the bar needs a French 95." Chris said walking with a handful of cards all in an order that he remembered which card belonged to who, placing them in the slits of his fingers looking like wolverine.

"Herd." Jackson said, grabbing two bottles that crossed one another in one hand.

Jackson tossed the freshly washed shaker up, spinning it in the air, catching it with and placing it on the bar mat. After pouring the first drink he picked up a bottle of lemon juice spinning it on his palm switching the direction of the spout pouring perfectly into the shaker. Snapping the bottle quickly to stop the flow of juice. Putting another tin on the mat in front of him then grabbing a bottle of bourbon from behind him on the shelf along with a bottle of simple syrup pouring them both at the same time into two separate glasses. He snapped the simple syrup first, placing it back in the same spot in the well. His other hand raised higher making a waterfall illusion of bourbon quickly bringing it back down to the shaker before snapping the bottle to stop the pouring. Jackson grabbed a jigger to pour a small amount of orange juice, measuring it meticulously then dumping it in the tin. Jackson lined up two tins and a rocks glass using close to a half a bottle of vodka on the drinks as he free poured. His tattooed hands grabbed the ice scooper, shoveling it right into the smaller shakers. Slamming the shakers into one another tapping it on the top he spun the shaker in mid air. After catching it then throwing it up with two hands past his shoulder vigorously shaking it.

    You could hear the ice being thrown back and forth from outside. Chilling the cocktail with his vibrating movement. Jackson poured the drink into a frozen martini glass that Chris placed on the bartop for Jackson. Jackson poured it into the martini glasses with flair tucking his body in as he poured knowing that Chris was coming around to drop off the checks to the man that took care of the drinks for the previous couples. Chris placed two more frozen martini glasses on the mat setting Jackson up for success. Jackson raised his hand higher till every drop came out of the shaker. Jackson finished preparing and pouring the rest of the drinks for Chris's guests. Jackson was shaking the last one up and Chris had the bottle of champagne in his hand and tossed it high in the air to Jackson. Jackson caught it with his free hand and spun on the sole of his heel toward the bar, popping the top off with his thumb. Pouring the chilly mixture of liquors and juices into the frozen martini glass topping it off with champagne. Jackson put the top back on and tossed the bottle back at Chris who put the champagne back in the fridge. Jackson sliced a lemon with a peeler and expressed juices into the martini before he dropped the lemon into the middle of the drink then finished garnishing the rest of the drinks. Jackson passed off the drinks to Chris's guests that looked impressed how delicious and quickly they all came out.

    Jackson examined the last martini walking over to the center of the bar, seeing thin ice crystals at the top of the martini built with perfection. Finally making eye contact with the woman in the blue dress Jackson stopped dead in his tracks when he realized who it was.

    Daisy sat there looking beautiful and smiled, her lips shined with maroon lip gloss covering her luscious lips, completely dolled up with her hair braided back looking completely different.

Changing his step, smoothly walking over with a boat load of confidence. Tossing a bar napkin toward her making it spin like a propeller in mid air floating down in the middle of Daisy frame. Jackson dropped off the drink then placed two small bar straws into the martini that dropped into the drink facing her direction. All she had to do was bend down and suck through the straws to quench her thirst.

"French 95, will warm you up on a brisk night like tonight." Jackson said leaning into the bar, noticing she was sitting in the same seat when he first saw her.

"Perfect but I went to a hockey game earlier. It was much colder in the rink, this is nothing." Daisy said as she pulled her martini in closer.

"Oh, you like hockey? My kind of woman."

"Nah, just there for moral support." Daisy said with a grin on her face.

"So you're taken then. If so, I'll stop flirting with you." Jackson said, taking a step back away from the bar.

"Not taken, you don't have to stop flirting." She said winking at Jackson taking a sip of her drink though the bar straws.

"Perfect, I'll come back and put the moves on you."

Jackson turned around, circulating around the bar seeking out who needed drinks next. Jackon moved around the bar like it was all his. Reading the people at the bar like he was two moves ahead. Watching him flow around the bar was a sight, with the other bartenders moving out of the way moving their bodies close to the ledges without directly looking at one another in such sync of instinct. They all worked together incredibly throwing bottles at one another, setting up glasses in line while another was putting together the ingredients into shakers. The flowed around eccentrically giving the bar a fun place to be. Joking around and talking to everyone, engaging multiple guests around the bar to intertwine conversations.

Jackson tapped Chris on the shoulder putting his hand up taking the plate from him. Jackson made his way back over to Daisy with an extra minute to spare. Jackson put the plate down in front of Daisy, sliding it on the bar top to her, grabbing a place setting at the same time putting it on the right side of her plate.

"This is me flirting." Jackson said leaving the food in front of her then walked away.

Daisy smiled, unrolling the black rollup, placing the napkin on her lap leaving the silverware tipped on the edges of her plate. The long plate had green sprinkled parsley all over it, bowned crispy cubes with a pink middle pink under a bed of leafy lettuce. A small glass ramekin was on the edge of the plate with an orange dipping sauce.

"Tuna tartare." Jackson said, walking back over watching Daisy examining the plate.

"I don't eat seafood." Daisy said with an embarrassed face.

"All good, it's all mine now. I guess I need to work on my game, I'm a bit rusty." Jackson said, taking the plate and placing it behind him, near the register.

"You have a game. Keep up the good work and I may give you my phone number." Daisy said loud enough as he placed his plate down playfully joking with him.

The couple next to them were enjoying the show Jackson was putting on. Jackson put the dish he got for Daisy in a to-go box, putting it in the corner bar with his name on it. Moments later a kale chicken caesar salad was placed in front of Daisy. Jacksons plan worked perfectly using his food to play with her because he needed a snack, really he wanted her to try it but for another time. Jackson had not forgotten their first date. Daisy did tell him she was not allergic, just didn't like seafood. He had a hard time forgetting anything about her since they met.

Daisy took a bite of the salad being blown away by something so simple having so much flavor. As she ate her chopped kale with chicken lightly covered by homemade caesar dressing she watched Jackson at work.

Daisy saw how good Jackson was at his job knowing the majority of people that came in by name. Often placing a drink on a bar napkin in an empty seat leaving new guests eyebrows to raise up. Jackson knew his clientele so well that when he saw them walk in from the parking lot he would make their drink by putting in their normal seat or an open seat on their preferred side. The guests appreciated it, making them feel like part of the bar. It was like a cheers bar where everyone knew one another largely having to do with having so many regulars, Jackon and the other bartenders engaging the groups of people into conversation. The vibe of the bar had a lot to do with it, the guests were treated with outstanding grade A service. Jackson was a natural, he enjoyed the flow of things. It was a sight to see him work the bar walking, talking and making multiple drinks all at the same time with such ease, not the least bit overwhelmed by how busy it was in the bar.

Daisy was impressed by how his brain worked, talking to many people before going to the POS system. Often grabbing multiple drink orders along with food orders without writing anything down. Quickly engaging then moving on till the task was done. When new guests sat down he would alway put out menus no matter how busy once they sat. Even if he was completely in the weeds he would start the service off promptly.

Watching him throwing in some conversation to each guest making them feel welcome by the end of the night they were like friends. Jackson knew when to pick his head up, when to make eye contact and when not to. When the bar was busy he did not make eye contact with anyone trying to get his attention if he maxed out how many things he could do at once. Then when he was free he was always on the lookout for anyone who needed a drink or something to eat.

 The shiny shaker flew through the air from Chris to Jackson, crisscrossing two bottles of liquor. They had to choreograph this and practiced a number of times to have it down as well as they did. Jackson put the tin on the bar mat once they were done showboating. Together they whipped the bottles around taking turns pouring into the same shaker elegantly. Chris filled up a small shaker with ice leaving it on the mat for Jackson to shake. Jackson shook so hard you could hear the ice disintegrating. Chris put a new frozen martini glass in front of Daisy so Jackson could pour it in the martini glass right in front of her. Jackson stared through the liquor downward flow of gravity right into Daisy's eyes. The pour slowed as the shaker grew dry only dripping down drop by drop. Jackson did not miss a drop nor break eye contact.

"Now about that number?" Jackson said tossing a white bar napkin like a frisbee landing directly in front of Daisy then he pulled out a pen from his back pocket and handed it to her.

    Daisy was incredibly impressed all day and night, she felt the impression tingling throughout her body making her nipples so hard she worried that it would be noticeable through her dress. Her legs crossed, holding herself on the verge of mentally erupting incredibly turned on by his confidence tonight. Jackson waited till she put the pen to the napkin before moving, as soon as Daisy put the pen to the napkin to write the couple next to her started to clap. Another woman on the other side of the bar clapped as well. Daisy finished writing and looked up into Jackson's eyes. Jackson put his hand up in the air, magically a bottle of champagne was put in his hand over his shoulder. Jackson walked over to Daisy to complete her French 95.

"My game must have improved quickly, eh." Jackson said, topping her martini off with some bubbles.

"You are a quick learner." Daisy said, handing Jackson her number on the folded napkin.

"I must be, I just watched a Youtube video on *how to improve your game* in the wine room after you called me out." Jackson said with a cheesy grin on his face.

    Daisy's lips were dry from breathing heavily using the martini as lubrication to satisfy her lips, luckily it was loud at the bar her loud breaths went unnoticed. She began to play with her hair watching Jackson work the room in his black collared shirt. Daisy stared down to his pleated black slacks everytime he turned around. When he was distracted she looked down at his zipper pressing her lips on eachother, her tongue massaged her lips. Releasing her urge, trying not to look like an aroused puppy dog when he looked over at her. It became more obvious with every sip she took as her body loosened up. The martinis had kicked in, having the devil on her shoulder starting to put dirty thoughts in her head.

The couple next to Daisy waved for Jackson to come by. They handed him their checkbook with a debit card inside. Jackson reached over to take it then the man pulled out a hundred dollar bill handing it to Jackson. The man's wife had been talking back and forth to Daisy since they sat down. The woman's hand was on Daisy's wrist looking like she was giving her a pep talk. It also could have been the truth talk or drunk talk, the couple drank two bottles of red wine.

"You take this pretty lady out. Make sure not to take her to a seafood joint." The tall man said sarcastically laughing, pulling the seat out for his wife.

Jackson and Daisy both showed their admiration for the kind gesture pleasantly saying goodbye to the couple.

"Pasta?" Jackson said, looking at Daisy waiting for her to answer.

"I love pasta." Daisy said, waving to the couple once more that departed, walking out the side door and the tall man grabbed the door for his wife.

"I guess we have to go out on a date." He said Jackson was lost in how happy Daisy looked.

Jackson began breaking down the bartop in front of her then went to the next station to break that down as well. The bar started to clear out in the next twenty minutes. The sound of glasses and plates surpassed the conversations that dwindled. The dishwasher was on repeat cleaning the glassware of every drink served in the entire restaurant. Daisy asked Chris for the tab while Jackson went to the back to restock beer.

"You dont have a tab." Chris said, shaking his head.

Daisy pulled up her bag to pull cash out of her bag. Chris shook his head putting his hand up, refusing the tip.

"You brought my boy back, I missed him. Worth more than any amount of cash Daisy." Chris said as he whipped the bar top near her.

Daisy thought of all the different things Chris could of ment by that. She turned her head around looking for Jackson. Wondering what had happened to him?

Her mind quickly changed, going somewhat blank when she saw Jackson appear through the swing black door behind her. Once she saw him he instantly smiled at her. Feeling honored that if there was something that happened to him that she can bring him out of the darkness. Healing the demons inside of him. Daisy thought about every smile she shared with him as a sigh of relief. Not knowing him well enough yet to know the facts. She was not nosey enough to ask or pry into his life. Jackson walked behind the bar with three twenty four packs of bottled beer. Dropping it on the cooler then catching his breath, putting his hand in front of his mouth covering his cough.

"What is that two or three people now?" Jackson said with his hands on his hips looking like Superman.

"We need to stop going out in public, sooner or later we're going to make the masses broke." Daisy said, raising her martini glass up to him finishing the last sip of her cocktail.

Jackson put the beers away in the cooler on the left of Daisy. They started to speak with only their eyes. Their bodies felt like magnets both feeling the pull toward one another with three feet of mahogany between them. Daisy's hands played with her hair, fingers going up and down her long strands of blonde.

"I'm going to take off, not going to be the last one left in here." Daisy said, pushing her hands on the bar forcing the seat to move back.

"I'll call you." Jackson said, pulling the napkin that Daisy wrote ten digits on from his pocket.

"Daisy." He said looking at the napkin then smirking at her like he had forgotten her name.

The clack of her heels amplified in the close to empty restaurant. While Jackson continued closing down the bar he was utterly distracted with each sound her heels made. Eyes were drawn in the direction of each echoing clack. The blue dress was tight in all the right places. Walking out the door Daisy looked over at him through the contemporary square glass wall tiles walking toward her car. Jackson was drying off glasses watching every step she took till she disappeared into the darkness of the night.

The night was very busy, lots of cash laid in the large glass bowl marked tips. The smell of beer from the drain started to stink up the place. The musty smell was a sign all in its own that the night was almost over. Hearing every word of the music as the bar continued to clear out. Jackson grabbed his phone connecting it to the restaurant's bluetooth putting on his own music while he finished up once it finally cleared out completely.

Chapter 5.

Ding....

"Up for another adventure?" Jackson texted Daisy a few minutes after the bar was empty.

Daisy was just walking through the door, a little tipsy, not hearing the phone go off. Throwing off her heels in the middle of the living room putting her purse on the couch. Daisy walked right to the refrigerator grabbing a bottle of white wine that was nice and chilled. Pouring a hefty glass into a wine glass, she then went to the living room and sat on the couch trying to make her mind blank, impossible after tonight's dream.

Sitting in the dark holding her glass of wine thinking of how sexy Jackson was that he got her number for the second time. Unsure of how he did it so smoothly, making everyone around them notice the spark as if it were the first time they met. Others want to add to their own flames trying to feed off them. Thinking what date would be next, what kind of surprises he had up his sleeve.

Regardless of that, a random stranger shelled out cash for them to go out on a date. Daisy began to long for him as she was getting used to that very feeling when she was not with him. Daisy looked into her purse for her phone to reread Jackson's texts to feel close to him.

A new message notification from Jackson was on her screen the moment she opened the phone. After reading it a full charge of emotion flew through her. Daisy sat up on the couch putting down the glass of wine between her legs.

"Yes." Daisy texted back, ready for the next adventure.

Ding....

"I'll be by in the next thirty minutes." Jackson texted back while he was counting the cash from the register on the bar top smoking a cigarette.

Daisy put her heels back on hoping they were sufficient for tonight's adventure. Jackson pulled up thirty minutes later to the minute with two coffees in hand. Daisy's head turned curiously when she saw the two coffees at this hour of the night. Becoming more suspicious shrinking her eyes when she noticed Jackson was in a completely different outfit also noticing he was not driving the same car.

Now he was in a navy tweed blue suit, cognac boots with a light blue long sleeve button up no tie. The top two buttons were undone exposing more ink that Daisy has yet to uncover. Each time they met she was electrified by new illustrations that marked his body. Waiting to see the whole masterpiece. Jackson handed over the coffee to her.

"Any fashion requirements for tonight." Daisy asked, leaning on the door frame still in the same stunning dress that left Jackson mesmerized at the bar.

"That's perfect, gorgeous. Are you ready for another adventure?"

Daisy eagerly nodded and put her pointer finger up then retreated back into the house to grab her nightly tablet, she stepped into the restroom quickly to make sure she was all done up right and grabbed her purse locking the door. Jackson took her hand guiding her to the passenger side of the blacked out truck. She needed to step on the running boards that automatically came down when he opened the door, Jackson helped her step up into the truck with her tightly fit dress. Daisy examined the vehicle thoroughly, the interior was a luxurious white leather on the seats, with dark hazelwood trim on the dash to the panels of the doors. Jackson shut her door walking around the front of the truck looking at her through the windshield then opened his door and got in.

"This is a new Escalade, do you sell drugs on the side or work your magic overtime at the bar?" Daisy said with both hands on her warm coffee waiting for his answer, noting in her head that she was also wearing all blue.

"Had to learn to do some other things, rather than be a career bartender. All you can do is survive with that kind of job." Jackson said starting up the ignitions with a touch of a button.

Jackon did not go into how, nor did Daisy ask. Now staring at his hands gripping the leather steering wheel wishing she could be the steering wheel, still feeling a bit tipsy. The heat transferred from the coffee into her hand, feeling the electricity form Jackson's subtle natural movements. Jackson jumped on the highway heading northbound aggressively moving past cars to get into the left hand lane. Very calmly moving his eyes from each of the three mirrors driving like he was going to be late for something with a heavy foot.

Daisy thought in her head he looked like the guy that kills people then goes and eats a steak. A natural protector persona, having higher laws than the man he projected. Jackson was sexy with a strong masculine, dark, mysterious, very put together and aware man. He didn't talk so much but when he did his words were thoroughly spoken. Flirting elegantly when he could fit it into any conversations, directly making her smile as often as possible.

Driving almost two hours away, listening to all different types of music. Jackson controlled the music on the steering wheel, a very eccentric taste in music played on the long ride. He only touched the phone twice to put on specific songs, not running a GPS the whole trip. Questions flew back and forth getting to know one another thirty minutes into the trip. Jackson was very brief with his answers, not going into detail about his past. Daisy knew that there was something that happened before she entered his life that derailed him a bit. Maybe that is why he is so reserved. There was pain in his eyes, he did not show much emotion except when he smiled at Daisy which was becoming quite often now. Jackson saw a sign looking intently, turning his head to look then getting in the right hand lane. Daisy tried to read the sign but it went by too fast.

"Know where we are going yet?" Jackson said, staring at the dark road in front of him.

"No."

"I need you to be my lucky charm tonight." Jackson said, putting his hand behind her seat.

Daisy bit down on her tongue not having any idea where they were going. Having a tough time putting together what was going on. Anxious and intrigued at the same time. Looking at Jackson curiously trying to figure out what he really had up his sleeve for tonight. Giving little information till now. Jackson pulled off the exit slowing down coming to the intersection. There was a big sign on the other side of the street that read "Hillshire Casino" with an arrow pointing to the right. Jackson slowed, then turned going in the direction of the arrow. A short distance drive then he pulled into the parking lot a mile from the exit.

The tires screeched with each turn up the car park, going up to the fourth level before finding a spot in the corner to back the truck into. Jackson grabbed Daisy's door and handed her his money clip directly after she stepped down from the automatic running boards. Daisy looked at the folded stack of cash bound together by a gold money clip. Feeling the weight of the cash in her hand filled with all large bills.

"Remember you're my lucky charm tonight."

Jackson grabbed her by the hand, the two of them walked toward the sliding doors to the elevators. Walking in the side entrance, they proceeded to head toward the main lobby. The lobby had vast wooden beams creating a triangular point like a teepee. There was a bar in the corner of the lobby; it was the only dimmed area in sight. Passing a few luxury stores on the way. Smelling charred steak from the steakhouse that was packed when walking by looking through the glass panels. Daisy said she had to go to the bathroom, after walking her to the nearest bathroom Jackson headed to the front desk. Once Daisy returned they headed to the underground casino, they were stopped before going downstairs by security that asked them to pull out their ID's.

After the handheld machine beeps flashing green allowing them entrance they both stood on the escalator descending into the casino. The lights from the machines blinked all over sparkling around the room, people cheered at the tables as they rolled the dice. Rows of people tapped buttons of the slots that sounded like a symphony. Smoke rose from people exhaling cigarettes on slots with drinks in hand. It was like a wonderland filled with opportunity.

Once they got off the escalader they headed straight toward the bar on their left filled with touch screen slot machines at each bar stool. On approach Jackson spun Daisy around spinning her around the floor like a ballerina tiptoeing into him. The blue dress Daisy wore flared out like an umbrella with each spin. Daisy's face lit up, Jackson pulled her in close in one swift motion. They were chest to chest, face to face, Jackson put his hand under her chin in the middle of the floor pulling her in for a deep wet kiss that melted Daisy.

Energy flowing all around the room, the blaring sounds of a jackpot ringer went off. People stopped to look at them in the middle of the room from every angle. Bells from the jackpot rang and like a tornado of eyes worshiping the lust that transferred between them as they kissed like no one was watching. Jackson pulled away from Daisy's alternate reality she was captured in and the jackpot stopped ringing. Jackson gave a light slap on her ass to go toward the bar with him then grabbed her hand.

Clouds of smoke rose from the cigarettes burning near the bar, the bartenders were busy shaking up drinks. The tins sounded like maracas as the ice slammed in the shaker. Jackson put his elbow on the bar leaning in to get the attention of the blonde bartender. Once she made eye contact with him he pulled her in with his brown eyes.

The bartender whipped them up two smoked old fashioned with giant squared ice cubes. Jackson handed Daisy a short rocks glass with smoke rising out of the glass. The smell of hickory smoke was inhaled, setting a precedent for her old fashion experiences. Daisy raised her glass as soon as he handed it to her. Now knowing Jackson would toast. Looking into his dark brown eyes she felt desired, the way he looked at her had her on cloud 9.

"To my lucky one." He said.

CLINK

A smile pasted to her face, impossible to remove. The suaveness of his deep voice complemented the words that came out of his mouth.

"Guess that was the end of our free drink reign." Daisy said then took a sip, her eyes widened once she tasted the smoked old fashion.

"Technically those were for free." Jackson said, trying to hide his smile with the glass.

"Technically?" Daisy said, raising her eyebrows, swallowing another little gulp at a time enjoying every bit of the drink in her mouth.

"Yes, the drinks are free here." Jackson said, moving his head in the direction where he was going, pulling her hand along with him gripping it tightly.

"How long do you think we can keep this streak up?" Daisy said walking on air.

Jackson spun her around again, then continued walking even after spilling part of her drink that began dripping down the side of her hand. Daisy was not phased by it. Feeling like a star between the bright flashing lights all around, her dress spinning in the wind and the eyes of strangers checking out the bliss that they shared. Jackson let go of her hand, leaned into her putting his hand around her shoulder and whispered in her ear.

"However long you want."

Daisy bit her lip as he dug his hands massaging deeply into her shoulders. An uncontrollable twitch consumed her body leading to the hairs on the back of her neck and arms to stick straight up like skyscrapers in a city. The goosebumps he gave her did not go away, he managed to continue to give them to her the more he massaged.

Walking through the casino on violet woven wool with gold abstract lines that made shapes at their feet. Hundreds of square 10x10 cut-ins lighted with fluorescents in the ceiling outlined by shiny gold trim making the room feel rich, an illusion of anything was possible. A row of marble columns went down the center of the room elongated throughout the whole casino.

The dice were flying out of a man's hand landing on 11 as Jackson stepped up to the table winning the roll. Daisy handed Jackson the money at his request. He began thumbing through pulling out three hundred dollar bills and handed them to Daisy to throw it on the table, the first one was the hundred that the tall man from the bar gave to Jackson. The dealer spread the bills on the table.

"Coming in at $300." The dealer yelled, then folded the money, putting it through a slot in the table that he then pushed through to a secret compartment with a wooden tool.

The dealer handed Daisy the chips. Jackson watched the first roll without betting. After a seven was rolled when the point was eight, the dealer had to pass on the dice to Daisy. Jackson whispered to Daisy where to throw down chips, she put them on multiple spots on the craps table. Jackson touched her hand with the dice in them holding them to tell her what to do. "Make sure you blow on them." Jackson whispered in her ear, then putting both hands on her hips centering her on the table.

"Owa." Daisy shrieked without thought as he put her in position.

Jackson stepped back watching Daisy throw the dice on the table like she was the only one there. Taking it all in, snapping mental pictures that shot in his mind. She had never played cramps before, playing it with excitement not fully understanding what was going on. Even though she had no idea it seemed from afar she knew what she was doing the dealer kept giving her more chips with every throw.

Jackson kept whispering where to put the chips as the dealer handed the dice along with her the winning chips. Their winnings continued to pile. The others at the table began to copy her bets. Tapping her on the shoulder with congratulations making everyone at the table money.

The cheers loudened drawing in the passing people to watch the show. Daisy rolled 11 winning passes in a row. A crazy run of luck made Daisy glow. The dealer used his metal dice stick to pull the translucent red dice toward him, handing them to Daisy once more. After all the applause was done Jackson tapped her when the dealer was waiting to pass the dice to Daisy. Jackson put his hand up.

"Lets cash out." Jackson said, making the cut off symbol with his hand moving them in front of his neck.

     Jackson took her by the hand with a pocket full of chips. He twirled her once more congratulating her in his own way, his arm went around her backside lightly pulling her hair with his hand forcing her to look up at him. He leaned down kissing her neck just below her ear. Sucking ever so lightly so it did not leave a hickey. Before he backed away he nibbled on the bottom of her ear, right below her stud earring. Jackson released his grip looking down at the glow of her. Daisy was stuck in another dimension, walking sideways as he led her. Her eyes completely shut, stuck where he had just put her letting him control her movement. Jackson noticed and stopped to wait, watching until she snapped back. Then after Daisy opened her eyes slowly she tried holding onto it as long as possible that feeling right before waking from the trans he put her in.

     Walking through the casino floor they began heading toward a red, black and green wheel that spun on a close to relatively empty table, only one woman was playing on the no limit table. The computer screen above it had a few different stacked numbers with a color in a column of previous winners. Daisy had seen this game but again did not know how to play nor the name. As they approached she read the gold badge screwed into the table that read *Roulette*. Once she got close enough to watch Daisy quickly grasped the concept of the game, understanding the numbers that took up the majority of the green felt board.that the odds were better if you picked the number and color. The game could also be played by picking the right color, odd or even without choosing a number.

"Pick a number." Jackson whispered in her ear.

"Take your time, no rush my lucky one." He said, rubbing the back of her neck.

Daisy watched a few rounds trying to see if there was a rhythm to the game. It was totally random. Jackson kept rubbing her neck, tickling her skin with his finger tips, completely relaxed her, his hand rubbed down into her spine.

The ball chased the numbers spinning on the wood board eventually slowing and the metal ball bounced from one circular groove cut out to the next until it found its home. Above each circular groove had a solid red, black or green circle with a number in the middle. First Daisy thought of the number 2, looking down at her hand in his tightly bound together. Watching the woman at the table lose constantly picking a bunch numbers spreading out her bets.

"I think we should get another drink first." Daisy leaned in, grabbing Jackson's other arm sliding her hand down to grab him by both arms to head toward the bar.

Jackson did not move, Daisy did not have the strength to pull him either. He created a backlash and tried once more to move the statue. Jackson pulled her in and she stumbled, Jackson gave her a kiss on the forehead then they headed to the bar on his lead. The same blonde bartender made instant eye contact with Jackson once they rounded the corner. The bartender nodded, grabbing bourbon after Jackson put two fingers in the air. Jackson then put his hand down covering his mouth coughing leaning on the bar to support his weight.

"You need to pick a color along with a number, or you can pick either of the two green zero's." Jackson said, speaking to Daisy but he was looking at the bartender making their drinks.

Daisy put her hand upon his chest, resting her head next to her hand hearing his heartbeat. Zoning out for a moment from the circus of entertainment going on all around them. She closed her eyes counting his heart beats completely relaxed. Daisy did not move until he kissed her on the top of her head for a few seconds. He then turned around to grab the smokey drinks Daisy released watching the smoke rise up out of the glass. Daisy saw Jackson pull out a

$10 chip from his pocket and flick it up in the air toward the bartender. Clapping with both hands the bartender caught it, then thanked Jackson.

Jackson sat down at the bar pulling Daisy's back side to rest in between his legs on the edge of his chair. They clinked glasses without a toast. Jackson only toasted one time, only the first drink of the night. Smoke entered their mouths as they took the first sip, the smokey wood chipped aroma gave the drink a more complex flavor that complemented the sweetened bourbon ever so beautifully. The giant ice cube corners botched inside the glass with every movement. The drink was so good that it could be possibly classified as addicting. After his sip Jackson exhaled and a bit of smoke came out. Jackson then pulled out the chair next to him closer then assisted Daisy up. After she sat he pulled the bar stool even closer to him. The blonde bartender walked over grabbing liquor bottles from the well nearest them, pouring them into the shaker her eyes got distracted from making the cocktail she was working on after hearing the screeching on the floor that the stool made as Jackson pulled Daisy in. Daisy noticed a gold charm with the number 11 that dangled off the bartender's neck when she looked up. The bartender finished adding liquor then bent over to grab ice for a drink she was making. "That's the one." The bartender said.

Daisy made her way up her charm with a blank face. Daisy's mind was stuck on the number 11. Again that number constantly recurring all over in so many different variations. "The drink, that's the one right there. That's by far my favorite drink here." The blonde bartender said.

"Yes it is delicious, this may be the best drink I've ever had." Daisy said, snapping out thinking that it would have been a grand illusion if she was saying *that's the one* to her thoughts about picking a number for Roulette.

Jackson sat like a statue in the bar stool, his head turning slowly. Daisy heard his neck that grinded, astonished by the heat of his eyes on her. Daisy smiled while taking a sip of her drink feeling like a demon was looking over at her in her peripheral vision. Drips of bourbon caught in his beard after abruptly falling down his lip, since he rapidly stopped drinking after Daisy's remark.

"Thank you, I'll be here all night! I'll keep em coming, good luck out on the floor." The bartender said going off to drop a freshly made screwdriver and some kind of martini off to a guest on the other side of the bar.

"I'm just kidding." Daisy said laughing out loud very close to making a snort noise putting her hand in front of her mouth controlling her laughter.

"I wanted to see your reaction. So stoic and adorable at the same time." Daisy said, her hand went up to whip the alcohol from his beard, she then stopped before it was gone and pulled him by his beard closer to lick it up instead. Jackson did not move until her tongue entered his mouth. He tasted the bourbon on her tongue that she just cleaned off him and then she pulled away.

Daisy licked the freshly wiped bourbon off her fingers, making sure to get every drop before pulling them out slowly glaring into his eyes. Jackson's eyes flashed over like a shark about to attack.

"I have every intention to bring you up to my room to show you how hard .... it will be for you to forget tonight's date. Let's go" Jackson said aloud once her fingers left her mouth.

"Your room?" Daisy said, stunned.

"Yes. We are going to go play roulette first." Jackson said walking away leaving Daisy no other choice but to chase after him.

There were more people playing at the table now. Only one space was open at the corner of the table, closest to the dealer. Jackson pulled out his money clip from her purse thumbing through the stack pulling a bunch of hundreds for Daisy, putting the rest of the cash into the middle of the clip then back into her bag.

"Put it all down." Jackson said, handing her a wad.

Daisy slammed it on the table, the dealer reached over and grabbed the cash lining it on the table side by side five bills at a time.

"Coming in three thousand," the dealer said when he finished counting.

The dealer quickly shuffled his hand through a pile of chips in his bank. It was like watching a magician stack all the chips in stacks of five. Jackson received thirty black chips worth $100 each. Daisy was too busy having so much fun at the other table throwing dice she did not realize how much money they won, the winnings were still in his pocket. Jackon grabbed the chips from the dealer, while Daisy watched as the ball spun around and around. Jackson then put the chips into his side pocket and slipped one chip into her palm, he rubbed his pointer finger along her hand.

"Pick a number, I'm putting it all in the center on a red, black or green. Then we go upstairs for the jackpot." Jackson said then backed away, slapping her on her ass as secretly as possible.

Holding onto the one chip, Daisy shivered looking at Jackson. Daisy tried to overcome her thrill by turning towards the table.

"Final bets." The dealer shouted.

Daisy's eyes were magnetized and frozen on one square that was screaming at her. Subliminally seeing it over and over since she met Jackson. Daisy was not the one to believe in anything magical, only facts and logic. Signs, supernatural or fate were not foreign to her; the concept never made sense. Nothing ever happened that made her feel like it was possible. Filled with insite of what to do, she knew where to put her chips.

"I know what number." Daisy said.

Jackson took the chips out of his pocket. Daisy put out both hands grabbing the stacked black chips looking at the square that she was going to put it all on, her intuition was steaming. The ball stopped, the game came to a conclusion. Everyone who won received more chips, the losers chips were taken and put back in the bank next to the dealer. Daisy reached over across the table trying to neatly pile up all thirty chips in the middle of the square.

"Final bets," the dealer yelled, spinning the ball around the wooden wheel.

The ball circled around at a high speed. There was a lot of money on the table, everyone watched intently. The ball started to slow, begging to bounce as the wheel twirled, lowering its speed the ball was ready to stop. The rest of the room was absent of all sounds. Hearing each tap of the ball on the wood going from groove to groove. Ahhs and ohhs around the table rose. The biggest hand on the table was from the most beautiful woman in the blue dress that sparked in the light. The ball slowed to find its final resting place, Daisy's hands were on her cheeks covering her face.

Before the ball stopped Jackson grabbed her hands off her face from behind and spun her around. Stopping her to look deep into each other's eyes while the rest of the table cheered. Daisy radiated with his hands on hers. The two were hardly phased at the outcome knowing that they won without looking at the table. Luck that it hit the black, or was it fate, number 11. Jackson gave her a long kiss then spun her back to see her fruition.

"Let's get one more for the road, gorgeous." Jackson said.

The dealers had to get the pit boss to grab more chips. The payout was 35:1 with a $3000 bet. Jackson grabbed twenty dark blue $5000 chips, the rest of the chips were $500. Taking them from the dealer, Jackson securely put them in his empty pocket leaving the dealer with a $500 chip as a tip before leaving. Jackson and Daisy's pinkies interlocked headed toward the bar. The same blonde bartender started making the two drinks without asking while they were sitting down at the bar all over each other like high schoolers. Jackson grabbed both drinks once they were dropped off. Taking out a $500 chip down sliding it to the edge of the bar toward the bartender and asked her for something before they left.

"Let's go upstairs." Daisy said, gripping her glass tight.

Jackson grabbed the bottle of champagne once the bartender returned, he then took Daisy by the hand leading the way to the room. As they waited for the elevator his hand gripped hers so tight holding his drink and champagne together in his other hand. The energy of their connection was pulsating, Daisy's heart began to beat fast with his fingers digging into her skin.

The bell rang, they were both so ready to be in the room alone for the first time. From the reflection of the chrome elevator they saw each other's smirks, intently looking at one another until the door opened. They stepped in and got close before the doors shut. Once their lips touched one another they heard the elevator ring again, resulting in the door opening back up. A hand appeared into the door that was opening back up. A frugal woman wearing pearls slowly emerged through the crack of the door. The door fully opened and the woman did not step in. "May I?" The woman asked, standing there.

Jackson biting his lip in agony, complacently nodding. Each floor that passed the tension arose. Jackson let go of her hand and side stepped behind Daisy.

His hand was still at his waist level then redirected to her arm to rub down her forearm with only his fingertips. Rising up and down to the mid part of her inner forearm down to her wrist. Daisy tried to keep her composure while being ticked. Pheromones fumed throughout the 4x4 enclosure. The sensation made her twitch, Daisy's eyes shut trying to hold it in. When Jackson saw this in the reflection of the mirror he barely grazed her neck with his lips smelling her perfume. Trying to keep the spark continuing even though they were interpreted. The lady in the elevator was either deaf, hard of hearing or was minding her business.

Finally the bell rang. The woman with the pearls prepared herself to leave. Jackson stepped up and held the door as she walked out. Once she exited the elevator Jackson held the close door button and waited looking right at Daisy. The doors shut and within an instant they were like a magnet their lips touched, saliva swapped, their free hands all over each other. Daisy's body was pressed up against the side of the elevator. Jackson spun her around forcing her fingerprints to paint the mirrors.

Pressing her up against the wall, he kissed the back of her neck. His fingertips in the middle of the back of her head, fingers under her hair scratching down to her neck. Jacksons lips moved around her neck, Daisy's urge to kiss him again turned into his lips. The champagne bottle hit the handrails of the elevator. They both heard the ring, the door could not have opened faster. Drinks were spilling the whole way up, they were all over one another bouncing from the elevator door to the side wall of the hallway. Till they got to their hotel room, Jackon fumbled for the key from his back pocket while they were still interlocked. Once the door flew open they made their way to the dresser. Jackson took Daisy's glass and palmed both of their cocktails, placing them on the dresser next to the TV leaving a water ring underneath splashing booze trying to put it down blind. He was biting her top lip in control of her every step, the chips jingled in his pocket. Jackson put her in the middle of the suite, stopping once she was in place. Holding her by the hips, he leaned in kissing her neck. Moving up her neck he exhaled, making her shake from blowing hot air in her ear.

"Close your eyes." Jackson said assertively walking behind her.

      Jackson grabbed her zipper located on the back of her dress, Daisy stood in the middle of the room. Standing posing like she was about to be painted. An uncontrollable chill went up her neck, her eyes were shut aimed at the ceiling after he pulled down on her hair. Her mouth was open, inhaling and exhaling heavier. Trying to slow her excitement down by taking multiple deep breaths. He pulled the zipper all the way down, Daisy felt like the air conditioner was on full blast tensing her body. Jackson moved both of her shoulder straps from her dress to the side. He had moved them to a position where when he let go the dress fell off in one motion. Once he released the blue dress parachuted slowly down her body till it collapsed on the floor. The cool air from the room changed her body temperature, her eyes clenched. She took a step forward, now she was only in her heels stepping over the dress assisted by his hand.

      Daisy trembling opened her eyes half way, feeling his lips on the back of her neck then down her spine. As he went down he paused and bit her ass, her eyes popped open. Jackson's hands continued south, fingertips dug into her ankles. His body came up, fingers rising up the back of her knee caps, rising more one of his hands went underneath her wetting his fingers.

Jackson's hands released from her body and he walked in front of her putting his wet fingers in her mouth. Daisy bites down on licking his fingers inside her. Jackson had to really tug to get his fingers back, he stepped toward the dresser grabbing the unopened champagne bottle. Daisy stood watching him pull the top foil off, popping the cork off shooting it across the room like a gunshot. Daisy did not take a step waiting for him to return.

Jackson approached her, taking a big swig of the champagne. Lowering the bottle to his hips he grabbed her cheeks mushing her lips into plato. Then his thumb on her chin Jackson pulled her mouth open. Her mouth widened, now open Jackson leaned in and spit champagne in her mouth. Once Daisy swallowed a large amount of bubbles the rest dripped down her chin and down her chest. Jackson put his thumb in her mouth, pushing on her bottom teeth, lowering her down on her knees. Jackson felt her smile on his finger pulling her down to the ground.

Jackson took another sip, swallowing as he crouched down facing her submission. Jackson put his hand around her neck squeezing lightly watching her eyes roll in the back of her head. Daisy moaned lightly stunned by another load of champagne spit into her open mouth. Swallowing quickly, making it possible to take in breath. She felt the excess flow down her body. Jackson released his grip a tad bit, pulling away licking her lips as he did.

Jackson put the bottle down still crouched and started squeezing, biting her lip, kissing her slowly full of passion. His hands felt how wet her lips between her legs were. Teasing grazing her, making his hands sticky. Jackson stopped for a moment, rubbing his fingers together in the air feeling only her in his hand as Daisy watched.

Daisy bobbed up and down on her knees, her tongue licked her lips watching him. Her back was arched leaning forward toward Jackson. His weight was on the tips of his toes crouched down at eye level.

Unbuttoning his sleeves looking at Daisy completely naked down on her knees. Her eyes closed shut with her hands on the top of her bent knees. After his shirt was all unbuttoned in the middle, he gently touched her cheek. Daisy opened her eyes gawking at Jackson's shirt fully undone patiently waiting to proceed.

Jackson stood up, standing over her dripping in ink for a moment for her to really look then he walked around her. Jackson reached down to move her hands from her knees to the back of her heels forcing her to grip the studs of her heels. Daisy complied, bending her back, her breasts in the air pointing toward the ceiling. Jackson pulled out a glass vile from his pocket unscrewing off the black top. Pouring a few piles of white powder on the top of her breasts. His face hit her tits sniffing up the powder and the small bits of residue that he licked up.

Daisy felt incredible being what he desired and submissive. The act he just did on her shook things up, sending electric sensations up her chest. Jackson's tongue was all over her chest and she was left with no breath, hoping this feeling stays up all night. That certainly was unexpected, the tingles spread. Enjoying how he was using her, giving her a striking demonic possession that heated her body to a boiling point. A powerful rush of sensitivity took her soul over. He continued his tongue all over her bent body.
"Anything you want to do tonight, I'm in." Daisy said, belting out breathing heavily, her hands gripping her heels.

Jackson was electrified, head rushed ready to rock her world, incredibly turned on by her words. Jackson's head rose up her body licking her breast then up her neck. Daisy's fingers rubbed vigorously into her heels, feeling the texture of the leather.

Jackson grabbed the champagne off the floor putting his other thumb back in her mouth. Daisy was forced to come forward, hands back on her knees. Daisy's big blue eyes looked up at his shirt unbuttoned. Jackson took a sip with his thumb still still in her mouth pulling her head closer to him, her chin resting on his belt. Daisy was licking his thumb inside her mouth, scratching her knees with excitement. Jackson leaned back pushing his hips into her face, his upper torso looked like a diagonal. Jackson raised up his arm bending his elbow back pouring the champagne down his chest, it continued down to her lips. Daisy on her knees trying to catch every drop with her mouth wide open, like a luge that ran down his tightened tattooed abdomen. Daisy gulped up as much as possible while the excess dripped down her chin proceeding to drip down her chest onto her stomach and all over her legs. The floor was wet and covered in champagne.

Daisy's hands elevated from his hips up to pull his shirt off as possible, never getting up from her knees. Jackson leaned back and the champagne luge stopped so he could take his arms from the sleeves. Daisy impulsively reached for his belt, ripping it off then unbuttoning his pants. Pulling down his zipper then down with his pants. She filled her mouth with his hard cock slobbering with the help of the excess champagne around her mouth. Drool dripped down her chin along the same as the champagne. Gagging when he pulled her in, he gripped her hair into a ponytail. Daisy almost out of breath. Jackson pulled his cock out of her mouth and helped her up, she licked all the way up his torso on her way up. Daisy tried to keep her balance even though Jackson was in control of her movements. Still in her heels that made her tall enough to reach up to his lips.

Daisy looked all over his naked body, it was fully covered in ink while Jackson kicked off his loafers then his pants stuck around his ankles. Daisy could not take her eyes off him, wiping the mixture of drool and champagne from her chin her hands descended down to her chest rubbing it all in. Daisy was soaked down to her body down to her hips, she felt every drop.

Once they were both completely nude Jackson picked her up carrying her a few feet to the couch. Gripping her tightly with his heavily tattooed hands holding her by her ass. Daisy could not keep her eyes off him in pure focus, without a stumble he made it to the couch. Jackson looked her deep in the eyes and turned around dropping his weight into the middle of the cloth sofa. Jackson teased her by rubbing his penis between her legs till she couldn't take it, reaching around her back to grip it and tried to put it inside her. It took a while for him to get inside of her tight pussy. Kissing in the meantime as Jackson continued to tease her slowly making his way inside, little by little she felt every inch.

Daisy rode him hard till her own liquid was dripping down her inner thigh savagely moaning at her climax. Right at that moment in her heightened state Jackson stood up with her, he was still inside her and walked her over to the bed as she screamed leaning her weight down feeling all of him. Jackson smiled and let her finish, then he dropped her on the bed and picked her legs up in the air. Jackson stood over her on the bed, he started thrusting and threw her legs over his shoulders. Daisy moaned as Jackson hit a new spot, her hand covering her mouth from screaming too loud after each of his powerful thrust.

The four walls shook with pain to pleasure, adjusted with wild passion. Jackson put his hand under her back picking her up, moving her to the center of the bed for him to have enough room to come aboard.

Daisy pulled a pillow over her face biting down concealing her loud moans of intense pleasure. Completely dominated from position to position feeling one after another powerful earthquakes deep inside of her. The cold air was on but both of them were doused in sweat, tasting the saltiness of one another.

Daisy's hands and knees on the bed she was gripping the sheets, he had a tight grip of her hair that wrapped around his hand. Jackson pulled her head up by pulling back on her hair, he gave her some slack as she leaned up and back into him and curled her head to the side. They were almost facing each other, Daisy's back was bent like the curve of the moon sitting in his lap. He released his grip of her hair leaning in slowing down thrusting himself inside her. Daisy turned so she could kiss him, her movements were controlled by his hands holding the inside of her hips. He sped up his movements and pulled away to spit in her mouth.

Jackson thrusted with such intensity randomly for just one stroke that made her shriek out cursing and craving more. He mimicked what her body wanted and gave it to her, she came hard again and again. Moving her body into different positions, he bent her over in a yoga pose. Daisy's chest was on the bed, arms out grabbing the edge of the mattress and her ass up in the air. Jackson switched his rhythm to different motions until he found the one she desired and finished her back to back in the same position while she drooled on the bed.

Jackson's hands moved all over her body each time she finished like he was prepping her for the next round. She enjoyed every second, Jackson pushed her into a new position noticing her body was weak, exhausted from his endurance. Daisy had finished many times each orgasm was stronger than the last. Daisy rolled over with Jackson's force and laid there on the pillow almost incoherent. Jackson rubbed her legs seeing if she had enough energy to continue to play, but she was ready to pass out with absolutely no energy left. He rubbed his hand all over her body, massaging every muscle in her arms, down her torso to her legs taking his time on each part. Massaging her body to rest, until she began to doze off.

Jackson laid down pulling her back into his chest cuddling her after putting the blanket over them. His arms tightened around her body holding her. His hips swayed guiding himself back in her, Daisy abruptly moaned as he slid it in, her eyes were still closed. They were like two lovers forever trapped in a tomb all night. Comfortably numb their breath synchronized till the morning light.

Daisy's hand gripped the sheets, the chill of the air froze her erotic dream in place. Moving her body back and forth with pleasure trying to hold on to it before waking up. Feeling a firm sensation with each of her movements. Daisy was awake and her head began to turn to see if the other side of the bed was empty or not even though she did not want to, just in case.

Daisy reluctantly opened her eyes and turned, pushing her body into him realizing she woke up with Jackson still inside of her, she stretched back harder pressing her body into him. That was the first time either one of them moved in hours. At last Daisy felt sane after what felt like another powerful dream, now he was finally by her side. She consistently grinded into him till he woke up, morning sex is the best way to wake up. The walls shook with the rise of the sun. They finished quicker than last night, getting a nice rush of energy as they climaxed at the same time. Daisy remained on top of him looking down all over his body.

"You have such pretty eyes." Jackson said, catching his breath staring up at Daisy still straddling him.

"Now I need coffee." Jackson said, rubbing his face and started coughing.

      Each time he coughed Daisy felt a vibration and trust together that made her eyes spin into her brain. It took a lot of will power for Daisy to get off of him, getting used to the feeling of him filling her up. They put on the same clothes as last night they put themselves together to go out in public, fixing their bed head and Daisy had to clean her body that was all sticky.

"I need to eat and a bloody mary." Daisy said, holding her stomach, putting her hair in a business bun, then stopped getting distracted by the symmetrical sharks on each side of his hips seeing it in the morning light shining in between the curtains while he pulled up his pants in the middle of the room.

      Daisy's mouth was open, looking at him shining in the sun completely covered. Seeing each chapter of his story that he permanently put into his skin. Jackson ordered another bottle of champagne for the table when they went downstairs for breakfast. They hydrated on mimosa and bloody mary cocktails. They were a bit tipsy first thing in the morning after a wild adventure. Once the plates were taken from the breakfast table Jackson pulled something shiny out of his pocket and it made a clunk noise as he moved it closer to her. The cold metal touched her wrist then the groves of the locks clinked until it firmly locked around her wrist.

"You're all mine." Jackson said holding her arm to put on the other side of the handcuff on his wrist.

      After dropping cash on the table they made their way back to the elevator keeping the cuffs on the whole time, her hand was in his with a firm grip. They walked chained to one another all the way to the room. An hour later there was a knock on their hotel door in the heat of the moment. The housekeeper opened the door before they said a word because they were into one another at that very moment. Jackson stood up fumbling to grab a towel that was on the dresser. Jackson made a noise trying to put words together and at the same time his hand was still bound to Daisy. The housekeeper walked in on Jackson standing there naked, handcuffed to Daisy and speechless. The housekeeper turned around and shut the door behind her, apologizing with her hands in front of her face. Jackson at that time used the key to release himself from Daisy.

"That just happened." Daisy said, covering the laughter with her hands, a dangling metal cuff hung off her wrist.

Jackson got back on the bed and grabbed her hands, putting them together. He put the other cuff on Daisy's other arm. Daisy shrieked as her hands were cuffed with one another looking up at the three x's stacked on top of each other below his waistline, his knees on each side of her head with him dangling in front of her face. She continued to look all over his skin while he hovered over her completely naked. The night before was so dark, seeing more of his tattoos for the first time as the daylight hit his skin in awe.

"We're already late checking out, mine as well as getting our money's worth now." He said, grabbing her bound hands.

Daisy's eyes rolled into the back of her head uncontrollably after he said that she was so ready for him to fuck her again. Waiting for the pleasure that he was going to give her, she was throbbing in anticipation. Now Daisy was tied up turning the spice up to a level she had never experienced. The cold metal on her skin made her body want him more.

They created waves in the bed once more. Breathing harder with each steady hip thrust. They shook the four walls, getting their money's worth for the night and day. When they finished Daisy wiped off her mouth that had a mixture of herself and Jackson laying there unable to move. They rested for about twenty minutes before Jackson looked at his watch. Once again they put themselves properly together to head back on their Sunday afternoon drive home.

Opening the door peeking out like James Bond checking for housekeeping. Jackson bent down a little waving for Daisy to get on his back. Daisy jumped on, a door near their room opened and Jackson took off down the hallway trying to avoid the peeping tom. A speedy piggy back ride down the hall left Daisy feeling like a bird flying through the air. Gripping his chest with both and holding on for dear life, hair waving back and forth. Perhaps the mimosas and bloody mary's did their job as Jackson's pockets jingled down the hall.

On the way back Daisy was exhausted with a beautiful glow to her and he couldn't get enough of it so he put his hand on her thigh. Jackson's hand lowered down to her knee where he pulled her dress up. Sliding her panties aside his fingers inside of her, he had a need to touch her more. Daisy leaned her head into the headrest and licked her lips.

It looked like they were about to be stuck in traffic, red tail lights in the distance, so they started to slow. Jackson pressed the breaks down till they were at a complete stop while his fingers moved and curved up into her. Rubbing inside of her driving a few feet at a time then hitting the break dealing with the traffic jam. As Daisy began to moan harder the car began to fog up, as the moans got louder and Jackson's fingers moved harder and faster pushing up toward her belly.

The car became humid, Daisy exhaled deeply and constantly. Windows quickly became completely fogged, Jackson had to turn on the defroster but did not slow the rhythm with his fingers in Daisy. Daisy leaned back in the seat, her legs were on the dashboard spread not aware of the traffic or the steamy windows. Her hand gripped the handle above the window on the passenger side of the door.

His aggressiveness started to rumble her body to convulse, the scent of her filled the car. Her other hand grabbed Jackson's hand inside of her to try to slow him down. Quivering with pleasure was so intense she couldn't take it. Daisy began to shake harder, gripping his hand trying to stop him, her body trembled as Jackson sped up. Daisy busts out yelling and screaming as she orgasm exploded inside of her like she had never felt before. Once she regained a sense of normalcy when he took his fingers out of her she sat enjoying her post orgasm ecstasy tingling.

Jackson gave her a second then began to rub softly in the right spot of her clit after she came, making her twitch feeling so good it almost hurt. She smiled but the feeling was too overwhelming she pushed his hand off. It was way too sensitive she opened her eyes pushing off his hand with both of her hands and might. Daisy smiled wishing she could have him continue but her mind was mush, feeling numb and having to focus on breathing. Licking her lips she put her hand on her head.

"Enough." Daisy said panting, eyes barely open feeling dizzy and unconscious.

"I'll give you a break. For now." He said with his hand up in the air.

Comfortably enjoying her after glory she looked over at him, she started to tingle once she saw his face. The windows were still fogged up, the windshield somewhat clear enough for Jackson to see the cars visibly in front of him. After a minute of Daisy enjoying the tickling that continued just by looking at him knowing what he just did to her. She pushed some hair out of her face turning fully in her seat to see what he was doing. Jackson put his fingers on the fogged window to his left. The traffic was barely moving, Jackson wrote on the window as he hit the gas then the brake, able to do both at the same time. His hand stopped moving, leaning his right shoulder back into the seat so Daisy could read. Jackson placed his hand back on her leg massaging it when he was done writing.

You're all mine!!

This is what Daisy was reading, sitting completely stunned but without words she felt what he wrote. Jackson continued to drive with his hand on her leg staring off into the road without making eye contact with her after that. Daisy read the note until it faded away after the windows were cracked open. Her legs were still on the dashboard barfoot now crossed, she leaned back in her seat with Jackson's hand remaining on her leg the whole way back. Daisy needed to take a nap, completely falling asleep after his words disappeared to regain her energy.

    The black truck pulled into Daisy's driveway, the bumps up the curb woke her. Jackson walked Daisy to the door after the long drive, she was still tired waking in her heels. Still in the same clothes from the day before having theirselves a dirty stay out. Returning in the evening, the sun was on its way down, night was falling upon them both. The pair stopped at the door, Jackson leaning in to kiss her goodbye. Daisy already had one hand on the door handle trying to pull him inside. Jackson released himself from her succulent lips, he backed away back down the stairs. Daisy stepped inside kicking her heels off. Looking out the screen door and watched Jackson walk back towards his truck. Once he vanished in the distance behind the truck Daisy pulled the door wide open.

"Wait!" She yelled.

    Jackson turned at Daisy leaning in the door frame, puppy dog eyes set on her face. She cocked her head to the side resting it on the brick in between the door opening. Daisy used his magic against him, communicating to him vividly without a sound with lustfulness. Jackson stood briefly watching her with a profound vision. Putting his pants hands in his pockets leaning to his left side watching her anguish in her spectacular blue dress. Daisy put her hand up signing for him to come to her, taking one hand out of his pocket he shut the car door then he walked back up the stone walkway. Walking with authority all the way up the stairs, wrapping his arm around her, picking her up once he got inside. Daisy wrapped around him like a claw machine going for a prize. Jackson stepped into the house propping her up on the couch right inside the door. She ripped his shirt off causing the buttons to fly everywhere, she threw his shirt behind her landing on the coffee table. One of her unlit candles on the coffee table toppled over. Daisy was oblivious, her teeth biting down into his chest. Digging her pearly whites deep into his skin. Jackson couldn't stand the teeth sharp like a vampire, he couldn't take it any longer pulling her fangs off of him. He put his two fingers in her mouth prying her jaws open to release her deathly bite.

"Where is your room?" Jackson said, after standing he pulled down her dress.

"Back there." Daisy pointed towards the hallway behind him to the left.

Jackson made his way toward her room, he stopped and propped her on the door frame before the hallway pulling back his hand smacking it on her ass.

"Ughhhh." Daisy gasped with a huge smile that crossed her face.

Pulling his hand back again he hit the same spot playfully. Daisy teeth dug into one another, he had a handful of hair in his grip. Daisy pointed toward the hallway to her bedroom, Jackson bent down and bit her ass like he was chewing a steak. Daisy reached back grabbing his hair to pull him back up with her head floating toward the roof. Jackson rose up slowly, licking all the way up her spine.

"Now, show me to your room."

Jackson stood up moving her in the direction of the hallway she was looking at and he watched her licking her lips. Daisy was already in motion then abruptly felt another tap on her behind, Jackson gave more of a jumpstart. Prancing eagerly to her room Jackson held only her hair like a leash to her bedroom. He did not move fast, he set the pace and pulled back as they were walking. Once they got in the room Jackson let go and smacked her once more in the same spot hard enough to nudge her toward the bed. Climbing up on the bed she stopped on her hands and knees, bending over on more of an angle slowly for him. Her ass had a red mark that perfectly fit his hand. Throbbing with sweet pleasure she put her weight on her elbows looking back up at Jackson, her feet up in the air waving back and forth.

Jackson was still at the foot of the bed visually fucking her with his eyes. Daisy felt like she knew what was coming, the heightened sense of pleasure began to run rampant in her mind. The thought of being thrown around wherever he wanted sent a rewarding sensation, she became aggressively wet. Jackson stepped onto the bed and went to work.

The hallways were not silent for long, soon after sounding like a stone dungeon hearing the echoes of Daisy's moaning orgasms that filled the house. Jackson got her off on how many times he brought her past the finish line resulting in her barely able to move once more. Daisy had no idea what was in store for her! The sun went down and his truck still remained in front of her house. Hours of grinding on one another left them tired and sweaty. Daisy fell asleep on his chest listening to his heart beat all night after passing out relatively fast, drifting off her last thoughts thinking how lucky she was to have the privilege of such a heavenly experience. Daisy was sprawled out in the middle of the bed almost horizontally, relaxed feeling like she was floating. Their two bodies were intertwined in the dead of the night till the sun appeared on the horizon.

Chapter 6.

At dawn there were no sounds from any roosters, just Daisy's alarm going off vibrating on the nightstand. Jackson did not move as she untangled herself from his webs that gripped onto her so tight. Reaching for the alarm she hit the snooze button then watched over him peacefully sleep. Her eyes were heavy, Daisy snuggled back under his arms trying not to wake him.

It was not a dream seeing him laying in her bed this morning. Eyes were barely open seeing Jackson, curling back into position nestling into his muscular body. So easily she could fall back asleep, laying there on him with her eyes drawn drifting back to sleep. Jackson was not awake yet but automatically cuddled her right back up, putting his arm directly under her body pulling her closer to him. Daisy laid on his chest, holding his hand that laid on his stomach.

Daisy moved a little to get comfortable and her hair caught on his nipple piercings snagging it in the process, Jackson woke with terror. Carefully pulling the hair out without ripping his piercing out of his skin. Both wide eyed and bushy tailed now, together they played a careful game of operation in the wee hours of the morning.

"Well I'm up now. Thanks for the wakeup call!" Jackson said, sitting up on the bed pressing his back upon the soft gray padded headboard.

"Sorry." She said rubbing around his piercings like nothing happened, making the cutest face.

"You're lucky and gorgeous, so you get one pass." Jackson said, pulling her over on top of him.

"I got more than a pass, do you remember how lucky I was last night?" Daisy said in her sexy voice grabbing the sides of his head leaning in to kiss him.

"Hahahahhahahahahahhahahahahhahahahaa FUCK!" Jackson burst out into laughter, Daisy let go and backed away from his face after his surprising outburst.

"We did not cash in the chips. So I have $100k worth of chips in my pocket," Jackson said, cracking up putting his hands on his forehead.

"Opppps. Wait how much?" Daisy said, rolling her eyes seductively, holding her finger on her mouth, cringing her lips wanting him to repeat the number once more.

Jackson moved his hands away from his face, looking over at Daisy naked. In a few moments he knew how lucky she really was to him in more ways than one and not just for making him six figures.

"That's right, we're not even yet." Daisy said, as if she was reading his mind.

Jackson smiled at how cute she was when she was genuine feisty, her true self was coming out appearing in front of him a little at a time. Jackson loved it when she was displaying full honesty with words or self expression. Jackson's hands began to wander up her body gripping, grabbing and massaging her. Then his hands made it back down to her hips where he picked her up straight off the bed shifting his back down off the headboard and lay flat on the bed. Jackson held her up in the air, he finally put her down her knees on each side of his head he buried his face in between her legs. Jackson began to lick composing a concert with his tongue. Daisy grabbed the headboard as his tongue moved faster looking down at Jackson underneath her. Daisy pressed her body down, she began biting her lip. Jackson sped up his movements, as a reaction her nails dug into his chest scratching him viciously. Jackson's tongue was like magic hitting the right spots very quickly with a perfect rhythm; her body reacted quickly to the finish line. After she let out a howl, he put his tongue inside of her as she screamed with insane pleasure.

"That should make us even!" Jackson said smugly, the muffled sound from underneath her then proceeded giving her another few licks till it became too sensitive, Daisy began twitching so fiercely that she had to get off of him.

Daisy put her hand on her head and laid back in dissolution. Jackson did not move, staring up at the intricate light fixture on the ceiling, licking her off his lips.

"Even? Not yet but you're getting there." Daisy said as minor tingles crept up her body, panting, dumbfounded and on top of the world.

Jackson put his hands under her pulling her next to him again just after she tried to scurry away from him making her cum again. He turned her on her side and they were now face to face. Their lips were bound to touch, like it was a prewritten deposition in time. Daisy could taste herself on his lips, turning her on a little more.

Beginning to spin getting into the moment they started wrapping themselves around getting knotted in the bedsheets, the alarm sounded off again. Daisy reached over, hitting the button to shut it off. Her hands stretching behind shoulder she raised them up to the sky.

"I have to get ready for work." Daisy said with a sad face drooping her lips, knowing she was a little behind her usual schedule.

"I have to work too, I'm closing up tonight then I have to go cash these bad boys in." Jackson said admiring one of the $5000 chips in his hand holding his full jacket pocket full of chips.

Daisy smiled happily that she helped him gain all those chips, but inside she was upset that she would most likely not see him tonight unless he stopped by before he left work past midnight. The thought of that causes an inner frustration, knowing she needed to catch up on her sleep. Daisy got up walking around the house naked going straight to the kitchen to turn on the coffee machine. Jackson's body was heavy, his brain was foggy and energy was low lying in the bed beginning to cough again. The aroma of burning coffee beans drifted through the house, Jackson rolled over knowing that is what he needed in his life right now, caffeine.

     Daisy entered the room with two cups of smoldering coffee trying not to spill them paying close attention to each step. The smell pulled Jackson up to a sitting position watching Daisy carefully deliver a black cup of roasted brazilian coffee into his begging hands. After passing off the coffee Daisy walked to the bathroom, turning on the shower.

     The open concept bathroom was all dark tiles on the floor and walls. A few white porcelain tiles made the illusion of the flow of the water from the spout, the highlighted white tiles flowing down the wall and down to the drain. There was a concrete bathtub flush with the windows with the white octagon shaped porcelain tiles surrounding it. The white floor tiles around the bathtub looked like it housed potential water if it overflowed from the tub. On the large wall there was a built in electric fireplace with a tv right above it making the bathroom seem like a spa oasis. Candles were on all the ledges all over, even in the corners on the floor. Daisy walked in with her coffee to grab a long lighter from the window ledge. Sparking it up to light up all the candles, never turning the lights on. Jackson got up butt naked with his coffee in hand to join her checking out the elegant bathroom design on his way in. Looking around the candled dim lit bathroom with his piping hot coffee, Daisy turned around beautifully as ever surrounded by fire with the lighter in her hand just after giving flames to the wicks.
"I try to only bathe in candle light." Daisy said, pulling her coffee cup up to her face blowing on it, the steam ascended to her face looking like some kind of mystical seer in the setting she was in. Smoke appeared to surround her feet from the water turned on full blast illuminating her body frame to perfection from the torched candles all over the room.

     Jackson almost dropped his coffee after seeing her in the darkness in her truest form. Her spirit came out showing him on a new level who she actually was inside, nothing short of a goddess. Daisy stood there luring him by standing up straight, leaning on one leg popping up her hip to emphasize her natural curves. One hand was on her hip, the other held her coffee close to her mouth looking sexy as hell, waiting for him to walk in.

Astonished how she was titillating so effortlessly, attracting every part of him down to his bones forcing him to put his coffee down instinctively. Daisy stepped back with every step Jackson took into the bathroom. Her heels hit the tub, she placed her coffee on the edge of the bathtub continuing to enchant Jackson. Once he stepped within arm's distance of her he pulled her into him making their way to the nearest wall. The tile was not warmed yet, the combination of the cold tile on her fingertips and the strength of him gave a shiver that shot up her spine. He blew air hot on her neck before sucking on her shoulders giving her even more goosebumps. The hot water rained only their feet, Jackson putting his hands on her inner hip and she naturally arched her body even though she had to work circled in the outskirts of her mind.
"I had enough this morning, I'm going to be late. I'll be weak all day if you fuck me again." Daisy said, closing her eyes, her forehead on the tile in desperation.

Jackson propped her ass up in the air, sliding himself inside of her. Thrusting hard, all the way inside her as she groaned, mouth wide open. He stayed in her, flexing his best muscle that pulsated inside of her. After about 30 seconds then he yanked it out spinning her back around into his chest.
"Fine." Jackson said.

Daisy grabbed his face with both hands shaking his head like a madman, sore and tickled. Her blue gem eyes were caught up in the artwork all over his chest, shaking her head filled with so many thoughts. Controlling her breathing, subsiding the dramatic thrill of him. The urge for him to continue was honestly the only thing on her mind burying her head in his chest talking herself out of it. The vibrations of her sighs made Jackson invigorated, he held her in his chest moving them both directly under the spout. The candle had flickered, the fire moving the shadows around the bathroom.

The hot water trickled down on their naked bodies, the fire barley lit the dark room. They shared the soap, rubbing it all over one another's bodies. Daisy thought even showering was a sensual experience for them when the only goal was to get clean. At least cleanliness was the only goal for right now, if she did not have to be on time for work they would have likely still been in the corner continuing to grind all over one another.

Hand's helped lather in fresh citrus scents into one another's skin. Jackson grabbed the shampoo from her before she poured it into her hand, he squirted it in his. He lathered it into her hair from behind rubbing his fingers deep into her scalp. Daisy began to feel light footed by his spectacular hands that rubbed her into another dimension.

Daisy's eyes began rolling into the back of her head, losing sense of gravity dropping down as her knees bet and body wiggled into jello. Jackson felt her drifting off catching her with his arms that wrapped around her, Daisy tried to fight the weightlessness. She couldn't because he began to run his hands from her scalp then pulling down to the ends of her hair, gripping handfuls of hair. Finishing off by pulling the whole lot of her hair down to the end, having nothing more to grab he went back up to the top of her ponytail held by his other hand to strain the shampoo out completely.

Jackson took pride and pleasure in it, she could tell by the manner in which he touched her. Once he was finished Daisy turned around looking into his eyes, pulling him back in to kiss him again, honestly not able to get enough of his lips on hers. The falling water splashing all over them as they swayed back and forth.

Dropping her head into his chest squeezing him tight Jackson leaned down, giving her a kiss on the top of her head leaving his chin on her head, slow dancing to no music on. Moving in the candle light for what felt like eternity. Shadows showed two figures combined into one unit, wet in the heat of water and faded smoke of darkness.

The shower finally stopped, the candles were blown out, bodies dried with the towels that were warmed on the towel rack that Daisy turned on before the shower. Daisy finished getting herself together as Jackson threw on the same suit for pretty much the third day. She was in a massive walk-in closet picking out one of her business suits for work when Jackson came in from behind kissing her on the back of the neck, scaring her.

"Have a good day, my lucky one." Jackson whispered in her ear.

Jackson held her for a minute not wanting to let go and turned around making his way out the door. Closing the door and walking down the walkway Jackson stepped into his truck then back down the driveway. Jackson tried to outrun Daisy who he feared would be in the doorway once more when he got to his truck to draw him back inside.

Daisy lingered in his kiss until she heard the door close, with one leg bent holding on to the hanger with a blue pinstripe suit and pants. It had only been moments since he left, already missing him. His touch, his voice, all the energy that surrounded his vast lust.

Daisy got dressed in her suit, put her makeup on and grabbed a coffee before heading to work. The day was long, she had to really focus on what she was doing all day. After a long day of work of trying to focus Daisy decided to relax and binge watch the new Lord of the Rings series that just came out. Stopping off to her favorite little Italian restaurant right by her house to pick up a burrata appetizer, a bottle of bourbon barrel cabernet and a slice of key lime pie.

Vito came out with a giant smile on her face, he was the owner who always took care of Daisy whenever she stopped in. Vito always acted like she was a part of the family the second she walked in the door. Sometimes sneaking a cannoli or piece of pie in her bag as a thank you for coming in so often. Little did Vito know that Daisy used his name often, not in the way he would have wanted. Often when there was a decision of food, movie, or multiple activities or any options in question amongst any group she was in she would Vito the ones she did not agree with. Saying Vito, Vito, Vito to all she did not want only to get her way. Every time she saw Vito she smiled to herself knowing she did this far too often and most people found it funny in a silly way.

Arriving home to her all plantation style brick house with her food smelling delicious. The garage door was going up and as usual she flew in the garage almost hitting the top of her car on the ascending door. Seems practice makes perfect but it was a cringing sight to see for the first time.

Daisy set her bag of food and bottle of wine on her ottoman, placing it neatly on the square serving tray. Coming back from the kitchen with her gold leaf plate, stemmed wine glass and wine opener setting everything up for the movie series on the television. There was a chill in the air on that brisk fall night, so she clicked the switch for the electric fireplace to ignite.

Daisy slipped off her pinstripe suit and got out of her silk blouse, putting them both on the chair in her closet. After unbuttoning her bra, it fell straight to the ground. Daisy stepped over it and grabbed a sweatshirt off the hanger. Exchanging her slacks for a pair of yoga pants and furry socks. Daisy began to walk out of the closet into her bedroom admiring the herringbone hardwoods that pointed North. She skated around on her fuzzy socks to her final destination. Once she entered the living room she was instantly distracted by a pungent smell that immediately made her stop in her tracks breathing in. Turning worrisome trying to find where it was coming from, wanting more of it.

She grabbed her sweater viciously sniffing like a baby wolf inspecting a carcass for the first time. On her shoulder was the area that she sniffed out, honing in on it. Closing her eyes and taking a deep breath once she realized that it was Jackson. Frantically wondering how his cologne got on her sweater. After the fresh oaky smell entered her nose she was reminded it was from the game where Jackson put his coat on her when she was freezing cold. Daisy grabbed her sweater rocking back and forth with her eyes closed in her own little world stuck in the hallway.

Walking over to the couch on clouds smelling the sweater like he was there. Her phone went off, the only letter she saw from afar was J before the notification went away. Rushing to open her phone thinking maybe he felt her thinking of him. Daisy opened her phone to open the text and it was Jameson, Daisy threw her phone down onto the couch upset, not even reading his text.

Jameson wanted to grab a drink, like usual. Daisy grabbed the wine bottle pouring to the top of her glass and took a big sip. Right as she finished her gulp she picked up the remote hitting the play button. Not only a second after hitting play her phone went off again, she looked at it on the couch thinking it was Jameson wanting her to go out.

Once she put her eyes on the television Daisy's phone began to ring, she picked it up without looking who was calling.

"Hey gorgeous!" A deep voice said Daisy gasped double checking the name on her phone. "Jackson, how.. how did you know... wait, you're thinking of me? That is so strange because.." Daisy stuttered trying to put together a full sentence.

"You sound absolutely adorable right now. I just took a break. All day all I could think of was you." Jackson said, cutting her off from her nervous hallucinative rant.

"That's ironic because I was just thinking about you for the past ten minutes before you called." Biting her lip and rubbing her head nervously smiling.

"You've been thinking about me for ten minutes, well I guess I should leave you thinking of me some more. I'm running up to cash in these chips after we close down and finish counting the drawer. Goodnight Beautiful."

"Goodnight Jackson." Daisy was playing with her hair, held on to every word he spoke and was not even upset he was brief with his call, feeling him smile through the phone.

After hanging up the phone she grabbed her legal pad. Writing down what just happened in bullet points. Daisy marked down all the times he texted her in the exact moments she was thinking of her since they met. In other columns writing down moments of extreme chemistry and moments of overwhelming intimacy. The list continued on, writing more at each line as she went down the page. Until finally she wrote on the bottom of the page in big letters and circled the question scribbling multiple underlines to finish it off.

"Is this for real?"

Daisy stared through the television, finishing off her burrata imagining that Jackson was the pillow next to her smelling him on her sweater. Daisy thereafter continued to drink another wine till the bottle was empty. Only paying attention to a few parts of the movie she was much too busy creating scenarios in her head, eventually closing her eyes and falling asleep with her wine glass attached to her hand.

Waking up to her 6am alarm, her phone sat on the ottoman violently going off hurting her head with its blaring consistency. Reaching over to shut it off she looked down, thankfully still holding an empty wine glass in her lap. Apparently she ripped off her furry socks in the middle of the night because they were on the other couch and an empty bottle at her feet. Daisy quickly cleaned up and yelled at *Alexa* to play music.

The music came on and she began vibing out to it even with a slightly horrific hangover. After turning on the water to the shower, Daisy began to undress. Taking a deep inhale through her nose before taking off her sweater, getting a whiff of his cologne before throwing it on the floor. As she stepped in the shower she heard her text tone.

DING…

Making an instant u-turn, the sound came from the living room and she walked back naked holding her throbbing head. Rubbing her eyes before picking up the phone she then put her finger on the button to unlock her screen. Swiping down on her screen to see the new notification, eyes too blurry to make anything out she sidestepped returning to the bathroom. Daisy's foggy eyes cleared once she rounded the couch, able to read the screen.
"Thinking about me again, beautiful?"

At this point she did not contemplate how? From anywhere he somehow could feel her delicate state of mind absorbing her emotions and thoughts. Admitting to herself it was a phenomenon that benefited her relishing in his ability. She had added another bullet point mentally to her list she started last night.

"Yes I actually was. But you're interrupting my shower." Daisy responded back covering up her chest with her arms that crossed unsure why she felt vulnerable.

She stood at the sink looking at herself bare in the mirror covered up waiting for his response before walking back into the shower. Seeing bubbles pop up knowing he was typing, they disappeared. It was blank for more than a minute. The steam began to cover her phone while she waited for a response near the door to the shower. She put her phone down walking toward the water that was beating down with tenacity, touching the water with her toes first to feel if the temperature was bearable. Daisy had just added her hands in the water, catching a puddle in her hands and splashing her chest with the warm water, then her phone went off.

DING...

"I have perfect timing, I'm outside."

DING...

"Come and get your surprise, clothes are optional."

Daisy thought he was joking, deciding not to look out the window and walked back in the shower not wanting to be let down by a joke. Once she extended her leg into the shower her doorbell rang twice.

Jumping out of the water like a cat, snatching one of the two robes on the hook. Putting on her dark gray bathrobe walking up to the front door like a tactical Tom Cruise from Mission Impossible. Tiptoeing to the door looking through the peephole, it was really him. She opened the door and Jackson smiled looking at her in a robe, her skin glowed at dawn. Daisy's breath was taken away, Jackson standing there with his dark brown eyes seductively aimed at her.

"You certainly give that bathrobe justice." Jackson said, moving his eyes down.

Daisy stepped back pulling back reaching for her robe belt. Twisting the knot undone and moving the sides of her robe, it swung open exposing her wet nakedness. Standing there waiting for his approval holding both sides of her robe open, all her weight on one leg.

"Well my day got a whole lot better!" Jackson said his hand on his chin surprised taking in the lovely view in front of him.

Daisy cheeks got red quickly pulling the sides of her robe back together covering herself up. It was very unlikely of her to act like that or worry about someone seeing because she felt like they were in their own bubble that was indestructible. She really didn't care about anything or anyone else when he was around.

"Hopefully this makes your day half as good as mine is right now." Jackson said, hands emerged from hiding behind his back.

Magically pulling out an iced coffee in one hand and a mixed assortment of colorful flowers in the other. It was a perfect combination that intoxicated her. Daisy grabbed Jackson by the middle of his shirt pulling him inside.

"My neighbors are nosey! I can't be half naked for them all to see." Daisy said, shutting the door behind her.

"Do you have a vase for these?" He said handing her the coffee brushing off his shirt at the seam line straightening out any wrinkles or any pollen on him.

Full of joy Daisy moved through the kitchen rubbing her finger on the shining marbled countertop before she grabbed the vase from the highest shelf for the flowers. Jackson took her coffee that she had put on the countertop taking a sip of the iced coffee. He watched her put the flowers in the vase admiring how she responded to his gift.

"Thank you! I'm not going to lie, I'm not sure who's morning is better now." Daisy said one hand on her hip looking up at him, her bathrobe was not tied up.

Jackson put down the coffee, he began stepping closer to Daisy. She was busy fluffing up the flowers in the glass vase half full of water in the kitchen sink. His hand grabbed her vase out of her hand and put it on the veiny grayed granite making it a beautiful centerpiece on the island. After turning back to Daisy he put one hand on the lower part of her back and the other stroked the hair out of her face resting it behind her ear. Feeling her tight body in his grip he pulled her close to him. Jackson's other hand went down on her neck and she turned her head into his hand like a kitten showing affection.

"Did I really interrupt your shower?" Jackson said tenderly his palm on her face transforming his vision into her eyes.

"Yes, I barely stepped in the shower."

"I could use a shower. I've been driving for hours and was up all night." Jackson said backing away brushing down on his black button up he had on since after work the night before.

      They reunited when Daisy pulled him back in acknowledging and answering his request. Once his body was close to hers he pulled the robe to the side, the center part of her frame was exposed. Her oblique abs widening with the robe sliding across her body, his hands explored around her smooth gentle skin. Then he slowly opened it further, the cotton getting caught by her firm nipples so Jackson pulled to the side a bit faster. Jackson's eyes did not move, they were locked on her beautiful blue eyes watching her reactions. Daisy consumed her bottom lip, her arms dangled down. Jackson took her robe off with such a sensual demeter she couldnt move, knowing the slow moving cotton grazing her fair pigmentation tickled her skin. Daisy felt a chill as the robe came fully undone, licking her lips looking up at Jackson's lips waiting for him to kiss her. Leaning up on her tippy toes into him whispering to him seductively.

"You definitely need a shower," she said, eyes flickering from his lips and eyes.

      Jackson leaned in, stopping just before his top lip was barely touching hers. He waited teasing her, his hand positioned behind her neck holding her in place. Daisy reached up grabbing his top lip by her teeth, she was done being teased. Having a firm grip on him, it was so intense he was overcome with an urge, grabbing her hips propping her body up on top of the cold countertop. Daisy smiled how he did it with such ferociousness, then she began to giggle and shake as she sat on the chilly stone. Jackson eyed her sitting on the counter top like a delicious treat that he wanted to devour. He leaned in to take a taste of her, Daisy legs spread. His hands on her knees hanging down as Daisy gripped the ledge of the countertop tensing her whole body leaning up toward him. After a sample, he wanted the whole thing so Jackson grabbed her hand helping her down off the counter top then whipped his face. As Daisy got down she knocked the coffee off the counter top, miraculously Jackson's reflex instantly bent down and caught the plastic cup. Unfortunately some spilled on his suit jacket sleeve but the brunt of the mess was in his hand, luckily there was no need for a towel to clean up the floor just to clean him. Jackson put the cup in the sink and grabbed a paper towel for his jacket and hands.

"Cranky, let's find ourselves a shower." Jackson said in an Australian accent imitating the late Steve Irewand.

    They started walking slowly down the hall. Jackson looked more in detail at her house not remembering how vast and iconic it truly was. He was taking in everything on the way examining everything from the style to her decor and even the paint combinations. Upon entering her room he looked around getting ideas of how to pleasure her. After partially hearing of the shower to the left, his head stopped looking in the middle of the room seeing the bronze mirrored bed set that was framed like a cube almost to the ceiling. His mind fluttered thinking that bed was perfect for restraining her in many different ways.

"I'll tell you if the water is hot or cold," she said walking into the bathroom au naturel.

    Daisy pushed the heavy solid cedar wood pocket door into the left making it disappear into the wall. Jackson stopped endearing what looked like a dark rainforest, all he saw was steam, black tile, and tall exotic plants in the corner of the walk in the spa. Maybe he was too buzzed or hungover last time to really take it all in. Perhaps his only focus was on the physical part of her, not understanding her by her vogue. Everything in the house matched Daisy, easy on the eyes. Daisy walked out after setting the water to the perfect temperature.

"You're hot, I mean you're sexy. The shower is hot now." Daisy said, mixing her words up, walking back in toward him.

Jackson was leaned up against the wall, distinct. Barefoot after kicking off his dark brown leather driving shoes. He looked at Daisy, having her undivided attention. He began to unbutton his shirt leaving her stunned seeing his tattoos that went down his toned chest continuing down to his stomach and hips, the light illuminated his ink with each button he pulled off giving her the whole show to enjoy. Getting to the last button, pulling out his tucked in long sleeve.

Mesmerized, Daisy took two steps toward him grabbing his buckle. Aching to feel him inside of her. A sudden halt, as she began fumbling to get his silver buckled leather belt off. Not understanding how it worked, she released her hand after about a minute of trying to break into his pants. Daisy's head pointed down pissed at what felt like a chastity belt, so she bent down to examine it further. Looking for a secret button or something so she could get his pants off, getting more angry as he pulled the sleeves from his shirt.

Jackson reached his hands down to the area in question with one swift movement unlocking his belt. Daisy quickly ripped the belt off his waist. Grabbing the top button on his pants then pulling his zipper down in a hurry. Rushing to get him undressed she looked up at him from her knees.

"I hate that belt!" She said standing up after she gave her honest opinion, pulling him by his member through the pocket door to the steamy dark spa.

"Thought you only bathed in candle light?" Jackson said, looking down at her hand holding with a solid grip.

Daisy tried to keep eye contact but her eyes looked down filled with a sense of wonder as she stroked his bulging cock. Gripping her hand harder she felt his veins pop out. Those blue eyes wandered all across his whole stomach, chest and arms that were covered in tattoos as they faded into the darkness. Daisy's body had an uncontrollable twitch, she released her grip on his wood.

Daisy continued walking backwards to further inspect him as they stepped nearer to the steaming water. She grabbed a box of matches on the window sill and lit a few candles, Jackson waited for her to finish before getting into the water.

The flames grew, she put the match box back walking back looking at him. The water began to drizzle all over the back of her. Daisy put her finger in front of her face, her pointer finger was the only one up she wiggled it toward herself telling him to come get her. His answer was obvious as he stepped toward her as she used the art of seduction.

They were both looking deep at one another more so than they have so far. He was overbearing, one big vein on each bicep popped out flowing down to a few smaller ones bulging down his forearm that trickled in the flames. She thought to herself he could squish me with his big arms. His chest was chiseled, nipples were pierced with gold. She stepped into the shower fully as Jackson followed, her hands touched his covered abs. Rubbing all eight of them, then grabbing his big muscular arms squeezing as they kissed. Hurting her hands doing so, not able to fit them around his arm. The water sprayed hot water precipitating down, the pressure awakened them in the heat of the moment.

Jackson continued to move forward, the black tiled wall stopped her when he invaded personal space she was defenseless and willing. Daisy thought to herself he can have her, all of her standing there against the wall wanting to be his good girl. Jackson picked her leg up in the air resting it on his arm, knowing exactly what he wanted. Beginning to play with her pussy, pushing his fingers quickly into her tight hole then pulling them out. Once her hips leaned in for more he rubbed her clit slowly.

Almost as if he was teasing himself as well, he looked like he wanted to growl with lust. Grinding his teeth he pushed his tight boney hips up in the direction of hers. He was on a mission, beginning to finish what he started last time they were in this wet abyss. Daisy took him in gasping, taking small tight breaths one leg up in the air on her tippy toe pretty much being held in the air by him.

The water fell down from the top of their heads, droplets heading in a downward motion on their skin. The bump of their eyebrow kept the water from blinding them, heads tilted toward the floor. Breathing heavily face to face Jackson stretched her leg further toward the wall, thrusting with a rough intent. Eyes were locked seeing the water pass between them as he thrusted, Daisy screamed with ecstasy.

Jackson allowed her to put her leg down back on the floor releasing it from his grip. She stood there in the middle of the hot water falling from the sky, legs numb and shaky. Jackson touched her body up and down. The steam was building up and the tile all around became foggy making the black tile appear gray in the candle light.

They were holding one another as the sun was coming up making its way through the charleston style shutters that were cracked open on a hard angle. Daisy grabbed the back of his head with both hands pulling him all the way in, she couldn't wait another second to press her lips on his even if her legs were not able to function correctly at the moment. Lightheaded, tingling and on the conquest for another explosion. Daisy's top lip was consumed by Jackson, he pushed her up against the tile leading the way to set the fire for another eruption. Their tongues wrestled with one other, saliva mixed with water filled their mouths forcing them to swallow. Jackson picked her up holding her up on top of him then stepped under hot water that hit her forehead dripping down her nose leaning forward kissing each other vigorously.

Eyes closed and fingers digging into their skin, they could both feel one another smiling as they kissed. As the sweltering water hit their bodies, Jackson controlled her movements on top of him as he kissed up her neck. Daisy's mouth was open, pointed toward the shower spout sighing aloud, filling her mouth and spitting out water. Her unrelenting sighs heightened to the point of finishing legs straddle around him. Jackson's arms were rock hard from bouncing her up and down with such force but it was worth it watching her cum.

Jackson let her down and pressed her against the black sleek wall spinning her around. Daisy's handprints were on the steamed tiles, she put her hands above her head bending back into him. Hands high holding her weight trying to grab onto anything because her body was spasming uncontrollably as she arched when he was thrusting from behind.

Daisy was wet in every sense of the word. Her mouth seemed to be numb from breathing so heavy, from the consistent vibrations as her moaning. Her moans loudened to screams close to her another climax, legs shaking harder. Daisy's teeth began biting down hard on her forearm as she felt his cock speed up inside of her. Daisy pushed hard against the wall and arching her back backwards into him tormented the good girl inside of her screaming in ecstasy.

All of a sudden Jackson stopped, Daisy could not feel him. Suddenly she felt him slightly digging his nails into her skin from the back of her ankles up, his teeth grabbed her voluptuous ass. Daisy spun and he began to work on what she placed in front of him. Automatically his hands rose up to her tits, squeezing hard and then letting go. Tongue continued to tickle her twine, bringing a new ray of convulsions to her spectrum. Releasing her nipple, then softly pinching it over and over she almost came. From above she watched his hands play with her, His mouth under her Daisy did not know this feeling existed she was completely consumed with arousal. She had a death grip on the back of his head pushing him closer into her as she leaned her head into the tiles looking up with her eyes shut.

Jackson slowed and looking up at her face he was turned on watching the pleasure she was overcome with, like her soul leaving her body. Watching the thrill of her face with such excitement and she had to control her breathing, gasping with her whole body tingling and shaking as the water hit her body.

Letting her catch her breath Jackson stood up turning the water to the left cooling her down. Gently rubbing her muscles that had been tight from the resistance of holding back the animal inside of her. Jackson was utterly stunned by her indescribable beauty. Eyes closed she

was panting, Daisy's body was twitching from aftershocks. The back of her skull rested on the tile as he softly rubbed her body as she settled down smiling at one another.
"I lied, my day got 100xs better." Daisy said, trying to stand up straight but was struggling to do so.

The cool water changed the mood, the same amount of passion changing the course they were on. Daisy opened her eyes, Jackson stood flickering in the darkness of the flames looking over at her. Her eyes started to tear up, senses pure fortifying her ultimate fantasies basking in this moment, he touched her with love and compassion.

Her dilated teary blues focused peering into his dark brown eyes and in a flash that sparked once she blinked she was gone. A reel in her mind time traveling in an instant from the first time she saw him at the bar to this very moment in the cold shower. The strangeness of how easy it was with him, feeling at home in her own forest of inner peace and safety having him there. Perceptive to each movement. Every action involving her was reckoned with a desired compassion. All the signs had appeared with a sense of universal motive, she opened her eyes on the verge of overflowing.

Jackson noticed her eyes begin to fill with tears. Stopping them with his curled finger before they fully eclipsed. Jackson bent down kissing her on the forehead holding her with tenderness , managing to subdue her gloom to a recession. Daisy's head was buried into his chest consoling herself, hiding the excess of tears that dripped down his chest camouflaged with the water from the shower. Jackson put his chin on the top of her head and held her as tight as he could. The two of them commended one another back and forth together for the next few minutes as the hot water sprinkled down on their skin. The steam wandered around the bathroom like a ghost watching this dynamic duo.

It was a beautiful moment between them, admittingly that they found something in one another that did not need to be spoken aloud. The connection was natural and pure speaking for itself. It was a fact out in the open, a certainty like the air that blew in and out of their lungs. A connection that sparked from the smallest smile from the faintest touch. A perfect fit that neither of them thought was possible. Love that is personified in the minds of millions was in the flesh here and at this moment flowing around the two like a limitless orb of intimate appreciation.

    The bold negative lines depicted two celtic dragons that flew across his broad shoulders. They flowed with symmetry, elaborated geometric shapes with spirals that looked endless, circular forms curved with his skin and not a straight line in sight. The dragon heads were fierce, mouths filled with sharp teeth pointed up his neck. She smiled as Jackson whipped the final tear from her eye while she got lost in his artwork trying to distract herself from her own thoughts. Daisy knew he was directly whipping the final tear that fell, not the dozen droplets of water from the spout that rested around her face.

    Jackson looked down with a worrisome face and his eyebrow wrinkled, knowing she was on the brink of saying what was on her mind but stuck in anguish. So he put his head down to the floor patiently waiting for her to speak.

 "Jackson, I need to tell you something."

    Retreating to where his eyes belonged, right into her beautiful blue lenses completely locked in once she spoke. Jackson stepped back releasing their skin that had been stuck like glue holding both her hands.

    Daisy looked up at the ceiling taking a deep breath out, the water hitting her head like raindrops on a cool night. Her eyes were shut, shaking her head like she was fighting a wild boar in her mind. Jackson stood patiently waiting for her to find her words seeing her struggle in her mind all in slow motion.

"Jackson." Daisy said, looking right at him, then her head dropped and she couldn't look him in the eye, staring at the drain.

"I." Mustering the strength to look at him in his eyes, bobbing her head up then right back down. "I dreamt you up before I saw you. Things feel too good to be true between us." She said, naked and afraid.

Some birds singing outside the window overpowered the shower. The moment was slowed down by his silence, time felt warped. Jackson grabbed the tip of her chin, lifting it up. "You're like a magnet, I felt instantly connected to you." He said.

Jackson looked at her then he looked over at the candle on the ledge in the corner. He looked into the flame like he was too burning with it, charging up his thoughts.

"You flipped a switch on that has been off for a very long time." Jackson said, both hands pushing down the water out of his beard to a point under his chin where his hands blended together taking a step toward her.

Unintentionally grabbing each other, their eyes sealed shut, the friction of their bodies heated each other's skin making sure they were in real life and not a dream. Daisy rubbed all over his tattoos on the raised lines and curves that were embedded in his skin.

Conflicted with the craze of doubt, Daisy remembered se la vie but in her head she could not believe it. Things like this do happen, some people settle and skate by life while some people are together for convenience or necessity. The crawling reality of her job helped make those facts clear. Her mind moved like the moon on a dark night, as Jackson's hands traveled all over her body shining with the light from the sun.

His hands grabbed in between her legs making her gasp, once he let go for a moment her thoughts flew away consuming her. Daisy thought about how many people are together because of an intense connection, an extreme love for one another was typically rare, especially in days of this generation then Jackson put his fingers back inside. Having his other hand on her neck he tried to relinquish her from her endless contagious reflections breaking her from her own prison.

Exasperated after a fulfilling orgasm, Daisy could not think anymore plopping into his chest. Jackson and Daisy stayed in the shower rocking, there was an absence of time. His arms were the only thing keeping her up, Daisy legs spasmed on her tippy toes leaning into him. The shower handle was eventually turned to the right. Their bodies were bound together the whole time. Skin on skin matching devotion with the final drops of water that dripped out of the showerhead. Hands intertwined with one another standing in the dark, Daisy put her heels down on the ground tingling, licking her lips as she stood on her own looking at him shining majestically.

     Daisy's hand went from his hips up to his abs that tightened, slowly digging her nails into his abdomen. Scratching so hard it began to distort the artwork on Jackson leaving multiple continued faint red lines as her nails scrolled up toward his chest. Looking at him as she did it, his face cringed. Her head leaned up biting his top lip, almost spying to see his reaction of forcefulness. The steam was thinning out but there was an unusual blanket of fog impairing them from seeing past one another. Neither of them cared what was beyond trapped in the dark tiled shower.

     They stood there wet and naked still holding one another playfully biting like lions would flirt. They couldn't break away no matter how hard they bit, breathing in steam and exhaling moans fighting for dominance. Jackson let her play until he had to exert his sense of alpha in one simple action. His arm moved quickly and his middle finger went inside her the rest spread out around her, Jackson lifted her up with one hand bringing her straight to him with his eyebrows furrowed and teeth clenched conveying his massive strength he had over her.

     Jackson propped her on his knees, Daisy in mid air as he repositioned to grab her with both hands then put her legs around his hips. Daisy's eyes were rolled, not in control of her own body while Jackson walked not too far out of the shower spa and put her up on the damp chilly countertop. Jackson yanked her hair back, her head jerked up and instantaneously her mouth open with a devilish smile looking up at him dripping wet. He licked from the tip of her clit all the way up to her chin. Spitting the water he gathered from her soaking wet body in her mouth. Daisy was flabbergasted and ticked at the same time. Jackson stared at her eyes screaming with enjoyment as she licked her lips and swallowed, opening her mouth ready for more wiggling her tongue at him.

Jackson grabbed her hand, helping her off the bathroom counter and brought her into her room holding her hand. Pulling her in close and picked her up again then he threw her on the bed soaking wet. Beads of water fell down on the cotton of the sheets and absorbed some of the wetness as they rolled around fighting for who was on top.

As soon as Daisy submitted to Jackson as he gained control and was on top of her, suddenly the doorbell rang. Startled, they both stared toward the conundrum. Instinctively Daisy covered herself with her covers. Jackson slowly got out of the bed, turning his head like a snake walking toward the door in a subtle fighting stance. Daisy ran into the bathroom grabbing her other bathrobe off the hook, also grabbing a towel and threw it at Jackson as she walked by. "Bullseye."

Daisy, like a ninja staying out of line of sight for the outside world retreating into her closet after hitting her target. Hearing some commotion outside Daisy put herself together quickly. Daisy's phone rang once while she disrobed. Once she picked up the phone she slapped the top of her head laughing hysterically pulling the phone away from her mouth so the person on the other side couldn't hear her hand over her mouth to control herself. Daisy was quick to get off the phone.

"What's so funny?"Jackson said, putting the towel tighter around his waist, whispering.

"I'm getting wall tile installed today going up the fireplace up to the ceiling in the living room." She said, Daisy stepped toward him pulling his towel off.

"Sorry to have interpreted you…" Jackson said, catching the towel from her hand, slicking his hair back with a slight lean back flexing as he stood naked in front of her.

"You can come interrupt me anytime you want, Jackson." Kissing him once more before she left the room to finish dressing.

"Do I make a dramatic exit?" Jackson said.

"Ughhhh no it's ok, finish getting dressed and i'll deal with them."

Gathering his clothes as she disappeared into her closet. He could hear a sweet voice faintly from the closet talking to the man in charge of the crew outside just called back, walking past to get his shirt on the floor by the sink. He drew on the mirror in the bathroom that was still completely fogged up looking over his shoulder to see if she could see him or not.

Daisy came out of the closet in an orange flower printed satin long sleeve dress with knee high boots putting her hair into a business bun walking toward Jackson who was not finished.

"Do you want coffee?" Daisy said, Jackson nodded.

Daisy saw him hiding something, intrigued she moved in to see. Daisy saw the writing on the mirror, Jackson walked toward her room right past her without a word.

All mine!!

Daisy's weight shifted to one leg, head turned back toward Jackson walking away biting the side of her lip smiling. She took a step, Jackson heard her boot hit the hardwoods and he turned, stopping in the doorway resting his elbows high on the door frame standing there like a wall that would not let her by him.

"Password?" Jackson said, taking up the exit.

Daisy touched the side of his cheek, rubbing her hand through his beard her lips neared his, once they touched it became the perfect key to get past him.

The smell of coffee filled the air through Daisy's sophisticated and exclusive walls as the crew entered the house bringing in various supplies. Jackson pulled up his slacks then sat on the bed to put his driving shoes on. Daisy walked back in and watched Jackson do this shirtless and as he put on his shoe, she could see his abs disappear then as he straightened back they appeared seeing each tight crease lines of perfection through all the ink that painted a picture all over the front side of him. Daisy had a cup of steaming coffee waiting for him to finish getting ready. Jackson grabbed his shirt that rested over his shoulder putting it on as he walked toward her.

"Steamy morning," Jackson said looking at the coffee in his hand.

Daisy smiled and rolled her eyes, quickly turning and went back to talk to the construction workers about the odds and ends that needed to be done in a particular way. Jackson finished putting himself together, looking like a million bucks with pockets full of cash prepared to surprise all of the construction workers setting up for the job. Each strand of his hair was perfectly placed and slicked back with a distinct style and his suit looked ironed despite being thrown off last night. He stepped out of her room and walked to the kitchen heading toward Daisy to give her a kiss on the cheek.

"I'll bring this mug back," he said, winking at Daisy then nodding at the construction crew walking out the door.

Chapter 7.

Finishing off her glass of red wine at the end of the night admiring the new tile stacked on her wall above her fireplace. The sweet, dark bold flavor eroded on the back of her tongue tasting the sweet bitter elements the wine had to offer. The room flared with massive Vita Bella polished porcelain tiles that became the new focal point of the room.

Looking at the sheer allure and decadence of the wall Daisy began thinking heavy before getting ready for bed. All this is too good to be true, something in her lobe was incapable of accepting the depiction of truth. She finished up her wine, continued to get ready for bed. After her teeth were brushed and her skin care was taken care of Daisy took off her clothes. Walking into her bed bare she threw the duvet cover over her and took a sip of an ice cold water that was always next to the bed to wash down her nightly tablets like every other night. Tonight, the orange bottle was never opened, out of routine they stayed in the back of the drawer. Drifting off into the slumber of the night a few minutes after her head hit the pillow.

Internally her body ached for his touch, missing him very much. Wishing that he laid next to her holding her tight all night long wanting to feel the firmness of his body traced all over hers and the heat of their bodies together. Her mind drifted in infinity of what if's that could happen in the future, overcome with rest her mind relaxed until it became blank.

Shifting her body to a state of unconsciousness, almost floating. Attuned by her weightlessness relinquished her body of all matter. The inherent nature of her lucid dreams had come in full swing. Flickering back and forth between the dream and her true mind that was completely blank, not in control but aware.

Lusting for the sensual energy that her body had been accepting in her subconscious. Apprehensive, wishing to be ticked by him, longing for his touch. A soft feeling on her ankle then something tickled her up her left leg. The coarse flesh continued scratching her skin. Daisy moved her legs up, rubbing them against one another, moving her arms to the center of her chest, eyes glued shut. A harsh breeze made her tremble. Infectiously she felt dry licking her cracked lips, moving her hands to her left of the bed and right looking for Jackson. Sensing someone near her but emptiness contained the context of her reach.

Again licking her lips that were uncomfortably dry, her tongue salted and completely dried out tasting of stone crippled her will. Tossing and turning in agony, her body became a fiery temple. Skin melting, she reached for the covers to whip them off her flaying body snapped back and forth unable to grip. Scratching her skin trying to grab the covers that disappeared into thin air. The disarray had her whaling horrendous cries for help that never came. Opening her eyes at last to the fluttering smoke that thickened submerging her spirit. Consumed by the dark clouds, burning skin that crisped with a frying coarseness set upon her. Scorching to the touch, the pain ran deep throughout her body down to her bones, canceling the courtesy of a good night's rest.

Fiercely fully woken from the vivid fileting she felt from sharp nails digging into her side. Ripping flesh down to the muscle, Daisy levitating was awake but unable to leave this realm. Receiving the duality cast upon her cursed with no further rights to pursue free will. The feeling of blood trickled down her ribs falling onto the sheets below, when she followed the blood she saw the bed was covered with slithering snakes. The open wound was instantly healed, the hand with the sharp nails vanished leaving an unruly scar that was sealed together with flames in an instant. The hisses sent fearful chills down her legs as she bent her body up in the air toward the ceiling. Not wanting to be touched evermore looking for an exit as she wiggled, Daisy screamed as loud as possible. In complete despair, hovering over the serpent's slithering down below, unable to hide from this shrilling setting.

Violent depictions of a figure surrounded her, the room blanketed by smoke and darkness terrifying her heart and mind. Spasming to the left and right, tensing her body so tight with massive jerking motions trying to get away. She flailed all around when touched by the demon that wanted to swallow her whole. Her soul in the balance of the figure slowly sucking the life out of her with its dark lifeless face as it fully appeared in front of her. The great power unhinged every part of her, the floor began to crumble as she spun slowly suspended as the dark figure moved her into position.

A provoking notion that this was punishment cluttered her beliefs and she closed her eyes. She felt drool on her chin dripping down upon her that oozed over its gruesome lips, turning her head to stray away from the saliva that felt like acid. The demon screeched something horrid and jumped away into the darkness. Daisy scanned the room to see where it was hiding, trying to muster the strength to fight it once it pounced back on her. A growing entity emerging from the destruction of the crumbling wood surface of the hardwood destroyed. Conceivably karma had finally found her, long searching through all frequencies and vibrations of depravity. Daisy's roots had sold her out to atone. The repulsive memories fluttered like snapshots in her mind, the ones she had long repressed deep down, locked behind multiple doors with locks stronger than the steel of the gods. Yelling and turning for help she tried to break free of this forcefield of evil. An enormous weight crushes onto her chest, leaving her incapable of breath.

      The sheer shock of these violent visions made her shake trying to fight the demon off both mentally and physically, spinning and tossing her body to rid the mysterious episode that consumed her. The weight of Mora was on top of her, claws hooked to her bones feeling like she was about to be ripped in half as it got a firm grip. Trying to wake up to get out of the wilderness of hell, the truest darkest part of her mind fueled as Daisy began gasping for air.

      Reluctant for one more breath grabbing the rotting skin to yank this beast from her ribcage. Daisy had unlocked her worst nightmares leaving her breathless, stuck in a carousel of panic that felt like death itself had personally called her out to suffer. Each time the demon touched a new part of her it burned, Daisy shook more and more uncontrollably as her flesh melted. Cut and scorn down her legs from the razor nails, the scars blossomed into rubber after squirting blood from her veins. The apprehensive horror took her by storm, taking away everything good she once had inside. The scorching howls of the demon petrified her ear drums while it yelled in valor. Echoing so loud she felt the energy of the vibrations crush her organs. Daisy tried to cry out, sadly unable to be heard. Her carotid throat hoarse from screaming at the top of her lungs. Her body was like a corpse spasming naked and afraid in a damp blank soundproof room.

      Bound in between the bronze mirrored fortress surrounded by smoke, her life remaining in the hands of the creature that had full control of her. The gallops shook the balance of the bed while Mora's movement dashed swiftly around the circumference of the room shattering her subconscious. In a ring of destruction summoned by the demon Daisy was helpless, the tormenting touch of the sharp nails up her back leaving a crooked trail of bloody scars with every pass of this monster. No mercy was being served tonight, Daisy was being flipped around the air like a rag doll shamed by the divinity of an evil presence.

A strange vague abstract painting on the wall caught her eye. Staring into it at first to distract herself from the pain and fear. Time passed and while looking at it long enough Daisy saw something deep within the ink. The paint collaborated together to communicate to her, two majestic twister's intertwined horrendously. The large piece of art gave her temporary great joy, with yearning regret and misery as it all started to make sense in her mind. Mesmerized by the shape, it formed by telling what she already knew about the past, that congealed into the present and molded the future that was laid out in front of her. The more she realized, the less Mora scratched and spun her around, high screech screams howled through the room like a dying ghost being sucked into its forever resting place. Trying to sound out the noise, Daisy continued to get lost in the vastness of the dark carbon ashes on the textured cotton paper, highlighted by a red shimmer that too once ran through her very skin. Halted in the collusion of the torment, the demon got off of her chest flying around her disinterested. Daisy closed her eyes tightly, telling herself this can't be real finally able to breath, she choked catching her breath and bringing it back to normal. Daisy opened her eyes expecting to see the dark figure but eventually after looking at it the canvas one last time the demon faded into the emptiness of the room in the infinite distance. Daisy looked over at the canvas on the wall and it turned to dust and smoke, the art vanished into a billion pieces of sand and her eyes shut with no hope.

    Wanting to wake up Daisy felt like this is life or death as her memory faded, if she did not move the right way down out of this nightmare onto the right path she felt like she could disappear into the great beyond. The visions relapsed in her mind all night, stuck in the demon's dungeon Daisy was captive but not being tortured any longer. Trying to find her way out of the dark cavern that she was tormented in. Stuck inside the juncture of misery trying to stay as quiet as possible. Encapsulated in the lucid excruciating and suffering from the demon's objective.

    Just as she let herself go, she slept, then was woken by the natural heat of the sun beating on her body. Controlling her breathing confused that there was no weight pushing down on her chest she could breath with right now with ease. Fearful to open her eyes, blinded by hours of torture, not knowing if it was a dream or reality afraid to fall in that dark place. The birds pleasantly chirped to her left, she lifted her head off the pillow. Daisy's arms moved, her fingertips felt her duvet cover's fluffy fur, the weight from the blanket on her chest. Coming to the realization that she was no longer floating, now she was on her firm mattress, gravity on her side now. Eyes weld shut, crust from the river of tears solidified her lids like glue. Her shocked shaking body vibrated her bed so much that the reflection of the sun scurried all over her room. Gripping the sheets tight hoping to wake up alone in her bed to the morning sun, not a pale room of grim darkness. Determined to decide for herself as a test of fate trying to ignite a flame to spark. The failure of her thought process was all that remained, resulting in a loss of depravity laying there as the birds sang.

  Pulling all her courage and might together Daisy finally opened her eyes. Almost as fearful as she was last night in an unenforceable nightmare that made her more frightened than she could ever imagine. There was no fire, smoke or serpents surrounding her confines as she frantically searched the room for any remnants of truth in the faded blackness from last night. Reliving it in the few minutes after waking up, remembering the force that shook her body along with the burning along her skin. Looking along her sides for scars, any markings that indicated the realistic series of events from last night. Pulling off the covers she saw nothing on either side, searching vigorously up her arms and legs. After finding no evidence she took a long deep breath in through her nose and out her mouth. Laying back down into her pillow staring up at her light fixture wondering why she was visited by this demonic creature. All that remained of her, left in wonder by a dwindled reality.

  Daisy felt something underneath her, something was definitely touching her skin. Her hand reached under her leg feeling her skin being grabbed. Picking up the covers and gripping what had a hold of her. Touching what was sticking to her skin, her hand appeared from the sheets, her hand was full of pills. Ripping the covers off her bed entirely and throwing it to the floor. Daisy looked at all the pills all over her sheets, she searched for the bottle but it was nowhere in sight.

Chapter 8.

Daisy kept her nightmare hidden pretending like it never happened thinking to herself she must have taken one too many pills and hallucinated into a downward spiral. Daisy got ready, her head down all morning. Hesitant to grab her phone, worried about texting him. She mustered the courage to compose a message for Jackson to join her for a homemade meal at her home later that evening. Daisy needed Jackson to bring her back to life, needing emotional support and a loving touch. Thinking of what to cook to help lock her memory up, repressing her nightmare behind everything else to build a huge wall. This was something she will hold to the grave, never want to discuss it or relive an instant of anything from last night ever again. Fearing that if she spoke about it, the demon would hear it as an invitation and return with a bleeding vengeance.

Jackson arrived promptly later that night at the time she specified to have dinner at Daisy's, he could hear some strain in her voice when he talked to her. Ever since she returned from the office she went straight into chef mode, slicing away at the veggies with sharp cutting knives while the potatoes rinsed in the sink. Daisy looked off into the distance smiling seeing the beautiful day come to an end through the window, despite the circumstances of last night she looked out with untenable hope. The irony that comes with trauma, a harmony that stands still once the clouds of a storm dissolves and all that remains is the fading light.

Jackson bought four nice sized lamb chops for both of them along with a bottle of wine. Daisy poured the wine quickly to help take the edge off. She totally forgot to give him a glass, lucky he was distracted. Jackson grabbed a pot full of water to throw on the burner then after grabbing a peeler skinning the potatoes going right into preparations for dinner. Daisy put together the seasoning for the lamb chops, cooking a herb butter gravy with a cast iron skillet and zested the meat with lime and orange. They continued to get things ready for dinner holding their own darkness close to the belt, the secret boiled hotter than the pot potatoes.

Frank Sinatra was playing in the background. The heat from the oven and flames took charge of the room while they finished their assignments. Daisy noticed the fact that she did not offer Jackson a drink. She finished her glass of wine like she was taking a shot then put it back next to the bottle and his empty glass like nothing happened. Playing it off cool and casually pouring them both then walking away like she was giving the wine time to breathe and continued on.

The phone rang at exactly 7:00pm on the dot. Jackson quickly hit the button to silence his obnoxious ringtone, walking into the office for some privacy. It was a random number but he had a strange premonition that he knew who was on the other end. Suddenly out of nowhere it seemed like the temperature changed as he exited the kitchen. Walking by the living room's vast windows the sun had gone down completely, the sky was completely black not a cloud in sight and the wind blew the trees powerfully as he made his way through the reflective shadow of the night.

"Hello, Jackson. This is Dr. White, listen I don't usually make calls on Sunday's but I got your test results here and I got to tell you."

"Go on," Jackson responded, pacing around Daisy's desk.

Jackson stopped, making sure that Daisy was not in sight. Twisting the door handle and pushing it forward to shut the door carefully, not making any noise.

"The results came back late last night and I checked my email a few minutes ago. There is no easy way to say this so I'm just going to be direct. The cancer sprouted again, sorry man. Now that we are positive about its growth we can take more of an aggressive approach since your recent remission. The two larger tumors are amassing and both doubled in size."

"Ok," Jackson said.

That overwhelming feeling of getting a prerequisite to death for the second time was not what worried him. Death was something Jackson never feared, moreso curious. He had already been through this once before knowing all the different variables of what is to come in the coming weeks. The simple fact that he just got everything in his life was going right back in order and on the right track seemed almost comical. Now Jackson got another bitter taste of Murphy's law, the only thought on his mind was Daisy and how she will feel once she hears about this tragic news.

"We have a few different treatment options that you will………..." The doctor continued in his ear, a loud crackling sizzle came from the kitchen that distracted Jackson turning his heavy head to the doorframe trying to see though the wood.

"Ok," not quite listening, Jackon said as the doctor continued talking about the workup that followed the prognosis.

The water was boiling over, from a distance he heard it overflowing onto the stovetop sizzling down the metal pot, trying to listen to what the Dr. was saying.

"The water is boiling!" Daisy her muffled irritation screeched through the walls.

Jackon pacing had increased around the desk in circles taking longer strides. It felt like the doctor was talking endlessly as he rounded the desk again and again. Daisy cut the gas to the stove off, looking around for him all over the kitchen, her eyes drifted down the hall and she saw the door closed to her office. Jackson heard her stomping grow as she made her way to the office, the door immediately flung open once her feet stopped beating the hardwoods.

"Did you hear me?" She yelled abruptly the moment she opened the door.

Jackson felt the breeze from the quickness that she entered through the doorway, he turned to her and put his one finger up in the air. Jackson turned around, slowing down his pace around the desk ignoring her looking stolid. Jackson heard her footsteps fade off into the distance, making a three hundred and sixty degree turn to shut the door.

Daisy back in the kitchen hearing the door shut, grabbing the wine bottle and pouring a half glass to avoid getting upset. Attempting to forget it so easily, the long sip did not help her from feeling that she was not being heard. Putting her empty glass down and pouring another identical glass. Spilling the alcohol into the stemmed glass she was hit with the intuition that Jackson was being sneaky, distancing himself from her and hiding in the office. Daisy did not know that the doctor was on the phone. After a few more minutes pacing around the desk Jackson interrupted his doctor mid sentence respectfully.

"Ok, now what do we do?"

"We will start chemotherapy this week. So I will have my nurse call you, tomorrow morning come in and we'll go over the game plan some more to get you all set up then sign a bunch of paperwork again just like last time," the doctor responded wrapping up his speech.

"Ok I will see you tomorrow then, thanks for the call doc and have a goodnight," Jackson ended the rant of information which he had already been well informed a few years ago when he was first originally diagnosed.

Jackson turned straight to the bar in Daisy's office and poured himself a hefty glass of whiskey, shooting it down in one gulp. Before putting the cork back on the bottle he poured another shot into the crystaled rocks glass finishing it off then cork back in the bottle. Once he put it back where it belonged he opened the door and looked out for Daisy, he saw in the kitchen dumping the potatoes into a cullender. Jackson stood in the doorway once the door opened, watching her for a minute. Taking a deep breath before taking a step toward the kitchen watching Daisy spectacular ordinary movements seem ever so breathtaking, the simple pleasure gave him the strength to reveal himself from the confines of the terror he was just informed of.

"Thanks for grabbing that flame. Can you toss me the wine key?" Jackson walked into the room speaking softly, conducting himself in an orderly fashion.

Daisy slid him the wine key from the other side of the counter without saying a word, her eyes told the story but her body showed him the cold shoulder making it known more ways than one that she was upset. More on edge then she usually was, Daisy began taking her frustration out on the potatoes, aggressively mashing. Her mind was stuck on the jester of his finger and actions of shutting the door the second after she stepped away, it was not how he usually acted. The whole day she had to force herself to smile hoping Jackson would bring her joy effortlessly. Their interaction was a bit off, Daisy started to get familiar feelings before she opened the door for him that grew once he stepped through the door. Feeling as hot and her lips dry no matter how much she licked them just the same as she did from her excruciating dream from last night and it put her in a fragile state.

Jackson stayed quiet about his call, still uneasy about telling her anything. Jackson grabbed his glass of wine ready to try to numb his body. Hoping that with the excess of booze he did not spill the beans of his call to Daisy after a few bottles. If she found out it would not be easy on her, in so many different ways, it would be a risk continuing a relationship with Jackson knowing the possible outcomes of his disease. Jackson had the lip of the glass in his mouth, Daisy already gave him a death stare. She walked over and picked up her wine glass getting dangerously close to him.

"You're really going to take a drink without cheering?" Daisy said with fury and guilt that flooded her eyes.

Jackson put the wine glass down, realizing he did forget because of the other things on his mind. Trying to think of a toast feeling out of sorts. He looked at her not lifting his glass yet. Busy looking at her face, it stopped all his other thoughts putting his mind at ease momentarily. Instantly grabbing her hand across the counter looking into the ocean in her eyes and his arm rose bringing his glass to hers.

"To you," Jackson said earnestly.

Daisy broke, her fury drifting out of her body thinking why was she even upset with him, he had not done anything wrong. She licked her lips tasting the residue of wine that left her feeling hypocritical, the anger inside of her subsided. The two wine glasses kissed, Daisy and Jackson looked at one another with so much more to say. Jackson wanted to tell her more but could not find the words. In his mind he was fighting himself between saying his goodbyes or telling her the truth about who called, realistically he did not wish to bring her on this journey with him as it ended poorly the last time. Daisy could see the reflection in his eyes of her inner thoughts holding the door to the darkness that wanted to be unleashed.

Daisy could tell in his eyes that he was most sincere, smiling for him then her lips met the wine. His genuine look dissipated after the wine slid down her throat. Jackson put his wine glass down, swirling his wine on the countertop after taking a big sip. He did not speak aloud or with his eyes but there was something else, she could sense it.

"You ok?" Daisy said watching Jackson was looking into his wine glass with sheer emptiness.
"No, I am very hungry." Jackson said, giving her the diluted truth.
"Volume up," Daisy yelled at Alexa, taking out plates from the cupboard she could feel the wine kicking in.

Jackson took a big sip of his wine then poured some more before grabbing the silverware to set the table properly. They both helped plate the delicious smelling meal in an assembly line fashion. Daisy's mouth was salivating putting the finishing touches on licking her lips, dropping fresh garnishes on the edges of the plate making more of a masterpiece. All the preparation paid off because it looked restaurant grade mostly because of how precise Daisy was of all the small details. Jackson grabbed another bottle of red wine unconsciously from the wine rack while Daisy perfected each plate, it was the same label as the last. With speed he popped the cork out and filled his glass after polishing off the other one. Daisy did not realize that the first bottle was gone already, Jackson put it in the box of finished wine bottles. He got in and out of the garage without getting her attention.

The lamb was piping hot, the mash potatoes steamed from the plates. Daisy put his plate down first then put hers in her usual spot. The plates were placed directly in the center of the gold textured placemats. Jackson put the fresh bottle of wine in the middle of them, then put their glasses on the right corner of the placemats. Jackson pulled a candle from his back pocket. He stepped away from the table moving toward the wall, he flicked the light switches down. It was dark, the mood was changing due to his choice. Jackson came back to the table taking a gold zippo out of his pocket, he began burning the wax on the opposite end of the wick. Daisy sat and watched intently, with confusion. Watching each drop drip onto the glass table one by one creating a pool of wax that certainly added some entertainment to the night. "Maybe you should lay off the wine." Daisy sarcastically said with her hand on her chin contemplating what the hell he was doing but turned on by the mystery.

He smiled as the hot red wax dripped on the glass top that rested on the solid oak table. Daisy watched him grin through the fire. In the dark it was only them back at last, their connection grew back to normal. Both of their separate subjects clouding their minds evaporated from the dining room. Jackson licked his lips smiling and stuck the bottom of the candle down into the wet wax pooled in the center of the table. After it was secure he ignited the zippo and lit up the candle wick. Daisy smiled and grabbed his hand that rested on the corner of the table as he leaned over making the candle a permanent part of the table.

The candle was the only light in the room. Daisy looked at his other hand that began reaching over toward her face. She could see wax residue remaining on his fingers. Feeling timid when his thumb rubbed across her cheek, her mouth was halfway open, ready if he changed direction.

Jackson bit down on his bottom lip, the lust boiled his blood. He took his hand off her face and shifted it down picking up his fork and knife after pushing in his chair. Jackson did not say much throughout the meal, nor did Daisy. Daisy enjoyed fully, savoring every little bite that she took. Surrounded in the darkness, it seemed to have helped conceal the problems in their own minds . Both of their bodies warmed, bursting in silence to the undeniable connection. Imperfection torched the inability, the lamb being pounded between their teeth juiced, saturating tongues. Ramming the salt of the potatoes all over their taste receptors. The simplicity of food sparked their untenable frail human nature, ignited their sexual desires into wildfires.

"Mhmm," they both grunted.

That was the only conversation during the meal. Finishing at the same time Daisy grabbed the plates and put them up. Once she dropped the plates down into the sink, the clash of the plates hitting one another captured Jackson's attention and turned halfway around. He could feel her through the walls.

"Come here," he said, tilting his head back ready to use his powers while he had them.

Daisy came back putting her hands on the back of his shoulders standing behind him massaging him apologetic. Daisy continued now upset she snapped at him for nothing, and she drank more than a glass while he wasn't looking. Daisy's little hands tried rubbing deep into his shoulders but there was too much bone and muscle. Her fingers dug with all her strength huffing and puffing from putting in so much effort. The front of her upper body was rubbing on the back of his head pushing her toes up and leaning her hips toward the back of his chair. He put his head down enjoying her pampering him, he took slow deep breaths to bring him to clarity now able to feel the room with his eyes closed. Daisy may have been more amused, she proceeded pushing her weight down into his shoulders bending over putting the side of her cheek in his hair. Daisy's head lowered more and Jackson was surprised when he felt her lips on his ear. "Sorry for my little rampage before I was hangry." Daisy whispered into his ear then kissed his cheek with a touch of sincerity.

Jackson grabbed Daisy's hand off his shoulder and moved her body a step forward, spinning her body in the process around like a twister. Jackson pushed out his chair guiding her pirouette giving her the room to sit down on his lap. Jackson got close putting his hands around her body, Daisy felt his breath graze her skin leaning one shoulder in pressing against his chest.

Jackson pushed his face into hers till their skin stuck together, his lips kissed the back of her neck thanking her for dinner. Daisy sitting side saddle on him felt him engorge gratefully. He put his hands underneath her knees slowly shifting his fingers stiff walking up her leg like a crawling spider digging deep down stretching her tight skin. Daisy looked down watching his hands groping up her body becoming more aroused the further they got. Once his hands disappeared under her backside she bit her lip. Stretching her neck backward eagerly, pinching her eyes shut when she felt his dominant grip on her hip bones. The dynamic pleasure tightened her body up, her mouth opened taking in air that funneled down her throat from a commanding inhale. Pricked by the full satisfaction of his touch, causing unintentional overflowing. Tingling directly by his rhythm of madness, eloquently making her body indirectly feel sensational the harder he gripped. Daisy's rapid convulsing instantaneously silenced by the shock by Jackson powerfully picking her up in the air. Daisy keeped her knees close to her chest as he dead lifted her, she spread her legs one on each side straddling him once he was fully vertical and sharply centered by his passionate force.

    Jackson sat down and they were now chest to chest, Daisy's legs hanging off the chair. Her hands instinctively rubbed up and down his arms feeling every divot and bump. Looking into his eyes she was brief, not quite sure she was prepared for what was to come feeling partly weightless. Off Balanced by their silent foreplay during dinner, isolating her expectations she looked down becoming distracted by one big veiny tattooed hand cresting the top of her smooth leg gripping her toned thigh muscles very tight possessing every ounce of her mental capacity. Daisy felt like a puppet, his metaphorical hand inside of her controlled by physical touch. His disorderly conduct had her body rocking, making her sweat. Sensually reasoning with the comprehension of his simple motions that felt highly illegal corrupting her liberty. Jackon improperly licks his lips using his mind control because Daisy telepathically knew she was in for some extra spicy action for tonight.

"I want dessert." Face to face, his deep voice shook her body.

Willingly looking up after hearing his horse words, Daisy smiled biting down on her tongue looking at his fingers that were about to move her like a puppet, a brilliant idea came to her. Putting her hand on his shoulder holding her weight turning around moving his glass over, then her arm leaned back to the otherside of the table.

"To dessert." Daisy said risqué whisper, holding her glass up voluntarily offering herself up.

    Jackson grabbed his glass that she teed up for him, he clinked glasses looking at his hot treat with a dangerous mystery in his dark eyes. Jackson exhaled heavily, sounding like he was growling at her eyebrows furrowed. Daisy grabbed his empty glass and turned, putting both the wine glasses on the side of the table. Eagerly spinning back to him she jumped at the sight of his face that was already waiting closer than she expected, he came straight in aggressively wrapping his neck neck into hers.

"I'm going to devourer you." Jackson said, grinding his teeth.

    Daisy was overcome with an electric reflex from his spontaneous action of standing straight up rapidly with his cake in his hand. Deviously wanting to fix the fact he took a drink without toasting her in the beginning in the evening in the office clouded his subconscious. Twisting his heels around with speed, resting her to sit in his chair. Jackson stood over her planning on repaying with nothing but pleasure then Jackson walked off, his footsteps faded to the kitchen. Daisy stayed still, the excitement that built up inside began to drown her, licking her dry lips. Staring at the fire from the candle rubbing the sides of the cotton cushion she was sitting on, hearing his steps grow louder she released placing her hands on her thighs.

    The thuds into the hardwoods came to a halt, Daisy felt Jackson grip her hair into a ponytail pulling it down like a pulley. Her head jerked up, placing her hands back on the chair leveraging her body weight up in the chair to compensate. Jackson let go once she was in a position to his liking. Daisy watched him upside down leaning her neck up and over the head rest. His hand pinched down on her lips, prying her mouth wide open looking for a moment then he closed her mouth shut.

His footsteps circled till he stood in front of her, stepping close to her in a wide stance bending down his hand to the small of her back and the other was up at her shoulder, with one motion he straightened her back like a needle. Daisy's back was no longer touching the chair, both of his hands went down to her hips grabbing her shirt. After throwing her shirt on the floor he reached behind her shoulders, his fingers trickled back snapping off her bra immediately. Once she was naked from the belly button up Jackson walked behind her and pulled her down by the ponytail putting her back into her original position.

The glowing of the candle illuminated her half naked body. A suspenseful chill blew across her chest making her body squeeze reactively.

"Open your mouth," Jackson commanded, grabbing the hidden item he placed on the hutch after returning.

"Wider!"

His dessert smiled with her mouth open as wide as possible looking upside down laying her head on the back of the chair once more. She was ready to obey, ready to be his tangible dessert. Feeling dangerous and sexy in the moment of anticipation leaning her shoulders harder into the chair toward him. Bending harder on her tippy toes, her bottom slid to the front of the chair. Jackson stood over opening her mouth to maximum capacity. Daisy saw a black plastic bottle in his hand that he put directly above her mouth two feet higher than her tongue. Jackson squeezed with two hands and chocolate syrup began to fall down hitting her lips, it was still cold since he just grabbed it a few minutes prior. The stream changed course, hitting her tongue pilling up in the back of her throat Daisy had one choice and started to guzzle it up. Jackson controlled it carefully he moved it all over dripping the rich dark chocolate slowly into her mouth stimulating her senses. Daisy swallowed the sweet taste of dessert with full compliance focusing so she didn't choke.

Jackson intentionally poured the syrup on her lips dripping to her chin then stopped, she licked the chocolate off swaying her body looking seductively into his eyes. Once her lips were clean enough he flipped the bottle over and squeezed, squirting the chilled chocolate down onto her breasts. Daisy shook, the tingles that erupted caused by the dripping of cold chocolate that covered her chest. Jackson stopped and put the bottle on the table reaching down unbuttoned her pants, he stood her up to pull her pants straight down. Standing there she could feel the thick syrup drizzle on her skin going in the direction of gravity. The syrup dripped down her chin, dripping down her legs and hitting the floor. Jackson was careful with his hands making sure they were clean, he put all his weight on his toes kneeling. His teeth grabbed her panties savagely ripping them off. Jackson tried to control his animal-like tendencies, controlling his fiercely breath manually. Still ready to attack and on the verge of gobbling up his dessert after decorating her with a delicious topping making her especially delectable.

    His tongue appeared from his lips, licking up her body catching the falling chocolate from her naked body. Jackson's luscious lips dripping in chocolate kissed Daisy, both sugar rushed sharing their homemade dessert cooperatively.

    Jackson buried his face into her shoulder right where the neckline started nibbling on her collarbone. Daisy's head raised up looking up at the white paint on the ceiling her body tingled with unfathomable euphoria. She was covered in chocolate feeling sticky and naughty watching him continue licking her and rubbing more syrup along her neck. Her nails dug into his skin so hard it drew blood on the back of his shoulder blades.

    Jackson turned her around, facing her towards the table he gently put her fingers on the table while he rubbed the chocolate in like a lotion. Daisy was in paradise feeling his hands massaging her and licking her lips full of chocolate. Daisy's body jolted when she felt his lips on her hips, when his teeth bit into her hips she shrieked. Kneeling behind her his head continued to her frontside heading toward her belly button, a sudden stop Jackson opened his mouth latching onto her hipbone shaking his head back and forth like a dog. Daisy moaned, grabbing his head putting all her effort into stopping him, tickled by the pain of his persistence. Releasing the pressure of his crushing jaw Jackson stood up behind her.

Daisy was bent on the table using her hands to keep her weight up, leaving handprints of chocolate on the glass top. Back was arched for him and she anxiously waited for his touch. Jackson began kissing up her spine. Daisy pushed back into his crotch once Jackson felt her ass he reached up grabbing a handful of her hair pushing her head down, Daisy's nose was touching the cold table.

"Lick." Jackson said, pulling down on her handful of hair.

Daisy's head turned, her right cheek was flush with the glass hearing the cap pop open. With his other hand Jackson started up the flow of chocolate that descended down onto her cheek widening her jaw listening to him fully as the chocolate hit her lips. Trying to catch the falling load of chocolate with her wiggling tongue that emerged from her sexy little mouth. Goosebumps rode up from her skeleton, sticking every hair straight up on her body. Daisy opened her mouth to the max, her tongue out and she began to lick the chocolate off the glass table even after he stopped pouring the thick sugary substance all over her. Jackson reached over toward the middle of the table, Daisy was successfully distracting her for a moment and he made his move for the candle.

Daisy smiled, exhaling unexpectedly. Electrified by a surprising hot drop from the wax that fell on her ass. An elongated loud squeal came out of her cute mouth as the drops continued. Biting lip Daisy put her forehead into the glass, licking the chocolate off the table enjoying the burn like a good girl. Jackson saw how much she was favoring this bringing out her sexual demon. Watching her clean the chocolate from the glass he stopped dripping the hot wax on her. Daisy blushing stopped licking, putting her chin up arching her back higher, waiting in suspense for more of what he had to give.

It stung with extreme startling pleasure, she was fantasized by his secret weapon long for another burning sensation. Her wish came true, the warmth fell on the lower side of her back and the splash of the heat made her wiggle. Then another hot sensation hit her spine, she reacted spasming harder with each drop that fell. The candle burned on an angle that burned the wax on a consistent basis leaving the control of each droplet in his hand. Jackson held it over her back angling the candle more, the fire burned the wax at a quicker rate. Seeing her facial expression was evident she was amused at the frequency she was scolded. Jackson watched her hips sway like a flag in the wind anticipating more of that scorching sizzle on her skin every time he stopped dripping it on her.

  Daisy took a breath feeling the wax go from liquid to solid solidifying on her skin. Moving her hips side to side controlled by the frequency of the vibrations that he generated. Daisy felt nothing, then a breeze streaming up her spine followed abrupt burns on her shoulder, leaning back into Jackson's body to feel what was in his pants. Grinding harder into him with each small drop of wax that hit the thin skin on the back of her arms. Gripping her hands tight into balls because where on her arm it was hitting, her chest rubbed on the table smudging the chocolate into the glass opening her mouth gasping.

  Daisy fucking enjoyed it, loving the surprises and craving more. Experiencing things that made her feel enriched with energy making her body want to do naughty things. Loving every second, dripping wet increasingly desiring him. Daisy pushed her backside into his hips wanting to feel him taking a full step back, her chest was now on the edge of the table. Jackson gave her a solid slap on the ass that made her eyes bulge open with excitement. He then blew out the candle and tossed it on the table, the clash scared her. It was followed by another clash of his belt hitting the hardwoods.

  Jackson grabbed her hips and thrust himself into her. Daisy moaned, feeling his cock deep inside of her, her whole body felt like a lighting bolt went right through her. Accepting what she lusted, thankfully panting, putting her forehead on the table feeling the dominos fall in all different directions inside of her.

  Daisy's body was like an art piece by the end of the night, the red candle waxes all over her shoulders down her spine and drops all over the floor. The front of her was covered with chocolate smudged all over her body. The combination of sweat and drool blended with the mixture, concluding all over her face it all dripped down her body. Catching their breath they looked at the mess they made, looking one another up and down knowing they needed to venture into the shower before a good night's rest.

The well prepared dinner was delicious and it filled them with fuel needed for creamy dessert, not many words were spoken during dinner but the dessert was out of this world, loud and erotic. They both were completely satisfied after burning off plenty of calories now needing to hydrate with another bottle of wine and a few cookies. Walking to Daisy's bathroom with drinks and snacks, they were both dirty, covered in wax, sweat, chocolate and bodily fluids.

Showering off the remaining chocolate that was not eloquently licked off. The steam fogged the room, the smell of sex and dessert intensified with the heat. They both shared the water falling from the sky with no lights on. Holding one another, wiping off the chocolate and wax stuck to their body in the dark. As they cleaned one another off they triggered another round that started in the shower and ended in bed for hours before calling it a night.

Waking up clean and intertwined with one another at dawn, the blaring sound of Daisy's alarm rang obnoxiously. Jackson opened his briefly closed eyes, he was up most of the night and after the alarm he jumped out of bed. He was off heading into the kitchen to make himself an Irish coffee. A jumpstart was needed to refuel, completely dehydrated, not sleeping and after four rounds from last night. Daisy fell asleep right asleep in her glory tingling phase pleasantly with him in her arms. Jackson could not sleep, he was busy on his phone researching some information. His insomnia had him stuck reading current news on new trials that had come on the market this year that may match with his very specific type of cancer that was currently growing inside of him.

On the way to the kitchen Jackson began chuckling while walking by the table noticing Daisy's body was perfectly imprinted from the chocolate. Jackson started the coffee machine then went back into the dinning room hovering over the table reminiscing while he wanted for the coffee to get hot. Jackson awoke Daisy with a fresh cup of spiked coffee. Daisy was dazed, having slept soundly all night. Daisy sat up on the bed covering her tits with the covers and grabbed the hot cup of coffee out of his hands. Daisy blew on the steaming cup, smelling it and she looked at him surprised to smell whiskey this early in the morning. Jackson had his glass up ready to cheer and Daisy carefully went to cheer him without spilling anything on the comforter. "I want breakfast." Jackson said before she clinked glasses and her cup stopped looking up at him.

Jackson clinked her glass and took a sip looking at her. Daisy imagined what was going to happen next, licking her lips she brought the coffee cup to her lips nervously trying not to spill it. Daisy blew the coffee hoping it had a cooling off effect so she could quickly swallow and have him bring her heaven. Putting their cups on the nightstand and proceeding to repeat their actions from the night before minus the syrup or wax. Daisy and Jackson were incapable of getting enough of one another.

Daisy woke up on the right side of the morning, getting a release of happy hormones at the crack of dawn making her more cheerful. Laying in bed rubbing one another's arms calmly focusing on the day that was ahead in their own minds until Daisy's alarms went off. Since they showered the night before they had some extra time to snuggle up with another. Finishing their coffee they both got out of bed looking out the window watching the branches sway from the breeze as the sun rays hit the grass. Daisy got dressed having a nice little buzz so early in the morning, slightly worried because she had never gone to work after having an alcoholic beverage. Jackson went back to the kitchen while she was putting herself together pouring himself another cup of coffee. The whiskey made him a little more alert, pouring some more in his coffee cup to combat not sleeping. Jackson went back to the room to grab Daisy's empty cup for a refill, he glared at her in the closet, her reflection in the mirror in purple matching lingerie had him at a loss. He watched her and became angry walking away to the kitchen with her empty cup. Daisy did not notice she was too busy pondering on what to wear to work, looking at her massive wardrobe with her hands on her hips pointing forward. Searching for her outfit playing with her hair she still felt as if he were inside of her, she stood there blessed by it.

After the feeling lessened Daisy picked and put on a luxurious dress with black stockings, solid black leather heels and walked to the kitchen to find Jackson as she put up her hair. Jackson handed her a fresh cup of coffee excluding the whiskey putting her in a better mood from his thoughtfulness.

"No booze in this one. You're a lawyer! No drinking on the job for you."

"Thanks, babe." Daisy said, her eyes widened waiting to see his reaction accidentally calling him by a pet name.

Jackson took a sip of his good morning coffee without a word getting a little more angry internally. He took a big sip of his very boozy coffee and started to walk moving right past her. He grabbed her hand on the way and pulled her towards the dining room needing a change of emotion that would put a smile on his face. Daisy put her hand over her face inhaling heavily the second she looked that way, looking at the sexy mess they made. She looked over at Jackson so innocently, smiling and chuckling like they were in trouble for what they had done. He took his hands putting them on the back of her neck forcing her to look at her silhouette imprinted on the table, she was undoubtedly turned on by the model-like painting in chocolate syrup of her. A random recall entered her thoughts, Daisy started thinking how good she would look on a canvas. Deeply imagining how sexy it would be if she bought him a giant canvas and covered herself in ink making it a permanent reminder on a cotton canvas. With his hand squeezing seductively into her neck she began fantasizing about rolling around and dripping in ink getting dirty for him. She pictured displaying it on Jackson's wall in his house, an one capturing the focus of the room. Realizing this is a place where she has not been yet.

Daisy was stuck on the fact that she had not been to his place yet, it's not like they have been together for that long but it was on the verge of being strange she has not been there yet. Daisy made herself upset thinking of this. Her mind started to wonder further down the rabbit hole looking at their mess of chocolate. The fact that they shared such a bond that it impaired her sense of reality, she turned to him and smiled giving him a kiss on the cheek and then went back into the bathroom to finish getting ready for work with her hot cup of coffee. Really she needed her own space to cleanse her mind before it ran rampant. Jackson came in to hangout with her as she finished getting ready sensing something was off with her, not prying since he was hiding something of his own.

  Daisy burned the tip of the charcoal eyeliner looking into the flame seeing a vision of last night's fun. Reliving it in her memory she began to contemplate till the lighter burned her finger. Daisy was sure of what she wanted, knowing he was good for her and that she was falling. He was sweeping her off her feet since the start, even though he was not very forthcoming with his emotions. Jackson made it clear with his affection speaking louder than words, he did not let her in and gave her a strange sneaky vibe yesterday when he went into the office. Daisy did not have a clue of the real internal battle that was currently fighting in his head.

  Sleep deprived, mind racing, body exhausted Jackson thought to himself of what to do and what to tell her all night since he first received the call. Honestly he had clearly thought through all possible scenarios knowing what one was best. The best option was not the easiest but most protective of Daisy. She walked out looking spectacular, Jackson smiled taking in her beauty trying to make his mind blank and fixate only on her.

  Jackson kissed her goodbye and headed to the hospital to go see the doctor, driving thinking of what to tell Daisy. The same answer lit up like Vegas he keeped on dodging it. Overthinking about so many things, the list went on and on. His calendar would have to be set up with finesse, that he would have to receive chemotherapy when she was at work so she would not notice anything out of the ordinary. The shrilling fact that last time the chemotherapy made his hair fall out. What would his excuse be for that? He would have to keep his medications in his car when he spent time with her. Jackson could not walk around with a medicine cabinet in his pockets. Reliving his past he remembered how he got sick quite often last time, he would have to blame the flu or some kind of cold or virus. His mind raced on the drive down to the city, speeding down the highway filling in first degree lies he was prepared to tell her.

Jackson made a cup of coffee in the quiet bleak waiting room. He sat down thinking maybe he could tell her the truth, beginning to cough loudly. His noisy raspy hacks continued switching thoughts that maybe it would work and he would get better, he did not want to lose Daisy. The woman at the front desk stood up offering Jackson a water to console him, hearing the pain as he hacked the flem from his lungs.

Each time he coughed it felt worse like someone was scratching the inner part of his throat. The nurse called him through the automatic glass door to have a seat as she prepared the butterfly needle and placed the stickers with his information on the plastic tubes. Slowly the red liquid flowed filling the tubed, the best answer recurred in his mind again. Jackson looked down at the purple bandage the nurse put on after covering the pinhole of the needle that drew out some milliliters of blood feeling it pulsate. Jackson sat in another office until he heard his name called. A small lady in blue scrubs yelled over at him, he was the only one in the waiting room. The nurse had high energy taking his vitals with a few shots of espresso in her morning dose. She wrote down his information then walked into another room. Jackson sat on the paper that crunched and they both started a long questionnaire, after they finished she assured Jackson that the doctor would be in a few minutes. Jackson alone in another waiting room began coughing again feeling like knives cutting into the back of his throat. After what felt like forever the doctor finally knocked on the door and came in. Jackson had been bored out of his mind pacing around the room and was washing his hands in the sink when the doctors entered.

After exchanging pleasantries the doctor began to give him the game plan of how to fight this thing, Jackson stayed relatively quiet nodding his head mostly. The long list of information went on, Jackson kind of zoned out. His selective hearing went in and out throughout the explanation of what they are going to be doing in the next few weeks. Zoning back into Jackson's ears began to ring.

"Your hair should not fall out this time with this treatment," the doctor said.

Jackson heard zoning back into the conversation momentarily, he realized the impact his appearance would change due to the medications. So it is a good thing that his hair should not fall out.

"That's quite a cough. I heard it while you were in the waiting room from all the way back here."

"I feel like a nuisance coughing like this in public places. I'd rather not but it feels like Freedy Krugar is slicing my esophagus."

"I'm going to give you something that should help," the doctor said while typing his prescription into the computer.

The doctor continued to explain the game plan, another doctor in training was sitting next to him and a woman who was part of the legal team was there with a bunch of paperwork for him to sign. The doctor explained the drugs, the process with times and dates for the medicine, it was a lot, Jackson was in and out listening. A lot of medicine needed to be taken and more that needed to be injected into his bloodstream just to keep him alive.

Jackson leaned back, the paper cracked as he hunched over. Remembering that it all was not too bad from the last time, but last time he did not go through the whole process alone. Well at least the beginning of the process. Thinking back the only part that really sucked was losing the hair, in all actuality losing of his beard was what pissed him off more. Jackson began to sign a bunch of papers, giving permission to start the process acknowledging the risks. The papers continued to flip from the woman from legal with multiple folders. Jackson signed his name page after page, his hand started to hurt. Spilling the black inkjet pen across each line he started to get the feeling that he was signing his life away.

Jackson did not say much throughout the visit. Doing what needed to be done ready to start treatment to get it all over with as soon as possible. The last bit of information he received he needed to fill out at home after talking with his insurance company. That was a major document that he needed to handle. Jackson left, thanking everyone in the room including the nurses behind the counter, he walked down the corridor to the exit folding all the paperwork in his hand thinking of Daisy. Accepting the fact that this time was going to be different, much more difficult than his previous encounter with death. Last time he had Stage 3 cancer, now it metastasized and was classified as Stage 4 spreading to multiple organs. Now it is more severe they have to take more of an aggressive approach giving him higher doses. This would make Jackson's body weaker leaving him with low energy. Most likely this imposing dilemma would stop him from working a few months. The outcome after he started his medicine would be very difficult to hide from anyone, especially Daisy. Jackson knew what he had to do, it was so obvious and reoccurred in his brain.

Chapter 9.

After a long strenuous week at work Daisy had not heard from Jackson. She did not know that he was stuck with the decision of two evils. Daisy called him a few times but when he picked up he was brief. Dodging any offer to see her, saying he was dealing with something and needed to focus on that. Daisy was troubled by this, she stopped dreaming completely and he was gone from every part of her existence. Every morning turning over in the bed to see if Jackson was there next to her. Intuition was telling her that something was wrong, sensing the feeling of a dark presence that was surrounding him.

Jackson was purposely distant with her due to his secret he held, he did not want her to see him in the state he was in. At first he felt fine keeping his same routine, he continued working at the bar and going to the gym feeling fine full steam ahead. Then out of nowhere it hit him like a ton of bricks, feeling his body break down into a weaker and more feeble man. Hiding the fact that all the drugs he was being pumped with changed who he actually was. The painkillers, nausea pills, nerve medicine, sleeping tablets, chemotherapy and the experimental drugs containing high radiation all made him a different person. Not wanting to expose her to any of it, choosing to remain isolated. He hated not seeing her, holding this burden that strained him more than the effects of the medicine.

Daisy sent him a long message stating she was confused about what was going on, she described vividly how she felt about him. All truths, Jackson read on and felt her pain but also thought he needed to set things straight even if he was going to end things. Jackson opened his front door and stepped out slamming it shut behind him without locking it, walking toward his car he called her. Daisy picked up on the first ring. She was both happy and frantic hearing his voice.

"Jackson?"

Before answering Jackson waited, listening to her breathe. He was a little high off the painkiller he had taken this morning feeling comfortable and partly numb. Brain waves moving in a different pattern trying to think of a practical and intelligent way to deal his burden to benefit the both of them not wanting to come off as an asshole. Listening to her breath he could picture her lips open, her chest moving up and down. Hearing her desire for him as she inhaled. He imagined the agonizing picture of her lovely face looking downward, sad, drooped over posture waiting for him to say something while holding her phone to her ear.

"Dinner tonight, I'll pick you up at 7:30pm and wear a dress," he said in a direct manner.

"Okay," Daisy said, a smile widened and her back straightened, feeling the water pool in her eyes glad to hear he wanted to see her.

Jackson hung up the phone without saying goodby and threw it in the passenger seat contemplating what to do. Still knowing what he needed to do, he asked himself now how to do it without hurting her.

Jackson accelerated running straight through a red light. Flying down the two lane road his head shifted from one side of the street to the next. Catching the sight of a sign that caught his attention he pumped down on the brakes, then turned into the parking lot. The wheels screeched, turning the wheel hard to the right.

Pulling directly into the handicap spot he then reached over at his pile of cancer paperwork and pulled a pass out of a folder so he would not get a ticket. Slamming his door, he walked with conviction right through the heavy wood doors of the restaurant on a mission. maitre d smiled at Jackson the second he walked in. He was in a gray suit with a cotton white button up, the top three buttons were undone exposing a chunk of his tattoos. The cute maitre d looked him up from the freshly ironed pleats in his pants all the way up to his collar that surrounded ink. Catching her in the act Jackson smiled intently looking at her eyes as he blew right by her walking straight up to the bar. Once the bartender approached Jackson looked up, knowing exactly what he needed in his life at that very moment in time.
"Whiskey."

The older bartender turned around, he didn't ask if he wanted it on the rocks or what kind of whiskey he preferred. The bartender approached with a bottle of Irish whiskey and an empty rocks glass. Without a word the bartender poured him a drink and walked away leaving the bottle right in front of Jackson.

Out of the corner of his eye before taking a sip he saw the maitre d walk to the back looking over at Jackson sitting at the bar before she went through the swinging metal doors into the kitchen. Jackson took a sip tasting the sweet floral notes followed by the smooth burn on the back of his throat. The burn felt different today, like a scorching flame after he swallowed. Jackson began coughing after he took a sip, having to hold back rather than continuing into an outlash in the nice restaurant. Holding his breath pushing his chest out trying to regain control, the pressure built and he had to hold his breath to seize any rapid expulsions of air that would tickle his through causing further irritation.

Jackson took another sip to console himself, once the whisky entered his mouth he was fearful that it would cause an episode spiraling into a coughing fit. The whiskey went smoothly down luckily with no problem. A few minutes later the cute maitre d came out from the back smiling flirtatiously directly at Jackson. Another woman followed her from the kitching smiling over at him. Jackson finished every drop of whiskey from the glass and poured himself another glass from the bottle that was generously left by the bartender.

    With a full glass, Jackson looked over at the different whiskeys, scotches and bourbons along the top oak wooden shelves. He admired how the bar was set up, it was aesthetically pleasing. The older bartender was polishing glasses with a towel over near the dishwasher one by one as they came out of the machine.

    The lights were dim in the bar area, the bar top was a dark maple with a polished bronze lip, Jackson rested his arms on the cold metal. He looked at all the details in the joint, rummaging through the decor that matched the European style. Moving his head around the room he was stunned, fixated on the shiplap on one accent wall helping draw focus on the red velvet drapes accents perfectly. His mind right now was relaxed, finishing off another glass of whiskey. Jackson reached for the bottle pouring himself one more, shooting it down in one gulp. Jackson waved to the bartender for him to tab him out, reaching in his pocket for his money clip waiting for his check.

    Jackson respected the bartender's ability to read him, properly giving him a drink he needed without being specific. Leaving the bottle in front of him was a pro move. Jackson paid the bill in cash leaving the bartender a Benjamin placing the hundred on top of the bill extra as a tip. Jackson put his hand through his hair slicking it back once he got up heading toward the exit. After slicking it back perfectly Jackson felt something that remained in his hair, he looked down and saw a clump of hair that just fell out. Jackson took a breath and headed back toward the bar reaching for a napkin, agitated, he wrapped the hair up and nodded over at the older bartender polishing glasses.

    Jackson made his way to the front looking over at the maitre d standing there with another woman giggling back and forth to one another making it obvious they were smiling only to get Jackson's attention. Approaching the front door he stopped before leaving at the hostess stand, startling the two women looking back and forth grabbing a to-go mint. The other woman suddenly left the front desk walking away in a hurry, intimidated by his confidence. The cute maitre d stood there back straight with an uncontrollable smile making her cheeks raise and eyes opened wide examining him inquisitively take the wrapper off the mint and fold it precisely into a perfect square. Jackson stood there for a second, making her nervous with his presence. She did not expect him to come by, in her experiences she came to the conclusion that most men are too afraid to hit on women.

"I'd like to make a reservation for two tonight at 7:45pm." Jackson said, sucking on his mint.
"What is the name?" The maitre d asked, biting her lip holding the pen to paper.
"King," said Jackson, winking, then walked through the doors back to his car.

      Sitting in his car with the air conditioner blasting and the music blaring, Daisy popped into his mind. His mind was already made up that for her sake he needed to end things with her and enjoy the last little bit of his life. She does not need to go through this with, he thought to himself cancer is difficult for everyone involved during a cancer diagnosis. Putting the car into drive, Jackson sped off down the road taking a left at the light then another left into a parking lot at the nearest barber. The barber took the buzzer to his head, cutting it all off, then the razor sliced it all off till there was all but skin on his head.

      Jackson went home and slept resting until 6:30pm when his alarm went off. He jumped in the shower to shine his head up, when he came out he pulled down on his beard styling it. Noticing that there were more hairs than usual in his hand, he would need to shave his beard but not tonight. He put on a suit and Jackson jumped back in his car to head to pick up Daisy. Pressing down on the breaks looking at her house hesitant to turn onto her block, hitting the gas he continued down a street of falling darkness. The clock struck 7:27pm on his dashboard pulling in front of her house, putting his car into park. Jackson took a deep breath before opening the car door trying to get his mind right, practicing his speech to break up with her.

The chill blew in through glass Daisy was waiting by the window. Perking up seeing his car she stood up right away to put on her coat then grabbed her stuff. Holding her oversized wallet that basically fit her phone, lip gloss, ID and a credit card after deciding not to bring a purse tonight Daisy's other hand was on the door. Watching him approach through the peephole, she opened the door once he stepped up the stairs eager to see him.

Daisy was stunned at how handsome he was with no hair on his head, she had not got a good look when she looked out the door. Jackson's beard was still intact, it was trimmed up a bit more than he usually kept it. It took Daisy a second to finally open up the screen door, still shocked and taken back by him looking like a totally different person.

"When did you do this?" Daisy said, blown away from his change in appearance.

"I lost a bet." Jackson fired back, rubbing the top of his shiny bald head.

Daisy leaned in to kiss him, they touched lips but he barely kissed her. Jackson was quick so she did not feel his cold lips, he grabbed her hand proceeding to the car. Jackson opened the car door, putting her in then rapidly shutting it right after she got in. Jackson did not look at her through the windshield as he walked by. Daisy knew something was the matter, it was bothering her. The lack of eye contact and physical touch threw her for a loop. He had a way of making her feel completely invigorated with just one look or touch and that was missing. She thought that he disappeared along with his hair. Daisy reached across the center console and grabbed his hand once he sat down.

"I missed you." Daisy said looking at Jackson, he genuinely smiled once she touched his hand feeling the pure energy and gripped her hand tightly not saying a word.

Jackson started driving down her block and began to cough. Trying to cough into his arm suppressing the hoarseness, he held his breath to stop it before it got out of control. Composing himself to seem like a normal healthy human. Daisy reached over to hold his hand with both of hers. Resting her weight on the center console as she rubbed his hands, her nurturing touch helped cool him off from the overheating that was going on in his head. Jackon realized how he was coming off as he acclimated to her presence beginning to second guess ending things with her.

"I like seeing you in a tie!" Daisy said she reached out to feel the texture.

Daisy grabbed the crooked tie to straighten it up so he looked pristine. Daisy's hand's both went straight back leaning over cheerfully smiling rubbing his hand trying to get him to open up. Jackson cracked the window open, the chilly breeze hitting his face. Inhaling the cold air that went down his sore throat. Jackson reached toward the cup holder grabbing his water bottle taking a sip to alleviate the pain and to prevent himself from coughing. Feeling refreshed he turned and looked at Daisy starting to relax. Her hair tied up tight on the top of her head partially curled, Jackson took in her divine beauty slowing down for the stop light that just turned red.

"I'm glad we're going out tonight." Jackson said, stopping fully, he leaned over and kissed her.

It was not just a peck, he crumbled from his original gameplan. Their lips naturally forming around one another, lusciously gripping ……..……..……the blaring sound of a car horn beeps behind them. The light had been green interpreting them, they were forced to release their succulent lips. They both giggled, retracting back to holding hands as Jackson sped off. He stepped down on the gas down the stretch of road gripping her hand the faster he went. Instantly they were back to normal, her eyes big and dreamy looking over at him accelerating the car drastically not caring about the laws.

Pulling into the restaurant Daisy was delighted when she saw where they were going, always wanting to try this restaurant but never had anyone worth it to go with. Daisy was eager walking up to the restaurant holding onto his arm enthusiastically in her red dress that had a cut out on one side exposing her shiny from her high thigh down. Using a piece of jewelry that she never had the chance to wear. The metal chain tied around her leg like a garter belt on her mid thigh. Using the advantage of her long legs to show off her unique fashion with the assistance of the fit of her dress. Jackson opened the door of the restaurant for Daisy and once he stepped in

out of the corner of his eye he noticed the same maitre d was there behind the host stand. Jackson smiled and winked at her with his hand on the backside of Daisy after he walked through the entrance. The maitre d smiled right back at him, her eyes moved to Daisy admiring how stunning she looked in the dress. She looked right into Daisy's blue eyes commending her subtly. Jackson watched the maitre d shift from looking down at Daisy's lips then back to her eyes multiple times. She straightened up her back presenting herself, putting her hands together looking courteous and professional showing off her white teeth with a beautiful smile.
 "Welcome back Mr. King, nice haircut. I have your reservation for 7:45pm for two."

      Daisy's eyes focused on the maitre d curiously smiling at her as she watched her glare back pleasantly grinning at Jackson and herself. Tilted her head to the side responsive to how she looked at Jackson. Daisy looked over at Jackson, his hand grabbed her ass causing an internal spark that lingered looking at both women. Daisy's eyes closed quickly then enjoying the squeeze, she got wet and her eyes widened enjoying his tight grip on her. The maitre d saw Daisy's impulsive reaction standing behind the host stand. With two menus in hand she directed the couple to her table, her hips wiggling back and forth walking like a runway model on the way. The couple walked behind her looking at her curves watching her movements on the long walk to the table located in an intimate area in the back of the restaurant. Jackson pulled out Daisy's seat, the maitre d watched his courteous manner, waiting for Jackson to sit down to hand the menus out.

"I'll take a dirty martini and Jackson will have..." Daisy said, but the maitre d finished her sentence.

"Whiskey, I'll let your server know. Your drinks should be right out, enjoy your meal tonight," the maitre d said with her cheeks raised then walked off rocking her hips from side to side.

      Jackson watched the maitre d walk off into the distance with wonder flashing through his eyes. Daisy turned also, locked in on her hips examining her curves that complemented the black high-rise modern trousers she was wearing. Daisy looked closer realizing she had the same pair in her closet. Jackson turned to pick up his menu, aware of where Daisy was looking he was filled with indecision.

The drinks were placed on the white table cloth Daisy's martini arrived along with his whiskey. They were both busy overlooking the menu to notice, mindful of the anomaly they just experienced.

Daisy paid close attention to his hands still on the menu, wondering if he was going to toast. Jackson carefully read the menu acting like he did not notice the drinks, he was thinking that this may be his last toast to her ever. Mind rumbling on what to say. The menu was blank to him just aimlessly staring, over the menu he spotted her blonde hair shift in a completely different direction. The cute woman was walking directly toward them, she had menus in her hand bringing another party of three to a table in the same section as Jackson and Daisy. Jackson put down his menu, not able to distinguish if his date was admiring the seductress that made eyes at him.

Stuck between a rock and a hard place, Jackson picked up his rocks glass ready to toast a goodbye. Unusually nothing came to mind, in his conundrum nothing held no meaning. She looked over at him with a craving impulse, words could not compare to the telepathy they exchanged. A martini glass floated in her hand wanting to speak for him of what he could not say. From a far one might think that there was a beautiful awkwardness transpiring at the table but there was so much taking place.

The server came up to the table interrupting them, going right to the explanation of tonight's features. Once the server pulled his face out of his server book he spotted the two had their glasses up in the air looking at him bothered, he quickly apologized and rushed away. "To us." Daisy said once they were alone at the table.

The two sweet genuine little words she spoke made Jackson smile. The confliction that was clogged freed everything he intended to say flushed down the drain. Modifying his decision to end things, unable to stray away from the magnificent sight in front of him. The connection charged up, coming up out of the ground sparking the room as they clinked glasses. Jackson took a sip of whiskey and began to cough violently. On the inside it felt like acid was burning his organs, hurting worse than she could possibly imagine but he played it off on the drink going down the wrong pipe. Jackson put his hand in front of his mouth, coughing into it he felt something on his skin. Looking down into his palm he saw a few red spots of blood pooled in the center of his hand. He concealed his stained palm quickly, rubbing it off the remnants into the black napkin that rested on his knee.

  Jackson felt a tickling sensation in the back of his throat, the pressure built up needing to cough more. A refreshing drink of ice water did not ease his pain, so he had to excuse himself to the bathroom. Once he walked through the bathroom door he released his pain, it sounded like he was choking on mustard gas. His body was bent over the counter his balance was off the harder he coughed, holding onto the walls to stabilize his outburst. The scratching feeling from the continuous coughing made it difficult to breathe, gasping for breath. Leaning over the sink splashing the cold water on his face. Hacking up and spitting into the drain nothing but filth came out of his body along with blood. Splashing more cold water, rubbing it on his bald head he took a second to console himself.

  Taking a deep breath then he started to put himself together in a speedy manner before anyone came in, if a stranger came in they might mistake him for having the plague. Looking hard into the mirror he saw his watery brown eyes in the reflection seeing nothing but a dying man. It was a sign that things were not looking the best for him, already feeling worse than last time. Why bring Daisy down a street that only ends in complete wickedness?

  Jackson walked back to the table, sitting right down picking up his menu like he was one hundred percent. The metallic lingered in the back of his throat, tasting it go down slowly after he swallowed. Daisy picked up her head looking over at him even though he was stuck in his own world. Scrolling through the menu in compilation, hiding his face in the two pages feeling her lingering eyes on him.

Under a whirlwind he released natural serotonin trying to make it easy to say what he intended. He put down his menu and grabbed his whiskey glass looking over with a flat eyes. Daisy couldn't help but notice the apprehensiveness of Jackson.

"Listen Daisy, I need to be honest," Jackson said, his head angled up looking past her and his mouth open pausing after licking his lips as he got the strength to say it.
"Daisy I can't do this anymore," putting his glass right down without a sip, hands disappeared underneath the table.

Daisy was about to take a sip before he spoke, she put the stemmed glass down on the table and her face turned down into a frown, confused and filled with anger along with a wave of sadness. Thinking to herself that this must be fake, no way this is happening right now. Daisy started pinching her leg underneath the table trying to wake up.
"Why?" Daisy whimpered.
"I'm not that guy. I want you to be happy and you won't have that with me." Jackson said with no remorse.

Daisy's heart dropped, she couldn't say a word she was so distraught she excused herself to go to the bathroom. Jackson went up to the bar once she left the table and ordered himself a whiskey neat. Drinking it quickly, throwing cash on the bar paying the tab. Jackson walked back to the table and sat back down, Daisy was nowhere in sight, still in the bathroom. Jackson began to drink the whiskey he had at the table while the coast was clear. Finishing it off quickly, signaling another whiskey from his server. Daisy came out of the bathroom and headed his way back to the table. She sat down and took a sip of her martini, staring at him trying to find the words.
"Jackson I don't understand. We are great together. What else do you want?" Daisy said..

The maitre d that had been looking at Jackson walked over past their table smiling. Daisy noticed how she was looking at him, just like the other women she caught staring at him everywhere they went. Jackson's head moved, catching eye contact with the maitre d trying to hide his smirk, this woman was the only one Jackson seemed to be phased by.

"You want her?" Daisy said slowly in a low voice, coming off extremely sexy to Jackson.

"You want her?" Jackson laughed, shaking his head putting his hand up to his cheek inquisitively.

"Fine, I'm game," Daisy responded leaning in, ripening her frown to a pleasing smile.

     Daisy continued to try to change his mind not knowing the grim reaper had come back for him. He was completely taken back, thinking it was a combative answer waiting for her to stop this character she was playing. Her lips pushed together moving closer enticing him, Jackson was not expecting this at all. Jackson had a confused look, staring at her captivatingly waiting for an explanation.

"You want her, fine. She is cute, she obviously likes you. I just want you Jackson even if I have to share."

     Jackson lifted his glass nodding his head in accord. He took a sip without a word, raising it up finishing off his whiskey.

"Let's finish our meal, then let's bring her back to your place." Daisy said, holding up her martini.

     Daisy eyebrows shifted up and she took a big gulp of her martini with charming admiration. Jackson grabbed her hand, about to tell her the truth but then the server came over at that moment. Jackson leaned back in his seat and ordered for both of them, looking at the menu and chose the first two courses that caught his eye.

"Daisy will have the short rib with the risotto and I will have the ribeye medium rare with a baked potato." Jackson said then passed the menus to the server.

     Jackson put his hands together locking his fingers with his elbows on the armrests like he had furth business to discuss but his lips were locked up not able to tell her the truth. One moment of readiness, but the server coming over threw him off thinking to himself now that the news would hurt her more than a breakup. Jackson was also a bit curious about Daisy's suggestion, taking that as a possible sign.

The two cesar salads came that Daisy ordered when he was coughing his lungs out in the bathroom, tensions had eased after her recommendation to bring the cute maitre d home. Eating their salads they fell back into suit ordering another bottle of wine. Jackson and Daisy flirted the whole night, their eyes radiating with copious amounts of lust. Jackson put his hand under the white table cloth and pulled her chair close to him. A poetic change of events they could not keep their hands off one another throughout the meal.

Daisy went to the bathroom again after they were done with the second course. Walking to the bathroom Jackson mentally recorded her into the harddrive of his memory. Daisy stopped in her tightfit redstripped dress to turn back and look at him. She smiled and winked walking through the bathroom door, Jackson closed his eyes to savor her beauty. He finished his drink and tried to time it so he was at the front of the bathroom to meet her outside when she was finished.

On the way to the bathroom the maitre d watched his every movement. Daisy walked out of the bathroom and Jackson embraced her beauty in slow motion, her plump lips, the little freckles on her nose, getting lost in the universe of her blue eyes.

"Jackson, it's you." Daisy said looking up at him, Jackson took a breath nodding and kissed on the head.

Daisy walked back to the table glimmering in her red striped dress with her heels clacking with every step on the hardwood, Jackson watched from behind. Following the beat of his heels, memorizing the way she moved so elegantly. Jackson veered off on his way back to the table toward the host stand.

"Excuse me."

"Hi Mr. King, how can I be of service?" She smiled, fingers playing with her hair, slightly biting her lip at the dashing fella.

"What time do you get off work? Would you like to get a drink with us?" Jackson asked directly.
"9pm. I can go get a drink with y'all when I get off, yes." She said playing with her hair taken back.
"Give me your phone," Jackson pulled out his phone and put it in her hand, her finger rubbing on his as she grabbed his phone.
"Go put on a dress when you get off before coming to my place, yeah." Jackson said smiling, the anticipation was painted on her face nodding with a bright smile.

   Jackon went back to the table to Daisy, being watched by both women. Finishing off the meal the sparks continued to fly through the air. To finish off the date with two red wines instead of dessert. Jackson raised his single long stemmed glass not to toast just to cheer her glass. After finishing their wine he flagged down the waiter to grab the check. The tannins of the wine tickled the back of Jackson's throat, he coughed heavily into his napkin. Daisy looked concerned after hearing him, remembering he had been coughing lately now that she was paying attention to it.

   Leaving cash on the table he grabbed Daisy hand walking her to the door. The maitre d smiled at both of them as they passed, nervously standing up straight.
"See you later!" Daisy looked at the maitre d who was grinning back.

   The two both walked to the car hand in hand, once she got in Daisy opened her window all the way down letting in the brisk air. Leaning back in her seat breathing in the fresh air staring up at the stars. Jackson moved his hand to her left knee, wanting her now urging his hand to stop. His hand went up her dress even though we wanted to grab her and put her on top of him. Daisy closed her eyes, seeing her own set of stars behind her eyelids. Her body leaned down into his hand pressing her back into the leather seat, she felt his fingers playing. One hand on the wheel and one hand tickling her making her squirm uncontrollably.
"Let's stop at my place first," Daisy said mid moan.

Jackson turned, going in the direction of her place taking a deep breath trying to control his urge. Pulling up to the house his hands were submerged inside of her. Daisy enjoyed it so much, pushing his hand off so she could get out and grab some stuff from her house.

Daisy ran in the house after correcting her panties that were pushed over by him. Waiting for her his phone went off, it was the maitre d texting Jackson asking for the address. Jackson sent the address, reminding her about the dress along with instructions to knock at the door three times loudly. Jackson watched the sky admiring the stars just thinking. Holding the burden of the truth looking into the vastness of space. Everything Daisy said at the restaurant replayed in his mind about just wanting him. Daisy came out of the house in a long overcoat jacket.

Jackson's hand returned to her leg once she got in, he tried to pull her overcoat open and continue to make her squirm. Daisy slapped his hand with the devil lurking in her eye. Jackson bit his lip, returned his hand to the wheel holding ten and two. Daisy's hand touched his leg making her way to his belt, knowing where the button was now and unlatched it without a problem. Daisy bent over putting her head down. Her soft lips clasped onto him, Jackson inhaled, gripping the wheel.

When they stopped in front of his house Daisy put her head, her finger touched her lip wiping the drool. She watched Jackson pull up his pants waiting to go inside his house. Daisy examined every inch of his place when she entered for the first time, figuring out quickly his style.

"Grab three glasses." Daisy said loving the layout retreating into the unknown to find his room, shutting the door behind her once she found it.

Walking slowly through his room, she looked around at his industrial modern style of the decor. There was a huge giant white canvas leaning up against the far wall, Daisy thought it was peculiar. She was drawn to it, feeling the cotton paper thinking she may have insight into the future. In the corner next to the blank canvas she noticed a large staff, the light color bark looked stained with a color that was indescribable. The top of the staff had a criss-crossed knot holding in a dark smoky quartz crystal, in the very center of the crystal it seemed to have a yellow glow that was all too mesmerizing. Daisy heard Jackson's phone go off. It was probably the maitre d so Daisy quickly rushed into his bathroom so she could doll herself up in the bathroom.

      Jackson grabbed the bottle of fine wine from his wine rack, pulling off three glasses that hung from his stand up bar. Naturally he made sure they were clean and polished, he then set the glasses in the middle of the island countertop. His phone beeped and vibrated in his pocket and pulled it out to open the notification.

"OTW to put on something! SEE YOU SOON ;)"

"We are waiting," Jackson responded back.

      Jackson grabbed a rocks glass pouring himself a proper glass of whiskey, then stepped through the living room and slid the door open to go outside. Fortunately enough he was not irritated by this whiskey, he looked up paying a blessing up above. Plopping down onto the outdoor vinyl mesh couch the cool air blew holding his full whiskey staring up at the beauty of the night sky. A few minutes went by enjoying the peace and then his phone beeped again. "OTW." He read her text and got up to go to the living room.

      He stopped by his hutch, fumbling through his records to put on some music. After he was not able to find an album of his liking he yelled at Alexa to play "Sunflower." Daisy walked out after the first chorus ended. Jackson turned around hearing her heels from his room, delightfully looking at Daisy in red fishnets with a matching floral lace cut thong and bra. Her hair was now in a high slicked back tight ponytail. Daisy walked over in heels to kiss Jackson. His hands went up and down her body feeling the texture of her lingerie, touching her skin though the lines of her fishnets. Daisy walked over to the counter, grabbing a glass making a sad face that it was empty.

Jackson smiled and pulled out the cork from the bottle, pouring Daisy glass first. Jackson finished pouring his and Daisy tapped his glass unexpectedly.   .

"For your." Daisy said she had been in charge of all the toasts for the evening.

Raising their arms up to their mouths they both took a sip, ready to pounce on one another. Enjoying the dark blend of grapes that swirl boldly inside their mouths, his hand continued to rub her. The blood was flowing quickly though their bodies making it surreal. Aroused and anxious Daisy stood in her erotic attire completely soaked more than she was in the car.

The door knocked firmly three times. Jackson winked, walking toward the door with a chip on his shoulder. A bit nervous Daisy inquisitively sipped her wine. The moment he put his hand on the doorknob all the things in his mind that were pestering him since his doctor called evaporated.

The door opened, the maitre d was wearing a beautiful dark blue dress accented in silver glitter, with flashy glitter heels. Her eyes were on Jackson as she walked brushing into him. Daisy stepped around from the other side of the counter in her lingerie and the maitre d mouth dropped seeing red.

"Wow, you are so hot." The maitre d uttered at Daisy dazzling.

You could tell her hands wanted to touch Daisy, her fingers wiggle with desire. Jackson poured her a glass of wine and put it in her eager hands.

"What is your name sexy?" Daisy said, her elbows crossed one arm lifted up toward her lips, the wine glass was inches away trying to conceal her excitement.

"I'm Claire." Looking with an ungodly desire that twinkled in her eyes.

Daisy tapped Claire wine glass first, Jackson moved with speed to tap directly in the middle of both glasses. After taking a sip Daisy leaned in very close, whispering in Claire's ear. Claire looked down at the kitchen tile blushing, cheeks raising to what Daisy was telling her.

Jackson took another sip of wine watching the two women flattered one another with ongoing complements, whispering back and forth. He stood admiring the two of them as they made each other smile he recognized how each female held their unique model-like features.

Daisy giggling looking right at Claire, Daisy leaned in to give her a soft slow kiss on her cheek. Claire turned into Daisy, locking lips with one another. Swapping their wet and sloppy tongues in one another's mouths. Jackson leaned his elbows back on the countertop, raising one arm up to drink more of his red wine watching two beautiful women makeout.

After watching for a minute he was filled with temptation, he couldn't wait anymore. He put his glass down on the countertop and joined in, grabbing them both. One hand on each of their hips inviting himself to the party. Both women looked up at him smiling, touching his hunky beard with their finger tips teasing him. Struck by the pure sexiness that sparked off their lustful faces. He carefully took Claire's wine glass from her, taking a sip before putting it down.
"Take her dress off." Jackson said protruding malice watching Daisy turned Claire around, helping her unzip her dress from the back.

Daisy seductively shrugged the straps to the side bringing them past Claire's shoulders and let go, she watched the dress plummet to her heels. Claire was wearing a hot pink bra with matching panties that glowed in the dim light of Jackson's kitchen. Both half naked women in lingerie and heels eagerly looked up at Jackson as he stood there impassively empowered. Taking them both by the hands to a more comfortable location, they stopped in the living room.

Both of the beauties overtook Jackson, both synchronized pulling his tie first, then his gray suit jacket was ripped off. Together they both started to unbutton his white collared shirt off taking turns smooching him. They took their time taking his shirt off eventually exposing all of his upper body. Claire gasped to herself seeing Jackson's whole torso filled with intricate tattoos. Claire's hand began rubbing them, feeling the raised marks from the needle that previously pressed into his skin, Daisy's hand was rubbing up on Claire. Daisy's hands squeezing deep into her tight skin grabbing her pink thong.. Daisy shifted over to him, digging her superior nails into Jackson's abs. Both petite women rubbed all over one another but their profound focus was on Jackson.

Jackson pulled his arms out of his sleeves, throwing his shirt off. Throbbing below, both eager women massaged him. Daisy began kissing on Jackson's chest grabbing Claire's head to tag team his body with her. Both women stroked making their way to unbuckling his belt. Daisy grabbed Claire's cheek and began kissing her as they fumbled to unzipped Jackson's pants.

Daisy whispered in Claire's ear and she got on her knees. Daisy held her head and reached toward Jackson to kiss him, releasing her lips from him she bent down. He had both of their ponytails wrapped around his hands. Daisy suddenly got up and walked away for a moment. Jackson saw her return with something hiding behind her back.

Daisy walked behind her and smacked Claire's ass, leaving a red handprint on her cheek. Claire's mouth was full but moaned feeling the imprint burn, she started drooling. Daisy exposed her other hand; she was holding a candle and lighter. Sparking the flame looking up at Jackson sparking up the lighter, the fire hit the wick creating a new climatic part of the evening.

Claire was oblivious to the sounds, eyes closed, head moving back and forth. The faint sound of Claire's slobbering mouth on his cock, her body tightened and leaned harder on an angle. The wax dripped on the lower part of Claire's spine, Claire swayed in a vertical motion. Jackson's grip intensified, controlling her movements.

Daisy returned to her knees, unstrapping Claire's bra helping her arms out. Dripping the wax up her back Daisy bit her lip, feeling in control. Dominantly rubbing her hands into the bone in Claire's hip, blowing air into her ear. Claire's body was quivering, drool dripping down her chin splashing on the floor,more wax hit her skin. Jackson was in disarray watching Daisy touch Claire like he had touched her. His hand grabbed Daisy's cheek, rubbing his thumb on her face. He grabbed her hair pulling her in closer to share with Claire. Jackson held each woman by their hair like he was directing a horse and carriage. Daisy stood breaking Jacksons grip on her hair, she rose to licking his lip leaving a trail of saliva. Preoccupied kissing him the wax dripped down on her fingers, the hot liquid caused her to draw from Jackson.

    Daisy stepped back and began dripping the wax on Jackson's chest. Jackson rolled his head back on the sofa, teeth locked. Daisy dripped more of the red hot wax on the back of Claire's neck smacking her ass again, holding on to it like a trophy. His hands moved to grope Claire's chest, pinching around the sensitive areas. Claire began to continuously moan harder and harder between the both of them arousing her together. Her uncontrollable quivers escalated. Daisy slowly rubbed her nails on her inner thighs as Jackson pinched harder, the wax continued to cover Claire's backside. Both Jackson and Daisy were in sync watching Claire at the verge of bursting. Jackson grabbed Claire's head controlling her movements once more. Daisy dripped wax down her back then on the backside of her legs finally on the bottom of her feet, twitching in sweet pain of the burns. Daisy's fingers spun forcefully inside her, putting the candle down to use her other hand as leverage.

    Suddenly Claire gasped trying to lift her head up, Jackson resisted, holding for the right second then released as Claire erupted. Daisy pulled the back of her hair pulling Claire back toward her. Claire's eyes were slammed shut and mouth wide open as she shook, orgasming with Daisy's sticky fingers inside of her. Daisy rubbed the inner part of her thigh that was now soaking wet dripping down the side of Claire's leg. Jackson bent down, his hand under her to rub some more. Claire began shaking her whole body more with just his two fingers gently tickling her. As he sped up she started to convulse. Daisy bound her arms from behind, Claire was on the road to the finish line again breathing heavily as her soul was leaving her body.

    Another burst of ecstasy, Claire grabbed Jackson's hand pulling it away from her with a huge cringing smile on her face shaking back and forth in a ringing rhythm. Claire finished moaning, her pussy was tingling and opened her eyes panting as the two released her from their seduction. Daisy leaned in and kissed her on the side of the neck rising up, whispering in her ear. Daisy licked Claire's lips, her mouth was open, Claire was unable to move her body.

"My turn." Daisy said standing up, Jackson sitting on the couch waiting for her.

    Daisy jumped on top of Jackson rattling the couch, her skin fluttering feeling the cold untouched spot of the cushion on the outer sides of his spread legs. Daisy rode him like a wild horse as Claire was tingling watching the two grind all over one another. Claire's body was drooped over the floor, her arms resting leather and her head placed on a pillow on the sofa. Daisy tucked her body leaning on an angle hitting the spot that made her finish rapidly screaming and squirting down her leg digging her nails into his ribs. He leaned over on the couch and whispered to Claire. Jackson's movements slowed after Daisy's climax but he did not stop, in first gear maneuvering inside. Claire pushed her weight down into the sofa crumbling the leather, her lips were freezing from breathing in and out of her mouth expeditiously licking them as she stumbled into the kitchen involuntarily lightheaded. Jackson slowly thrusted with Daisy on top of him, two inked up hands compressed into her hips getting her ready for round. Claire came back with Jackson's tie creeping through the living room on her tiptoes. The second he saw her feet hit the carpet, the gestures of his body indicated where Claire needed to fasten the tie. Jackson trickled her hands behind her as he propelled in an upward motion to the soothing rhythm that kept Daisy tranquil. Jackson's firm grip clenched her wrists together picking them up, the two worked together to chain Daisy's arms together with his cotton tie. Daisy's keen voice screeched pushing her weight down into his tattooed hips. Claire finished giving him a wink for the go ahead to continue pleasuring at his own ambitions, her tempting smile made Jackson force Daisy closer with his hand on her back leaning off the sofa. Jackson continued to lean up and forward to grab Claire by the back, Daisy's appealing moans aroused the other two amplifying their sweltering make out session.

    Jackson quickly began to push his body up and down quickly, Claire did not back off she was drawn further into him, twisting her tongue inside Jackson's mouth bending over. He had to shift his hips to continue messing with them both at the same time. Claire grabbed Daisy's bouncing body, resting her palms on his knuckles. Her fingertips could feel the bulge of his veins on his hands, while she helped alter the gravity of Daisy vigorously fuck his cock.

To the neighbors the sounds that belted out of Daisy's would have been misconstrued as sounds indicating deep suffering, deep yes but on the contrary. Jackson leaned back releasing his lips from Claire, patting the cushion next to him for her to sit down as he pressed his shoulder blades into the furniture frame. Letting Daisy regain her breath he too took a deep breath, head pointed up toward the sky as the two gorgeous fatigued women laid. Claire watched him illuminate, it was so dark she could not see him moving. Claire watched waiting for her turn, intently noticing each nuance Daisy expressed. His slithering hand went unnoticed until a swift strike down there and her knees touched at lighting speed. Her breasts jolted making them fuller after the shock of his accurate attack on her libido.

Making both of them scream with pleasure simultaneously, he began to break a sweat. Claire reached over, scratching the wax from his chest, she grabbed his beard pulling him into a kiss.

Within ten minutes, Daisy finished four more times one after the other. Jackson picked her up and put her down on the couch still bound, he grabbed Claire and propped her on the couch. The sweat drifted down his body, breathing fiercely. Endurance continued to excite whoever was in front of, bent over, or on top of him even though he spent more time with his woman.

When Jackson finally finished Daisy was barely keeping her eyes open. Jackson was out of breath as he untied Daisy's arms, his arms slipped under her legs on the rug and around her back. With Daisy in his arms he waved his head from Claire to come follow.

Come she did, her excitement arose watching the power of Jackson's body walking into his bedroom. Claire's eyes grew heavy watching him gently put Daisy on the bed. Claire's intent was crystal clear, capturing his vision once finished what he was doing. Her body was primed, standing at the foot of the bed ready to have uninterrupted one on one time with this man she had just met a few hours ago.

Jackson rounded the corner of the low solid oak wood framed bed, when she was within his reach he grabbed Claire by her ponytail pulling her to his side of the bed. Jackson let go of her hair, instantly latching onto her hand before getting into bed directing her to get on top of him. Claire smiled filling her firm, her legs were now on both sides of him shimmying into position to be entered. The stimulating sounds of Claire cumming hard infatuated Daisy began helping her regain her energy. Jackson got up with Claire still on top of him, leaning back on an angle. His knees sunk into the mattress with Claire straddling him. Daisy opened her eyes, watching how deep his strokes hit. She got up and crawled behind Jackson, rubbing the surface of his traps before kissing the side of his neck. Changing her attention from him to Claire, struck by the ravishing hourglass shape wiggling her hips in a seesaw circular pattern. Each woman was more envious of the other watching with envy.

His stamina was off the charts, relishing in the fact he made them cum harder the next time. This went on for a while, until Jackson fired the last shot to conclude the evening. All of their bodies had a glaze of sweat that layered on their skin, Jackson hair was damp from putting in so much work all night.

The two ladies together had enough after a night of their bodies plowed like a contortionist. Laying down cleaning themselves with a towel Jackson threw on the bed before walking out of the room. He returned with a Waterford rocks glass filled with tequila, going to his position on the empty side of the bed.

Hydration was much needed, with the help of smooth tequila to quench his thirst that in this instance was more pure than water. A delicious sweet flavor profile to end a sweaty night looking at the women that were already passed out cuddled up to one another naked on the gray silk sheets of the king mattress.

Parched Jackson left the bed walking in the direction of the bar in the living room to pour himself another glass. Once his crystal glass was filled with the golden yellow reposado he stepped outside and stood among the stars. The agave lingered on the back of his tongue after taking a sip. Jackson sparked up a cigarette in only a towel, stretching his spine up to the sky as he released the smoke from his lungs increasing the v shape in his hips. His mind contemplated what to do with the undergoing problem he was dealing with, trying to figure the words to say. The speculation into his future, if he was to bring a woman through the valley of the shadows of death after tonight Jackson knew she fits the position much better than his previous endeavor.

Knowing it would break her heart to hear the news that his time on Earth was potentially limited to under three years if the medication did not function as intended. His mind raced, the predicament sprung him into an orbit of paradox thinking. The images of his ex filtered, her elegant beauty bewitched his envision. The enchanting trip down memory lane undertook the moment he quit his job after becoming weaker from the chemotherapy radiation and the dozens of other medications in his bloodstream. Reliving the final chapter of his last relationship, the one that ran its course longer than it was meant to.

For the reason that their outstanding physicality was never an issue it took more time for the unrecoverable blip to materialize even after having the knowledge of her betrayal. The confusing induced state of his mind left him to believe that their love was pure even after finding out that she had been seeing someone romantically just before his treatment started. Addicted to painkillers and grand illusions was a deadly mixture. After coming to the realization he eradicated the viciousness from his life accepting the loss for a lesson. Jackson reached up, squeezing his eyeballs to seize his thinking. Helping him halt all further thought of his past indiscretions.

While under the moon that shined bright Jackson contemplated how to form the sentence that could come to change everything, his words were mush. Jackson continued to drink till the bottle went dry. Feeling a strong buzz he looked for a formidable sign in the stars.

After an excessive amount of alcohol he did not sleep a wink, steadily overthinking till the sun cracked into existence. The stars faded and the yellow of the horizon strengthened, birds began to softly chirp. Jackson got up to get back in bed and after laying next to the two beautiful women for thirty minutes he got up to make a pot of coffee to slow his speeding brain.

Filling the house with a gentle aroma from the kitchen shirtless he scooped the grinds and heated the water. Daisy and Claire woke to the smell of dark Colombian roasting beans. Both women came out in Jackson's hockey jerseys forcing Jackson to lick his lips naturally. Daisy walked up to Jackson giving him a kiss and accepted the cup of coffee he prepared for her, just the way she liked it. Jackson admired watching the oversized jersey cover Daisy's naked body.

"Can I get a cup to go?" Claire said, holding her matching bra and panties that she picked up off the floor.

Claire was brief, feeling out of place first thing in the morning. She quickly got dressed, taking her cup of steaming hot coffee and said her goodbyes. The door slammed shut, pure silence.

"I'm going to take a shower, you're welcome to join." Jackson whispered into Daisy's ear feeling her cheekbones rise, she stood up on her tiptoes.

"I'm just going to grab something to eat. I'm starving." Daisy said, she stood in place watching Jackson walk down the hallway.

Jackson began coughing, he reached into the shower pulling the handle to the right to make the water hot. The steam filled the air brushing his teeth. Daisy was finishing up putting the cream cheese on her bagel and her head turned hearing Jackson start violently coughing. Restraining himself, he held his breath, stepping in the water. The water hit his face while he controlled his breathing hoping the steam would console him. Sadly he began coughing again, so hard he had to put his hands on his knees to balance. With each his body convulsed, the verge of his back being thrown out coughing with such force. His hand tried to grip onto the wall facing the floor. He continued to cough until his balance broke, falling to his knees.

"You ok babe?" Daisy yelled into the bathroom from the kitchen.

"Too much booze." Jackson muttered.

Listening to the continuation of wheezing Daisy wandered into the bedroom and stood by the door listening to him cough up a lung. Jackson coughed so much he began to feel sick. He began throwing up and blood covered his tiles. The water hit the white tile clearing up a dark red stain that came out of Jackson. Daisy popped her head in thinking he was hungover, but his coughing sounded painful.

"Jackson? You ok?"

"Daisy st-- ughh - stop." Jackson said in the mists of covering the floor with a puddle of blood.

Daisy witnessed a crime scene when she walked through the door to the bathroom. Jackon was on his knees throwing up blood, it looked like a murder scene and Daisy's cup of coffee fell from her hand. Coffee spilling as gravity took its course, shattering into a million little pieces. The rest of her bagel followed down to the floor watching the blood spew from his mouth. His bloody hand on the glass door trying to stop her, too weak to stand.

"Jackson, Jackson, you need to go to the hospital," frantically watching him heaving in severe pain wiping the excess blood from his mouth.

Jackson eventually stopped throwing up, losing at least a pint of blood. He continued coughing trying to catch his breath. There he was sitting on the floor of the shower with his back against the wall. The water cleaned up the pool of blood that eventually swirled down the drain.

"No, im fine," Jackson said, putting his hand full of blood though slicked his hair back trying to compose himself.

Finally Jackson had the energy to stand up. He swung open the door grabbing Daisy's wrist that were shaking, tears falling from her face, he pulled her in the shower with the jersey still on. Holding her, the hot water hit the two of them and small spots in the corner of the shower were remnants of blood. The steam rose to the bright bathroom lights as the two sat on the shower bench. Jackson's body fatigued, trying to muster up the words to say for Daisy in the twilight of his fearful endeavor he was faced with.

"I don't want you to worry, I need you to calm down. This is just a result of my medicine."

Daisy looked at him confused. Looking at him with teary eyes trying to wind down, Jackson took a deep breath looking at the drain pulling back the hair that was in his face.

"Daisy, I have cancer. I've had it for years, it was too soon to tell you. Now it just started growing back again and I started treatment last week. Why I've been so distant. I didn't know how to tell you."

Daisy fell into his chest crying. Jackson sat with her on the tile feeling her tears hit his neck. Daisy was devastated, but it was much worse witnessing the complications of the medications had done to him.

"Jackson, you threw up so much blood."

"Perhaps it was too much alcohol, not a good mix with chemo." He said in a joking manner trying to lighten the mood a bit.

"It's going to be ok, it's going to be ok." Daisy said holding on to him saying it over and over repeatedly, her voice lowered the more she said it. Jackson turned off the water feeling the tears fall from her face, as they sat on the shower bench.

The drips from the showerhead being the only noise aside from her sniffling. Jackson got up putting all of his weight on the wall to assist him standing up. He grabbed a towel wrapping Daisy in it, walking her over to the bed. He stood over her giving her a kiss on the forehead dropping down to a knee, pressing his forehead to hers.

"It's going to be ok, that's an uncommon side effect." Jackson said, looking dully down at the ground in sorrow.

"You don't deserve to go through all this." He said reluctantly, playing with her wet hair.

"Is this why you tried to end things last night?" Daisy asked knowing the truth now of what was truly bothering him, maybe her awful dream was a sign.

Jackson grabbed her hand, holding it so very tight. He went into detail to Daisy how this had happened before, going into depth the chaos his ex caused out of spite. That his perspective on everything and everyone changed, his trust was hard to earn. Realizing that the true colors of others were shown for the best. He continued describing that aside from cancer the other things in his life that first year nearly destroyed him.

"I can't put you through this, it will not work out. Lets cut the head off the snake before it's too late," Jackson said, still focused on the floor.

Daisy's eyes focused on Jackson's side, a gray washed grim reaper with a sickle slicing a rose stemmed with the shape of a ribbon. She looked up his arm, the story was inscribed the more she looked into the scars that protruded with such beauty deeply drawn into his skin. She put her hand over it to cover it, understanding the meaning that the piece displayed.

"Jackson, I'm not your ex. I'm not going anywhere! Never! No matter what!"

Jackson took a sigh of relief, her words caused an insurrection of his negative thoughts. He took a long hard look at her, harping on her words. Looking deep into her soul in great compilation, seeking trust with his empty gaze. He put his weight on the bed rising to his feet, then he hobbled back to grab a towel for himself leaving a trail of water. Jackson started coughing violently again, luckily making it to the bathroom in time without throwing up all over the floor. Once he stopped he slammed the bathroom door, then rushed back to the toilet to throw up blood. Daisy heard the pain though the walls.

Jackson cleaned himself up, stepped out of the bathroom after taking a line walking straight to his closet with conviction to put on clothes. Fully dressed with Daisy naked in his bed he went over and kissed Daisy on the head.

"I have to go." Jackson said directly walking out of the room when his lips left her forehead.

Daisy had no words, the tears ran down her cheeks into the pillows hoping he would realize she was being honest. Jackson got in the car whipped out of the driveway driving straight toward the interstate. At the stop light he pulled out a glass vile, pouring a bump of powder on the top of his hand. He snorted it from the dip in between his thumb and pointer finger. Once the light turned green he was off squealing the tires. He flew down the exit ramp pressing his foot down to the floor hitting over 100mph before merging onto the highway. Once on the straightaway he continued to accelerate reaching top speed.

Screaming at the top of his lungs as he passed 120mph, feeling the scratching feeling on the back of his throat ready to cough more.

Closing his eyes in his lane counting to 1-2-3 -4. The picture of Daisy lying down in his bed lingered in his mind. The repeated memory of her silhouette in chocolate on the table from the other night.

5-6-7-8 he counted eyes still closed, the napkin with her name and phone number vividly resurrected from his internal memory hard drive.

Trying to vision the first time he laid eyes on her, but could not remember. Foot all the way down to the floor. The car was rumbling, feeling the vibration while he gripped the steering wheel.

The engine maxed, RPM in the red. Unable to hear the sound of her voice 9-10 he screamed.

BOOM!

    Jackson's eyes opened, hitting a wall in his mind. At the next exit he veered off to the right again and again till he found a nearby park that overlooked the water with a sandy beach. Sitting in the parking lot, he stared up at the sun making its daily routine of rising. He began thinking of last night's fascinating paradox that left his mind boggled.

    The foundation that they have built was already stronger than anything he had been a part of. Basking alone in the sun with the realization that a strong foundation would not matter if this new medicine he was currently taking did not work. The dilemma had him stuck calculating every different situation.

Dirt followed him back from the trail, turning the ignition over to drive back to the house to talk to Daisy who was still laying on his bed naked waiting for him to return. The conclusion of the decision will change his life forever. He unlocked the door and right back into bed with her. After getting comfortably in bed he started to explain to her the game plan set out by the doctor.

Daisy expressed how she truly felt for him, laying naked in bed. Daisy was willing to take the risk of losing him while he battled instead of losing him now. Jackson laid with her and listened, she had apparently been looking up different options of what to do in this situation to help patients heal. Explaining the natural remedies she wanted to try with him to combat his cancer. Wanting Jackson to go on a carnivorous diet, eat apricot seeds and do multiple parasite cleanses. Daisy talked about cutting sugar completely out of their diet going into grave detail.

Jackson looked at her knowing deep down in his heart he did not want her to leave even though that was probably the smartest idea. He did not say it but he felt that Daisy understood his disposition. Her striking beauty stalled his negative thoughts as she explained all the different ways they would try to improve their health together. She tried to unpuzzle the horrid situation, Daisy continued to formulate a plan of action to make it work.

Chapter 10.

The chilling air of the hospital consumed Daisy as she stared at the nurse putting a needle in Jackson's arm. Good thing he did not have a fear of needles; this was one of many. He had spent over two hundred hours in the chair being painted. His face did not cringe when the needle pierced his skin, but it felt like a thousand shards of glass all at the same time, his veins tried to hide from the thin dense metal.

The all white rooms were sterile, the cold blowing from the vents helped make that to be sure. Scents of alcohol from nurses and doctors rubbing their hands filled the hospital. It helped postpone the scent of death that lingered in the beds.

Jackson and the nurse were going back and forth about their favorite hockey teams, talking about the game from the other night. The hockey season had just started and the excitement flew from his mouth talking about something he loves. This made Daisy happy to see him smile in a hospital wing that was filled with sadness and death. You can feel and see who is going to make it and who won't. The majority of the people hooked up to the chemo machines were older, at least fifty years old plus. Most brittle and weak, some with hair others with none. Many had blankets and hats, the heating blanket was best for sleeping. Quiet in desperation, dreaming as poison is injected into their system. All trying not to think of the negatives of the inevitable.

"Ok well you're all hooked up. In an hour I will come back with the chemo after the immune therapy is done. I'll be here all day so if there's anything you need let me know." The blonde nurse said.

As soon as she left the room Jackson looked over at Daisy and smiled rubbing his stomach.

"I'm hungry too, let's go see what snacks there are or do you want to get lunch?" Daisy said, watching him continue to rub his belly she already knew the answer.

"I'll go upstairs and get a sandwich for us." Daisy said, chuckling.

Daisy gave Jackson a kiss and went to find some food. Jackson turned on the TV searching through the channels. After scouring through he found the NHL channel and kept that on, watching highlights from the night before. He began coughing hard and each one louder than the last. Daisy could hear his pain from the elevator.

The doctor had explained the process and different routes they could go just a few minutes before he was all set up and specifically asked to talk to Daisy alone. He explained more to her because sometimes in these experiences, patients were too overwhelmed with everything going on. It is easier having someone else to understand and help guide the patient. Daisy was holding herself together with chewing gum and chicken wire trying not to crumble. Shaking as she stood in line waiting for their lunch, maybe it was from the caffeine or the fear of the situation. Putting on a strong and happy face, telling her mind that everything will be ok.

      Daisy heard coughing once she got on the fourth floor. She returned with food listening to him try to impossibly cough out the cancer. Another nurse came in as Daisy walked in, she asked Jackson if he needed medicine because of how awful the sound echoed through the sterile walls of the chemotherapy ward.

"Yes, that would be lovely!" Jackson said drinking cold water to help prevent his scratchy throat, feeling somewhat of a nuisance.

"I heard you from three rooms away, and I remember that cough from a few weeks ago when you were here. You must be in a lot of pain, I can recommend to the doctor a morphine lollipop and cough suppressant to make you more comfortable."

"Oh all right," Jackson said, smiling at the nurse.

      Jackson opened his bag of lunch up. Grabbing his chicken sandwich and fries from the paper bag, two sides of buffalo sauce and a lemonade. They quietly ate, after they were done eating the nurse in blue scrubs walked back into the all white chilly room.

"The doctor approved it, I'll go grab it for you when the pharmacy has it ready." The nurse stated, checking his machine..

      A few minutes later she came back with his medicine. In her hand was a lollipop covered by an orange top. Jackson perked up on the bed ready for his treat.

"You don't like sweets!" Daisy sarcastically remarked to Jackson.

      Jackson ripped off the orange top the plastic off the lollipop sticking it in his mouth like a child wanting a sugar rush.

"I have a sweet tooth today." Jackson said with a huge smile on his face.

"That may make you a little sleepy and more relaxed, since you'll be here for a while. A nap might be a way to kill time." The nurse said no pun intended.

The nurse walked away and Daisy's curiosity grew wild. Watching him eating his lollipop like a ten year old kid.

Within twenty minutes Jackson was sleeping. Daisy saw him passed out with a needle in his arm, a shaved head peacefully sleeping, the lollipop was in his hand. Daisy got up to grab the lollipop holding it close to her mouth ready to try it then quickly put it on the table after hearing quick footsteps approaching.

Daisy turned around and shut the curtain. Jackson's hand was ice cold when she pried the lollipop from his fingers, Daisy grabbed his hand to warm it up as he slept. She took off her shoes and got in the bed with Jackson touching his shaved face. Moving the IV line away trying to not get anything tangled. She snuggled in with him in the small hospital bed pulling the covers over the two of them and laid on his chest. Hearing the muffled breathing constricted by the disease that congealed in both lungs.

Daisy's hand warmed his back to a normal temperature, now rubbing his frigid fingers back to life watching the liquid chemo drip into his IV. It was like watching paint dry, but much worse when it was someone you care for. It was cooler in the hospital but Jackson was unusually cold even with hoodies and blankets over him as a result of the medicine. His body temperature remained one degree lower during every checkup during the treatment. Daisy watched the medicine pump into his vein time after time seeing the medicine's side effects occur. Daisy looked at Jackson, he was weak from enduring all the medicines mixed along with the disease that had him on the verge of lifeless. Feeling the faintest feeling of death that surrounded him. The poison that coursed through his veins was killing him to make him better.

Daisy would fade off to sleep but awakened by his coughing, to Jackson it became so regular he stopped noticing. Her head rumbled with every cough as it rested on his chest. Listening to his body try to get everything out was one of the worst parts.

Nurse's would often pop their heads in after hearing him. Once they saw Daisy in the bed with him they would nod, closing the curtain behind them. Every half hour or hour his machine would beep precisely once the clock ran out. The nurses would come in and out taking the old medicine, shortly after resetting the machine then bringing in new drip bags. After hitting a button nurses put on gloves, another nurse walked in wearing a protective suit when dealing with some of the bags of drugs. The biohazard symbols on the bag always gave Daisy a fright.

Jackson coughed himself awake, surprised to see Daisy on top of him half the time. Dazed he looked around, Daisy wiped the drool from his mouth.
"Where is my loli?" Jackson said barely awake.

The two chucked, Daisy always took care of it when he fell asleep. Jackson was kind of zoned out most of the time but in good spirits laughing at the little things. The medicines all combined together, putting him in a fog. Feeling like he was both floating and burning up at some points. Freezing body filled with chivers and extreme pain as he coughed scratching his throat. Waking to scorching joints and throbbing bones that lasted for hours, the morphine could only do so much to help him feel better.

The two gripped each other tight and continued to joke back and forth each time. Once his loli was in his hand he did not put it down, even when he grabbed the coffee thinking it would keep him awake. Not the case, Jackson fell asleep after some more of his lollipop and Daisy did her job protecting it. Beating his body of all the contractions for a while, Daisy was understanding of how uncomfortable he was.

The days in the hospital were long and dull, seemingly never ending with nothing new but medicines or what was for lunch today. Last time Jackson did this he went through almost all of it all by himself, which made it easier because it was all on him once his ex disappeared. He kept it a secret from everyone he knew, few knew only after months of it being in a remission state a year later.

It was better with the company, but having her see him weak put a heavy burden on Jackson. Each treatment flew by faster and faster until finally the bell was rung. The ringing of the chrome bell was the end of this part, now they had to rely on the medicine to do its job in the coming months.

Dismal frequent visits for scans to make sure it was doing its job. As long as it did not continue to grow was the goal. It got to a point where the doctor's office became a job for them, deciding to break away from the string that bound them. They both changed some things in their lives a bit after he got sick. Changing everything about their lives together both on the same page. Daisy began to work remotely, Jackson invested some of his casino winning and watched the interest pile up.

Over the next few months anytime they had the chance they would go away, feeling like a fantasy. Until they came to the crossroads where they both quit their jobs, living on their own terms. Staying in different luxury hotels or camping out in nature and always finding new places to explore. They ate a variety of different foods along with one another as often as possible. Using the cash Daisy accumulated for him picking numbers and rolling dice. She continued to do so every time they stepped into a casino anything and everything was possible being his lucky charm.

Every day rolling the dice, in and out of casinos both at home and abroad. Their passports were kissed by the different stamps, the ink bleed through the pages and soaked in champagne. Drinks continued to flow, never forgetting to cheer for what they had both not ready to cash in their chips just yet.

The sun rose through the solstice, the orange rays in the Indian Sea they watched. Moving from the Pacific to the Atlantic, currencies were exchanged along with commodities. Goods were gathered as needed for the day, fire slow cooking dinner on beaches. The moonlight music played to dance them to sleep.

Taking a boat out to sea at random. The spray of the ocean waves flew, tasting salt from the great sea. The navigation was wide open anywhere they wanted to go, the waves splashing against the sides. The all dark green boat bounced from one wave to the other, throttling the engine to shoot through the water in the fast vessel. The wind blew from the west, the flag on the front of the boat flickered in the breeze. The murky water was dark in the sun's light but changed with the clouds' contrast.

Hiking up to the upside of mountain tops. Falling waterfalls created pools of fresh water that got stuck in between the curves of the rocks, higher elevation of the mountainside overlooked a large valley of water. The rocks and dirt provided natural minerals making it a good place to stop when parched. If the area was secluded enough then the two undressed for a dip into the cool springs for dessert.

Fresh food from local markets filled their bellies, enjoying every meal. Picking up different recipes from place to place depending on the culture that surrounded them. It all went by as it should have, never feeling like the day would end. When it did end it ended in the same way every night, under the sheets that ruffled for hours. Juices from fine wines were used to hydrate after the two bonded. Fire warmed their naked bodies glued to one another as they cuddled. Recapping all the pleasant fictions Daisy looked at her left hand and was ready to make it official.

Chapter 11.

Daisy gripped the sheets, holding on as she was swallowed whole in the breaths before waking. Her body curved, eyes shut, not fully conscious. Inhaling deeply she opened her eyes looking out the window to a stormy dawn. She closed her eyes, resting her body to a numb on the gray sheets. Calm, she began dreaming of her fairytale wedding day with a smile on her face.

As promised he was to put his signature on his wife. She had agreed to her first and last tattoo and Jackson would do it himself once she said I do. There was one reason she would allow for this. To be the one and to be the only, it was because he asked her to be his. He wanted to own her not as property, he wanted her soul and to have a true life tie with someone.

In order for him to want and need her forever, this is what he needed. Every breath, every move, every thought he wants to be a part of. Everything that had to do with her he wanted. The ink would be a key to unlock another realm, a reminder of absolute commitment to one another and a symbol of unfathomed infinity.

Once one experiences what she shared with Jackson there is no going back. It's twenty one, blackjack, it is game over! Love flowing like the waves of the shoals bringing the current in from the swells to land to one another's arms.

Laying in her bed gripping the sheets remembering the cold breath vapor from every word and every howl from last night vividness. Blankets, dessert and wine. The fur of the blankets were made from bear, elk and fox. The wine was bold and spicy. The taste of tannins elapsed in their mouths. They prepared quenching the celebration on their tongues. This was a ten year old batch that they had been saving for a special occasion, a delicious bourbon barrel blend of wine. The two glasses remained partially full, stemless glasses stood dancing in the lonely night on a freshly cut log. They used the log as a table, a sharp ax stuck in the heartwood in between the glasses right in the middle of the seemingly endless rings of the tree.

It was close to what felt like freezing, goosebumps were common. The embers glowed a bright yellow light. The carbon burned creating the ashes to make black pigment for tattoo ink. Staring at the fire long enough you can see it all. Almost as a sign, that turns into a story that was untold. The element burning down presents the future. The number 11 was seen in the fire and their hands tightly gripped one anothers.

The mire movements of the tree leaves swiftly flowing in the wind. The smoke drifted over giving the wine a smokey complexion then the smoke drifted up toward the moon. A flash, a long shooting star jetted across the peaceful sky. The bright moon was so close you could reach out to touch it, Daisy understood the unspoken words from the Earth. Her eyes attuned to the fire, hearing the soft crackling that tuned with the howls in the distance.

At the rare moment, sensing the strangeness of reality Daisy awoke. Looking outside the window at the stormy gloom she quickly pressed her eyes together to return. She was back under the stars, smoke flowed and the smell stuck to both of them. Warming themselves in the cool night transferring body heat warmer than the fire. Their naked bodies rubbed together all night and she howled louder than the wolves.

Jackson prepared the ink, compressing the charcoal down to dust with a stone. The ink was dark as he stirred it in with gin, the black pigment sparkled in the bowl. It was handmade, one of a kind all natural ink made from the carbon of nature just like the same carbon that dwells within us.

Daisy was ready after saying *I do*, her pants were off, along with her delicate red lace panties. Jackson positioned her in the chair to his liking. Her hands on the headrest of the black leather chair. Needles quickly went under a layer of skin in such a fast manner it was undetectable by the naked eye. Once a line was finished he wet a paper towel and wiped off the excess ink. The towel turned black, the room was silent when the vibrations of the machine stopped.

Daisy's goosebumps rose up the small hairs on her skin, her anticipation was still there knowing it was not over. The sensations heightened, the excitement remained. No words were spoken looking up in the mirror at him. He then continued with his signature on the right side of her butt cheek. The arch of her back curved to almost a 90 degree angle in anticipation. Her glossy maroon bottom lips were consumed by her top teeth digging down into the skin.

This was the only part of Daisy's body that was tattooed. Her entire body was blank, absolutely beautiful and perfect. A blank canvas, now glorified into a masterpiece. The one who changed her mind about getting a tattoo stood over her with the tattoo gun making sure it was perfect.

Jackson cleaned the excess ink off of her and then the machine. He took off the latex gloves and grabbed her by her hand to help her out of the black leather chair she molded down into. The leather chair had scratches from her nails. Daisy was on her feet eager to see, she turned her body to see the finished work in the mirror. She felt his hand on her neck then a squeeze that made a tingle go down her spine and she knew they'd meet lips. Jackson spun her around by his hand before she got to see his finished work flying into his arms.

She always told her friends he had a way of speaking to her without speaking. He spoke with his body, by his eyes, and by his touch. Daisy leaned in to kiss him as she was commanded. If he was not holding her, she would hit the floor. She was weightless, deeply kissing with the absence of gravity. All of this was way too perfect, too perfect to be she thought.

Jackson grabbed her panties and pants that were neatly folded next to his suit jacket. Daisy put them on without looking in the mirror, much too busy watching him put his suit jacket on while he stared right back at her with desire pooling in his eyes. Jackson took her by the hand and led her out the door once she was fully dressed. Everything got blurry, darkness clouded the room.

The storm had worsened the longer she drifted back to sleep. Daisy gripped her hand hard into the silk sheets during the last part of her lucidness. The images flickered through her mind. She tossed and turned, imagining Jackson. His broad shoulders, how his hair was always slicked back and each shade of ink on his chest.

Daisy smiled hearing Jackson saying *I Love You* for the first time before she opened her eyes. Waking up to the same reassurances, the feeling of Jackson being with her. Basking in the moments before she completely forgot what she was thinking about. Naturally she turned over to pull Jackson in close to her. No one was there, turning back to reach to the other side of the bed having the same result. Daisy grabbed her head, feeling in a fog. Breathing heavily she got off the bed to go rinse some water on her face. Looking in her reflection to a few more wrinkles on her face. The cold water dripped down off her cheek helping to console her a tad bit.

Fully awake Daisy got dressed going straight to breakfast. She pointed to the scrambled eggs and bacon reaching her plate up to receive her scoop. Daisy went to her usual table pulling out the solid wood chair and sat down.

Daisy walked back to her room after breakfast and sat down on her rocking chair looking into the large abstract black ink in the canvas on the wall. Thinking of when the two were *Dripping in Ink* creating it. Her imagery disconnected by a knock at the door. Daisy tried to ignore it looking into the canvas vastness. Daisy was handed a small plastic cup and a glass of water. Throwing back the white tablets and a sip of water to wash them down, she handed the plastic cup back to the nurse.

The painting made her lost, reliving the acute moments she had developed towards Jackson. Rocking back in her chair holding on to the lucid memory of him she was mesmerized by the large cotton canvas. Being hypnotized by the work's consumption, an overwhelming feeling of a presence in the air. Hearing the whispering words I love you again. She turned around to the empty room.

Daisy got up and a gray haired woman looked back at her in the mirror. Deep in the reflection, the painting grew behind her and started to obscure her vision like it was possessed. A figure was seen in the red ink of the canvas blending into a depraved face that gave chills that crawled up her body, a scorching sensation that she had felt before. His three words repeated from all areas of the room. The black smeared ink was her new depiction of reality. Enchanted by the unfortunate sense from the malicious creature motivated to terrorize her, it distracted her from looking anywhere else she could not move. Festering with anxiety and the unwilling capability to move trapped in dormancy. Trying to focus on the mirror knowing what she needed to see to face her sanity.

Shunning the power of the demon in the artwork she tried to break free of deep energy restraining her soul. Locking on the edges of the cheval glass to shield her eyes from the fierce tantalizing agony that had a hold on her unbreakably. Exercising all her strength to rotate her neck down a few inches, squinting to limit the visibility of her perfiles. The abstract paint spun into a twister on the surface of the canvas discouraged her sense of stability.

Reaching down with her hands pulling her pants down she constricted her muscles at maximum power demanding to see the 11 letters that Jackson rammed under her skin to permanently mark her body with ink. The end of the possessors clinging clutch was almost broken as she fought for free will, she heard his words repeat like a broken record player. Daisy strenuously continued to move her eyes down, wanting to see the spot that caused her both pain and pleasure. With all her might she got into the perfect position, the force released a little to allow her to do so. Her eyes broke the demon's magnetic pull, looking in the reflection her body felt like it was hit by a thousand shards of glass. Daisy's eyes stalled fixed on an unbelievable

blank

section

The End

Dripping In Ink
Dr. Humpry

The second book will be a prequel based in the first hundred years of a new age of AD. More of an understanding of the origin of Daisy's condition will be explained. A group of battle hardened warrior vikings jump on a longship and head to the island with tales of power one could only dream of. Heading to the biggest island (Ireland) before the eternal sea that no one had found land past. The warriors of Ireland help to defend the Druids who kept this magical staff. Protective magic combats fury and tactics intertwined to make this next novel to be quite the adventure.